The Insect Farm

The Insect Farm

STUART PREBBLE

ALMA BOOKS

ALMA BOOKS LTD
3 Castle Yard
Richmond
Surrey TW10 6TF
United Kingdom
www.almabooks.com

First published by Alma Books Limited in 2015
This mass-market paperback edition first published by Alma Books in 2016
Copyright © Stuart Prebble, 2015

Stuart Prebble asserts his moral right to be identified as the author of this work in accordance with the Copyright, Designs and Patents Act 1988

Printed and bound by CPI Group (UK) Ltd, Croydon, CR0 4YY

ISBN: 978-1-84688-389-7
eBook ISBN : 978-1-84688-361-3

Prologue

There was no particular sense of urgency about the first call that had come in. The duty sergeant's log said that an unpleasant smell had been reported coming from a shed on a site of allotments, and that the caller had been advised to contact the local council. It was not until three days later, when a complaint was received from the head teacher of a primary school situated next to the allotments, that any notice was taken. A supply teacher who had previously served in the army had mentioned it was a smell he had known before, one he associated with decaying flesh. Even then, it was coincidental that the Chief Inspector of the Serious Crimes Unit was within hearing distance when two constables were being briefed to go to take a look.

"What did the original caller say it was?" asked one of the constables.

"An insect farm, whatever that is."

The unfamiliar phrase triggered a distant memory in the Chief Inspector. He asked if he could hitch a ride.

Thirty minutes later the patrol car pulled up at the allotments. Already parked outside were another police car and a van from the Environmental Health Department. In the middle distance, beyond the wire fence and padlocked gate, the Chief Inspector could see the outline of the building, which was surrounded by half a dozen men dressed in over-alls and a policewoman.

It took a few moments for the policewoman to unlock the gate, and all four officers set off towards the abandoned shed. Ahead of them they could see that two men from the council wearing what looked like bee-keeper outfits were just about to open the door. The Inspector winced as the rank smell of rotting flesh was picked up by the breeze. On one side of the path he noticed a man wearing working clothes.

"That's Mr Bolton, who reported the problem," said the policewoman. "He says the shed has been here since well before he took over his own allotment from his father years ago. He first noticed the smell at the weekend and reported it to us and the council on Monday."

"What made him call us?"

"I think everyone was a bit freaked out by the stench. Shall we stop them from going in?"

The senior officer shook his head.

At first it seemed as though the door had been holding back a mound of powdery soil, which was now spilling out onto the ground in front of the shed like waves on a shoreline. A few steps nearer, what had appeared to be a swamp of inert particles was now a growing mass, swirling and churning within itself. Close up, it became clear that the rising tide was made up of hundreds of thousands of tiny insects, crawling *and tumbling over each other as if they were a moving sea-scape. The officers took a step back.*

"What the hell?..."

The two men in protective clothing waited for the initial surge of tiny bodies to subside and then edged forward through the open door, wading above their ankles in the teeming creatures; multitudes of them, all shapes and sizes, still being driven outwards by the pressure of their own weight. Minuscule red ants were clambering over larger beetles, which scrambled across the backs of grasshoppers and cockroaches. Mixed in haphazardly were worms and moths, all spreading out like an oil slick. Millions of legs waved wildly in the air, as though trying to gain a foothold.

Within less than a minute the men re-emerged, in a state of agitation and trying to kick off the insects still clinging to their boots. They struggled to remove their face masks, as though in panic, then bent over as the masks fell to the floor, coughing violently and gasping for air. After a few seconds one of them straightened up and turned towards the police officers.

"You need to get some of your people to look in there." He was still trying to catch his breath as the other man removed his helmet.

"I think there are two of them, but there is just about nothing left. Two human skeletons, both picked almost clean."

Chapter One

If you have been lucky enough to be able to tell the truth for most of your life, you probably cannot imagine how exhausting it is to spend forever living a lie. The never-ending necessity to police the gap between the thoughts going on inside your head and what is being conveyed to the outside world by your words, your actions and your eyes.

From the cheating wife or husband who spends years in the most intimate relationship with their spouse while living a parallel life with someone else, to the double agent whose safety depends on appearing as one thing to one side while being entirely something else to the other. In the end, it's usually the sheer exhaustion of it which is their undoing.

In my defence I would say that the effort has been hard for me, because deception was not something which came naturally. I had to learn how to conceal the appalling secret which I have kept for all these years, and I made many mistakes along the way. As for my brother Roger? Who knows? Who could ever really know what was going on in the mind of Roger?

Roger was six years older than me, and a six-year gap normally means you have very little in common with your older brother. No shared friends, toys, mysteries or secret camps. The ten-year-old will have defrocked the tooth fairy before the four-year-old has lost his first teeth. The twelve-year-old will be wondering where Mum and Dad have hidden the presents, while the six-year-old is expecting them to arrive down the chimney. The fifty-year-old isn't far from the forty-four-year-old, but the sixteen-year-old is a whole generation apart from his ten-year-old sibling. Normally.

But Roger was never like any ordinary kid. I always knew that, though at the time I had no idea of why or how. These were the Fifties and Sixties, and while it's true that Roger always was a bit difficult to categorize, if pressed to put a label on him, most people would have chosen the word "simple".

I remember forbidding hospitals with long echoing corridors painted green and cream, and smelling of the unequal battle between stale urine and antiseptic. We waited for many hours on hard chairs in cold rooms, with posters on noticeboards warning of everything from tooth decay to rabies. I watched from a distance as my beloved brother crouched over wooden shapes set out on a small table, trying his best to piece one to another. I saw the tiny lines ploughed in his forehead as he struggled to understand what it was that was being asked of him, and even then, when I was maybe two or three myself, I broke loose from whomever held me to rush over and hand him the round wooden tube that so very obviously was designed to go into the round wooden hole.

I remember our mother sitting on the long bench seat at the back of the 54 bus on the journey home, her self-control faltering as she struggled to make sense of it all. Her whispered conversations with Dad behind closed doors, a mix of frustration and despair. "Why us?" and "What will become of him?"

From my own point of view though, any awareness of a problem relating to Roger was way in the future. All I knew was that I had an older brother who was much taller than I was, but who liked to do the same stuff I liked. I was far too young to worry about what would become of him – I just loved that he did not treat me with the same contempt with which most older brothers treated their younger brothers, and that he was happy to play the same games that I wanted to play.

Roger was content to take all the turns at being Silver, so that I could take all the turns in being the Lone Ranger. He was happy to be the camel so that I could be Lawrence of Arabia. He would blunder around for hours with a scarf tied around his eyes, while I shrieked and ducked and weaved as though one touch of his outstretched fingertips would spell instant electrocution.

Photos taken at that time show two young boys, one tall and gangly, the other smaller and with more puppy fat; obvious siblings, one just a newer imprint of the other. Without exception they show two lads with smiling faces, perhaps carrying buckets and spades, or sitting side by side in a dodgem car or on a carousel, often with the bigger boy's arm draped protectively over the shoulder of the younger.

There seems to be nothing in those fading photographs to give any hint of what was to come. Here we are, Roger and I, sitting on the bank of a river holding fishing rods made out of bits of bamboo with a length of nylon attached. Here we are again sitting astride a concrete lion guarding the gates of a stately home. Two lads, one aged maybe four, the other ten, floppy haircuts and floppy limbs, neither with a care in the world.

The younger brother in the photographs is undoubtedly the less good-looking, unquestionably the less athletic of the two. His beam into the camera is more guarded and less unswerving than the clear gaze of his older sibling. Though it is not comfortable to admit it, if forced to identify the retard in this picture, it is hard to escape the conclusion that the average observer would choose me.

Of the two of us, I was the one who thought it a good idea to use my colouring crayons to join up the polka dots on the wallpaper in the bedroom we shared, while Roger confined his involvement to a fit of giggling. I was the one who experimented with the possibility of human flight by jumping off the garage roof, breaking my ankle in the attempt, and leaving Roger collapsed in tears on the grass as the ambulance took me away. And I was the one who took our home-made go-kart and careered within inches of the path of an oncoming bus.

One day I was playing hopscotch near our house with three friends of my own age when a bigger boy who lived nearby decided to wreck our game by rubbing out our chalk lines on the pavement. Brian Maddox was the same age as Roger, but far bigger and stronger. More important than that, members of the Maddox family were used to fighting in a way that we were not. We were not soft, but neither were we quite that sort of family. Not like the Maddoxes.

Brian pushed me to one side when I protested, and in a moment of recklessness much like the one which had propelled me off the garage roof and into space, I summoned all my strength and shoved him backwards. He regained his balance quickly and came back strong and hard, lashing out with closed fists. Instinctively I fought back, but I was no match for him.

I still remember the look on Roger's face when I came into the house, shedding floods of tears and bleeding from scraped knees. He seemed in that instant to become another person, someone I did not recognize, and I watched in amazement as he strode along the street towards a group of boys which included Brian, and attacked without pause or hesitation. There was a brief whirlwind of flailing limbs as Roger advanced and more or less fell onto the bully, both of them thudding down onto the concrete. It took three kids to pull Roger off the boy, who limped away with a stream of blood and saliva flowing from his mouth. After that, no one in the area bullied me again.

Even in those earliest days, though, Roger had his softer side. I remember that we were driving one day to the seaside in Dad's car, singing songs and generally having a good time, when there was the sound of a splat on the windscreen as a large flying insect met a dramatic end. Roger suddenly stopped singing.

"What would happen," he said after a few moments, "if enough cars drove along enough roads and killed enough insects?" He paused. "In the end, would there be any insects left?"

There was silence as my mother tried to formulate her answer.

"I don't think there is much danger of that, Roger. There are so many fields and hedges and forests where there aren't any cars," she said, trying to sound reassuring. "But it is a pity—"

"Yes," my father interrupted her, "apart from anything else, they make such a bloody mess on the windscreen." I was ready to burst out laughing, but just in time I saw a look of sadness in Roger's face which I don't think I had seen before, and had to make an effort to suppress my amusement.

So yes, even from the earliest days, Roger and I were inseparable. If Roger was a problem, or had a problem, or caused a problem, then none of these problems were mine. All I had was the sort of older brother that everyone would wish for: bigger than me, stronger than me, and who would do anything for me, as indeed I would for him.

It was only a matter of time before some busybody – maybe a doctor or a teacher or a social worker – suggested that it wasn't good for me to spend so much time with Roger. It was nice that we were so close, but perhaps I needed some other friends of my own if my development was not to be impaired. No doubt the idea of two kids with restricted development so alarmed our parents that they were thrown into a panic. For several days there were whispered discussions which were said, when I enquired, to be "nothing to do with you". It turned out that they were everything to do with me, because the upshot was that in the summer holidays of 1959, when I was eight, my parents made me join the local cubs, and I was packed off on the annual camping trip to Torbay.

A more loyal fellow than I would be able to report the distress from missing his older brother and only true friend, every hour and every day, and of pining for the opportunity to make an early return. However such is the promiscuity of youth and the enchanting nature of anything new, that I should admit that for most of my time away I hardly missed Roger at all. The novelty of cooking our own food around campfires, of going on treasure hunts, building rafts and sing- ing songs to the accompaniment of out-of-tune guitars, and all of it way past my usual bedtime, absorbed my small life.

Once we had made the phone call to reassure our parents that we had arrived safely, we were encouraged to contact our homes as seldom as possible, and in my case this involved an occasional brief call on a crackly phone line from the red telephone box in the nearby village. My memories are all overlaid by the smell of damp cloth and canvas. Damp socks and sleeping bags. Damp grass and plimsolls. If I was missing Roger, I don't think I sent a message to say so, and if he was missing me – well, the unattractive truth is that I hardly gave it a thought.

Time is distorted in the young mind, and at this vantage point I cannot recall whether I was away for as little as a week or as much as two. Whatever the case, I know that it was not until the end of the holidays, as we were packing up our soggy clothes into sodden bundles and pledging lifelong allegiance to the new friends we had made over burnt sausages and dew-soaked sleeping bags, that my mind returned to my family. Only then, as coaches departed en route to Basildon and Dagenham and other places on the periphery of my tiny universe, did I give any thought at all to what had become of Roger during what seemed to be a long absence. For all this time I had enjoyed constant entertainment and companionship, while he, I had little doubt, would have had few activities provided for him, and few if any friends to play with.

Before leaving for the six-hour bus ride, we were instructed to make one last phone call home to confirm our expected time of arrival. Having reassured my mother that everything was fine and that I was looking forward to seeing her again, I asked:

"How is Roger?"

"Roger?" she said, as though she didn't know whom I meant. "Oh, Roger's fine."

"Has he been missing me?"

"Yes, I suppose so," she said. It was obviously not something she had thought about. "He hasn't mentioned it."

In my self-centred world, for a moment I was hurt not to have been missed, and thought nothing of the fact that I had hardly missed Roger either. "Will he be there?..." I began to say, but she was gone.

The journey back from Torbay seemed to take for ever, and was only punctuated from time to time by some half-hearted attempts at singing the songs which had sounded so melodious when sung around the campfire.

After the hilarity of making faces and V-signs at passing motorists wore off, some of us went to sleep and others retreated into our own thoughts. Eventually, any feeling of guilt I experienced at not having communicated with the brother from whom I had been all but inseparable, gradually gave way to anxiety to see him; an anxiety that grew as the miles passed by and the thatches and hedges of rural England merged into suburbs. Though I hadn't missed him at the time, I now missed him awfully in retrospect, so that by the time the bus neared the gates of the school where we were due to be met by our families, I found myself craning my neck to catch an early glimpse of Roger among the gathering.

"Where's Roger?" I asked. The look on my mother's face was enough to tell me that the more diplomatic thing would have been to express joy at seeing her.

"Oh, Roger's at home. He said he'd see you when you got there," she said.

I was disappointed. "Didn't he want to come to meet me?"

"I don't know," said my dad. "He was preoccupied."

"What with?"

It was clear that my parents didn't want to talk about Roger. They were eager to know how their younger son had fared during his first extended stay away from them. But at that age you don't care about the stuff that has happened already; that was great, but it's in the past, and what's the point of going over it with someone else who wasn't there? So I didn't tell my parents that I had had a great time but had missed them both. I didn't mention how much I had missed my mother's cooking and a goodnight cuddle. Now that I think about it, I don't think I ever got round to telling my parents properly that I appreciated them, or that I knew what they had done for me. By now all of my attention was focused on Roger, on seeing him again and finding out what he had been doing. How had he coped without me?

Our family home was a small terraced house in Croydon, south-east London, though if anyone had describe it as "terraced" within earshot of my mother she would instantly have put them right. She preferred the expression "one of three" which meant that we had a semi on one side of us and a semi on the other side of us – leaving our house most accurately described as "terraced", but not to my mother. The house was one of those between-the-wars mock something or other, with fake timbers embedded in pebble-dash, which characterized the southern suburbs of London and no doubt many other towns and cities.

"Where's Roger?" I said again as we got out of the car and he was nowhere to be seen. I thought that if he couldn't come to meet the coach, he might at least have been waiting at the window, but there was no sign of my older brother, no twitch of the nets to indicate his presence. When I burst through the front door in late August of 1959, it took me all of forty seconds to put my head into every room in the house, and to reach the conclusion that Roger wasn't in any of them.

"Where's Roger?"

Considering that the purpose of my banishment to summer camp had been to loosen my ties with my older brother, my mother and father now seemed to take pleasure in my enthusiasm to see him again. Which parent of siblings would not take pride in such closeness?

"I guess he's in the shed," said my mother. "That's where he spends most of his time lately."

There was a tiny garden at the back of the house laid to lawn with a few ornamental flower beds carved into the soil and filled with specimen roses, the names of which were written in black magic marker on yellow labels affixed like a dog collar to the stems. Beyond the boundary fence there was a garage which was designed to accommodate just one car, but was filled to the rafters with my dad's tools, offcuts of timber and some garden equipment. Next to that again was a large wooden shed which had been allocated to Roger and me for use as a den. Over the years the shed had doubled as a cave (in our Batman and Robin phase), as a stable (in our Wyatt Earp phase) and as a spaceship (in our Dan Dare phase).

"What's he doing?" It had never occurred to me that Roger could effectively occupy himself without me. I was thinking of all our games together – most of which involved an inseparable pair. "How can he be spending time in the shed when I'm not around?"

Roger had his back to me when I yanked open the shed door and threw myself in. Just beyond him I could see what looked like a pane of glass, all smeared and dirty, with a bank of soil behind it. The atmosphere smelt of the damp and dank of wet earth, the smell you associate with nightmares of being buried alive.

"What's that?" I asked him.

"Oh, hi, Jonathan," he said, more or less as he would have done if I'd popped back to the house five minutes ago for a glass of orange squash. "It's my insect farm."

"What's an insect farm?"

He hesitated, as I might have hesitated if someone had asked me what the moon is. As though the answer is obvious, but you want to find the right words which don't imply you think the person asking the question is an idiot.

"It's a place where you keep insects so that you study them." Roger still had not turned to look at me.

"What kinds of insects?"

"Well you can keep any kinds of insects you like. All you have to do is to create the right conditions for them to live in. These are ants." Roger stood back to allow me a better view through the gloom at the installation in front of him. It looked like an aquarium that you might use for tropical fish, except that the panes of glass were only an inch or so apart at the width. "Come closer and have a look."

I did, and on the edge of my vision I caught a glimpse of Roger in the half-darkness. It had been only a week or two, but something about him seemed older. Or if not older, then perhaps more mature or in command. That was probably the first time I noticed a little bit of downy fluff in front of his ears and across his top lip. Roger was fourteen and entering puberty, but at the time I didn't know what puberty was, and was much more interested in examining whatever had preoccupied him so thoroughly that he hadn't had the chance to miss his younger brother and only real friend. Still, the only thing I could make out was a mass of what looked like soil, squished up against the glass.

"Closer still."

It was not until my face was a few inches away and my eyes began to adjust to the gloom that I could identify anything other than the sludge. Gradually I began to focus, and I could make out tiny avenues carved into the soil, little thoroughfares in which I detected the shapes of tiny creatures. Dozens and dozens of them slowly materialized, scuttling backwards and forwards, tripping and clambering over each other, apparently oblivious to anything other than whatever was their task at hand.

"Amazing," I said, and it was true. Obviously I wanted to be nice to Roger about his new preoccupation, but I genuinely did think it was amazing. "What are they doing?"

"Look even closer and you'll see." Roger handed me a magnifying glass.

"How come Dad let you play with this?" The magnifying glass had belonged to our grandfather, who had died a decade ago. It was understood that it now belonged to Roger and me, but we hadn't been allowed to keep it among our stuff because Dad said it was too expensive to be used as a toy. I remember feeling a sting of resentment that Roger had been allowed to use it without me being there.

"I'm not playing with it," Roger said. It was a distinction which carried a lot of importance at that age. "I'm using it to study the ants. It's what it was meant for."

I already knew that the magnifying glass wasn't meant for melting toy soldiers with the focused beam of the sun, as Roger and I had been doing when we were first allowed to try it out. I took it from him and drew it backwards and forwards, Sherlock Holmes style, attempting to focus on the glass frame.

"Keep watching carefully," he said, "and you'll be able to see what they're doing."

Chapter Two

As the years went by, and my older brother and I passed through our childhood and into adolescence, Roger's preoccupation with his beloved insect farm expanded and grew, just as did my interest in music, fashion and, of course, girls.

I always think it's implausible when characters in police dramas seem to know where they were on the night when the crime was committed, but I can remember vividly and in detail the occasion when I first met Harriet. It was in the end of the autumn term between my first and second year in the sixth form, and I recall it for two reasons – one was, of course, that first sight of her. The other was that it was the evening of the farewell concert by the band Cream.

A ramshackle group of us had arranged to go to the concert, and I was there with Angela, who was my girlfriend of the moment. Angela was fabulous, or certainly I thought so at the time. Long straight brown hair, as thin as a rake, with tiny, scarcely budding breasts, and those dark shadows below her eyes which we associated with late nights and soft drugs, and which later came to be toughened up by fashion and labelled "heroin chic". Angela knew the right places to buy the right clothes, was always on the crest of whatever was the latest wave, and somehow managed to be wherever it was "at".

Harriet was also with a boyfriend on that night, although she told me later that they were just mates and were not sleeping together. I took some comfort from that, until I realized that this did not mean that they were not having sex. To Harriet, sleeping with someone would have involved a whole level of intimacy that merely having sex would not have come near, but all that represented a dimension of her that it was way in my future to learn about.

I was besotted with Harriet from the very first. It's a rarely used word which sounds like something out of Jane Austen, and ordinarily you would never use it or think deeply about its meaning. In this case, though, "besotted" is the right word for what I was. It even sounds like it. Being "sotted", to be "sotted" – somehow the word suggests that all reason has been lost.

My most vivid first memory is of the view of her from the south-east – one row back and a few seats along – the back right-hand side of Harriet's head. The fine silhouette of her chin, partially obscured by her long and curling brown hair, a few stray strands stuck in place by perspiration to that tantalizing area of skin just in front of the ears. Even in the multicoloured glow of psychedelic lights, Harriet shone pink and white.

No doubt the passage of time filters any negatives from the memory, but I do know that it was not only I who recognized that Harriet was unlike those around her. For one thing, her look was unique. When everyone else of her age was wearing dungarees or tie-dye, Harriet's big-print floral dresses marked her out from the crowd. When Dusty Springfield wore spiders on her eyelids and Kathy Kirby's lips shone like a warning to low-flying aircraft, Harriet remained unmade-up. When the world was going barefoot, Harriet delighted in wearing wool socks pulled up to her knees.

My girlfriend Angela dressed in variations on the theme adopted by all the girls of the same age – flowing clothes, patched jeans, tumbling tresses, tassels and beads in multi-colours. All the other girls were cool and sexy and slightly exotic and certainly desirable, but Harriet was not one of them. Where Angela and her friends were of the moment, Harriet's look seemed timeless. While their femininity was just being discovered and then reinvented in the spirit of the age, Harriet's brand of sexiness would have worked its magic in any decade past or future. Something about her had a particular way of reaching out and taking an intensely discomforting grip around your groin. To see her was to want her, and it was on that day in November 1969 that I saw her.

After the concert we all headed onto the street. Angela went into a huddle with the other girls and I stood on the fringes of the group. We discussed what to do next and I saw Harriet hanging back, not quite part of the inner circle. Had she noticed me? She said later that she had, but there was nothing at the time to suggest it. As we reconciled ourselves to the fact that the pubs were closed and we would soon miss the last train home, I tried to make it seem an accident that I fell in alongside her.

"Some concert, huh?" Her smile was a tiny flicker of warmth, but she said nothing.

"I don't like to talk about it." I expected her to continue, but she did not.

"Don't like to talk about the concert?"

"Not for a little while, no."

"Oh," I said. "Is that just this one, or don't you like to talk about any concerts?"

"I don't like to talk about rock concerts," said Harriet, "because everything that everyone says about them seems utterly facile, and somehow talking about it devalues the experience I feel I've just had."

"I think I know what you mean," I said, but I didn't really, and I hadn't often met people who used words like "facile" in ordinary conversation.

"Some of us are going back to my place," she said. It sounded like a statement of fact rather than an invitation and, in my adolescent infatuation, I failed to understand.

"That's nice." I felt like an idiot. *That's nice?* I sounded like Alec Guinness.

There was a pause.

"You could come too if you'd like."

It turned out that she lived above a shop in Carnaby Street, and she said it with an interrogative in her voice which seemed to question whether it was possible to live anywhere else.

CHAPTER TWO

A dozen of us ended up walking the couple of miles or so from the Albert Hall to Harriet's flat in the West End. There were far fewer cars on the road in those days, and by now the streets were emptying fast. Angela was immersed in conversation with two friends, and so seemed not to notice my instant infatuation with another girl.

We were headed towards a flat above a clothes shop, halfway down the street, and next to a pair of red telephone boxes. Despite being one of the most famous streets in the world, at that time of night it was all surprisingly quiet. I learnt that the place belonged to Harriet's uncle, who lived in the country and used it when he was in town on business; I cannot now remember the actual words she used, but they were designed, I think, to give the impression that he was some kind of a spy. Certainly Harriet's father worked for the Foreign Office, and he and her mother were on a temporary posting in Hong Kong. They had left Harriet to finish at boarding school. The uncle was on an extended trip somewhere far away, and so she had been allowed to stay in it long term. Seventeen years old, with independence and her own flat in the West End of swinging London.

The decor and furniture looked and felt like something out of a 1950s film set – a bolt-upright sofa and two armchairs, a small Formica-topped table with four wooden chairs, standard lamps with shades made of discoloured fabric. Someone began playing 45s on the record player and someone else started rolling some joints. It was a small work of art to paste

23

together three Rizlas and roll up the end of a cigarette packet to make a roach, and it was an art form we had all practised. Angela and her friends went into the kitchen to make tea, and I did my best to position myself as close to Harriet as I could, while seeming not to do so.

I have now had many years in which to turn over in my mind the conversation I had on that evening with Harriet. So frequently have I done so that I believe I can recall it – if not precisely word for word – then as near to accurately as makes no difference. Since I have recalled it so often, what she said has gained the sense of the everyday that comes with familiarity, and so now I have entirely lost any perspective I may ever have had on how weird or otherwise it must have appeared at the time. She had a glass of red wine in one hand and a joint in the other, but seemed to be neither drunk nor stoned. I, on the other hand, had by now had too much to drink, which no doubt added to the mesmeric effect of her words.

"I am not all that good at drinking alcohol or taking drugs," she said, as though continuing some earlier conversation of ours without a pause, "but at the right volume and in the right place and time, rock music can do something for me that no narcotic can." It was as if she had been thinking about this for ages, and had decided that this was the moment to express it. No doubt her mood was partially drug-induced, but still there was something within and about her that made what would usually come across as pretentious rubbish sound real.

"Music comes into your body through the ears, right?" She raised her eyebrows in enquiry. "But in a weird sort of way I also feel that somehow it comes in through my eyes, my nose and through every pore of my skin." She paused, her pupils darting left and right and joining the dots between the silver stars upon the purple sky of the ceiling, searching for the right simile. Then she seemed to find it. "It's like the lovemaking between two people who have come to know each other over many years. A little stimulation here, a hint of a caress somewhere else, the brush of lips across your skin. The music has the power to join all my senses together, each one overlapping the last, to build me up and up, finally reaching a level where to go forward would tip you over, but to go back would disappoint. And to stay there, for seconds, maybe minutes, before being taken gently or convulsively back down to earth."

Maybe it was just adolescent rubbish, but I didn't think so then, and I still don't think so now. What I do know for sure is that Harriet wasn't like anyone else I had met before. Leave aside what she said about the music: I was seventeen for heaven's sake, and here was this wonderful girl talking about soft kissing and experienced lovers and caresses on the skin.

"I love the opera," she continued, "and in the right time and place I love jazz. But there is something about rock music the way we heard it tonight. Something about how those guitar notes seem to come from a union of the soul with the instrument, and flow from the musician to the hearer like the bolt of lightning passing life from God to Adam." I know, I know, but this is what she said. I was lost. Lost for words, lost for an appropriate reaction, lost in Harriet.

The Carnaby Street flat was small and there were probably a dozen of us, and so, even if it had been anywhere on her agenda, there was no chance that she and I could have been alone, and that's not to mention the matter of my current girlfriend. Harriet and I were sitting on the landing on the stairs just outside the door of the flat when Angela put her head halfway out.

"Aren't you supposed to be doing something with Roger?"

Oh God! I was supposed to be home for Roger.

In the year since I had started studying seriously for my A-level exams, the duty of taking care of Roger had fallen entirely on my parents, and the strain was showing. This is not to suggest that I had been of all that much help before, but just the fact of having me around, able to go with Roger to the cinema or to the football, gave my parents an occasional break from the otherwise continuous responsibility.

The point was that, on this summer's evening when I was lured by the unique charms of Harriet, Roger was due to return home from a trip which had been organized by a group at the local church. I don't remember where they had been or for how long they had been away. All I recall is that Roger was due to arrive home in Croydon by midnight, and that I had promised to be back before then to be there to make sure he was OK. My parents had said they would like to take the opportunity to go to bed early, and I was responsible for ensuring that Roger was safe and settled.

"I have to go," I said, dragging myself to my feet. "My brother Roger needs me."

Nothing in Harriet's face gave a clue as to whether she regarded this as good news or bad news or even particularly any news at all. What was perfectly clear was that she by no means shared or even sensed my desolation. What appeared to her to be no more than a casual meeting for me was an evening that was to change my short life.

Chapter Three

Just how strange is it to become as obsessed as people do? Just how potty can you become? Little wonder that it has been the cause of wars. Even now I recall pondering for many hours the configuration of three honey-coloured freckles on one side of Harriet's nose, which to me looked as though they had been painted on in watercolours by some marvellous pre-Raphaelite artist. I remember the exquisite thrill arising from the ever-so-faint suggestion of the rise of her nipples as seen through a thin woollen pullover in pink. I still get a visceral charge from calling up the memory.

I cannot now remember whether Angela finished things with me or whether I finished things with her. There was no row or break-up, it just seemed that one day we were and then one day we were not. Maybe on my side it was to do with my new-found preoccupation with Harriet. Who knows what it was on hers – probably she just got bored.

It was scarcely a couple of weeks after that first party back at her flat in Carnaby Street when I contrived to call on Harriet, apparently by chance, while browsing around shops. I don't imagine that she was fooled for a moment, and she seemed to be amused as she held open the door in welcome. The flat smelt of the recent smoke from marijuana, which felt in contrast with the operatic music that was playing in the background. I caught a glimpse of the album cover, but quickly decided against pretending more knowledge than I possessed.

"*The Pearl Fishers*," I said. "Do you like this kind of thing?"

"I like it sometimes," she said. "Like now. I love to listen to music when I'm reading, but if it is something with words I recognize, I find I can't concentrate on the text. Anything sung in a foreign language works well for me."

We drank black coffee and smoked a little bit of grass I had brought with me, and we talked about ourselves and our ambitions. She spoke more about her love of music in terms as weird and unworldly to me as those she had used following the concert, and then I asked if she played a musical instrument herself.

Harriet – of course, it must be obvious from what I have said of her already – played the flute. Perhaps the impact of the sound upon me was so great because I had not heard the music of a solo flute before I heard it played by Harriet. I still recall in microscopic detail watching her as she opened the black wooden box and assembled the instrument from three pieces, carefully adjusting the fit so that the mouthpiece would sit at a precise angle. I remember the dull silver plate and the distorted reflections of stars from a chandelier. She placed the rim of the mouthpiece against the top front of her chin, just below her lips, which formed into a chaste kiss. As she prepared to play it was as though her whole body animated, and she seemed hardly to breathe into it, but rather to become the instrument. The sound was forming all around us, not from her mouth or the flute itself, but from the walls and the furniture in the room – anywhere but from this small being and this thin metallic tube.

I could not wait for her to finish the closing bars of the piece, but leaned towards her and took the flute. For a second she resisted, but I felt the warmth of the instrument in my hands and suddenly it made me more insistent. Her slight wrist was in my grasp and, without speaking, I led her down the corridor. The bed was covered with a blanket that her uncle had brought back from a trip to India, and the thick lace curtains filtered the sunshine which threw patterns of light across the floor. Harriet wore a white shirt made of fine cotton, with a multicoloured design crocheted into a one-inch-wide stripe on either side of the buttons at the front, allowing tiny glimpses of her flesh beneath. She looked at me steadily, never taking her eyes from mine, and I unfastened the tiny white pearl buttons, one at a time. At one moment she covered my hands with hers, as though unsure of whether to allow me to proceed, but I shook her away. I did not feel able to stop and was glad when she acquiesced. Now her shirt lay open to her waist.

I have the clearest memory of her softness, of smooth and perfect skin, and I placed the palms of my hands on her hips, level with the top of her jeans, and pulled her towards me. Her face was just a breath away from mine, but now, once again, she pulled back, but was no longer resisting, rather seeming to prolong the moment. I could not, and I pulled her harder towards me and we kissed a kiss which threw me down the well into Wonderland, falling headlong and not ever wanting to reach firm ground.

Chapter Four

"Tell me again about Roger."

It was a Sunday afternoon and my parents had gone for a drive in the country and were not due back for several hours. Since I was constantly preoccupied by the question of how and where to have sex with Harriet, I imagine the thought must have been somewhere in my mind, and I'd probably used the idea of getting Harriet to meet Roger as an excuse to bring her to the house.

In some ways, the fact that Roger looked perfectly normal was a disadvantage. It meant that people made no allowances for him. Had he had the familiar look of Down syndrome, then probably no one would have jostled or cursed at him when he was unable to make up his mind, at the last minute, whether or not to board the bus he had been queuing for. Had he walked with the awkward and staccato gait of the cerebral-palsy sufferer, it is unlikely that people would have become irritated as he fumbled at the supermarket checkout. But Roger had none of those characteristics. He had retained the good looks he had as a boy and, dressed as he was by my parents and therefore in their taste in clothes, he came across as a very straightforward and normal bloke in a world where the generality of youth had apparently gone crazy.

Over the years of living alongside Roger, I think I must have seen every variation of reaction to him, from confusion and awkwardness at one end, to pity and patronizing at the other. I'd seen it all. In a cafeteria where the too loud voice of the six-year-old would ring out, "What's the matter with that man, Mummy?" only for the child to be shushed and dragged away to another table. In the supermarket, where the vacant or benign expression on the face of the checkout girl would scroll within about five seconds through curiosity to concern to pity. The "I've seen it every day" routine of the professionals who talked about the need to behave normally, but then gave their advice at a speed just a little faster than dictation to an arthritic short-hand typist.

What I had never seen, even from my own parents, was anyone who treated Roger just exactly the same as they treated everyone else. No better, no worse, with no apparent consideration for any perceived limitations on his side, and all without any evident effort to do so. That was to be the unique quality of what would turn out to be the special relationship between Roger and Harriet.

I opened the front door and went into the hallway. I had never been sure about the best way to describe Roger and his problems to people who were due to meet him for the first time, and so I have very little idea what Harriet might have been expecting. I had done my best to describe the insect farm to her, and Roger's growing preoccupation with it, but in the end decided it was better for her to see it for herself than to try to make sense of my inarticulate ramblings.

"Are you OK?" I asked her, maybe worrying that perhaps she was hiding her nerves.

"Sure thing," she said, bright and breezy. "Any reason I shouldn't be?"

"None whatever, it's just that..." I trailed away. Of course there wasn't any reason why she should be anything other than perfectly relaxed. It's just that other people in the same circumstances frequently were not.

There was neither sight nor sound of Roger in the house, and already I knew that he would be in the shed at the back of the garden where these days he spent most of his time. Having been studying hard for much of the autumn term, I hadn't actually been inside the shed for some months. The last time I looked at the insect farm, it consisted of a crude structure made of wood and glass, enclosing an inch thickness of soil in which a variety of grubs of one kind or another did their thing.

"I hope you don't mind worms and creepy things," I warned Harriet.

"I put up with you, don't I?" she squeezed my arm.

I stood at the back door of the house and hollered, "Roger, are you in the shed?" There was no reply and no sound of movement, so I told Harriet to wait in the kitchen while I walked down the garden path towards the garage. "Roger, are you in there?" I knocked on the door and pulled on the handle at the same moment that Roger was pushing from the inside, as a result of which he came close to tumbling out onto the path. He had no idea that I was bringing anyone to see him, or indeed any idea who Harriet was at all, but as always he was pleased to see me. At five foot ten, Roger was still a couple of inches taller than me, and he put his arm around my shoulder just as he had when we were aged twelve and six. "I've brought a friend to meet you, Roger," I said, and at the same time beckoned Harriet from the kitchen.

Seeing my signal, and without hesitation, Harriet strode forward, touching and adjusting her hair briefly as she walked, just as she might when meeting any other boy of our age on whom she wanted to make a good impression. By the time she reached us, she had her hand outstretched for a manly handshake, another of the many little ways that made Harriet not quite typical of other young women of the time.

"Great to meet you, Roger," she said. "I've heard so much about you."

I'm not sure whether it was because few people had ever greeted him for the first time with such warmth and apparent ease, or because she was so lovely – but Roger's face burst into a sunny smile which I had rarely seen since our carefree days as kids at the seaside.

"Lovely to meet you too."

Would you have been able to tell from those few words, if you hadn't been warned in advance, that Roger had problems? I think that maybe his voice was just a bit more of a monotone than one might expect, but probably just a fraction. I think that perhaps there was just a slight lilt in his tone which indicated delight more suited to a small boy, but probably just a trace. Just possibly his eyes moved the smallest bit more slowly from object to object, as though the process of registering what they saw took a fraction longer than it might for you and for me. A combination of tiny signals, none of them decisive on their own, but taken together in a package producing an overall effect which transmitted something. This person is not quite one of us.

If Harriet was picking up those signals, there was nothing whatsoever in her manner or response to indicate it. I know that I was always a bit tense when introducing people to Roger for the first time. Who would be embarrassed, or do or say something inappropriate? So when it was immediately obvious that no one was embarrassed and that no one was going to do anything inappropriate, I felt a wave of relief flow through me. A wave which no doubt further contributed to my already totally out-of-control feelings of love and lust.

"What are you doing?" Harriet asked, peering into the darkness behind Roger. His face fell momentarily into confusion, as it might if she had been asking him the square root of pi, but she was undeterred. "In the shed. What have you been doing in the shed?"

He seemed to hesitate, but then suddenly Harriet made this unexpected movement that I had not seen before, wiggling her head from side to side like a comic caricature of an

Indian manservant. At the same time she raised her eyebrows in the interrogative. Roger seemed delighted, and he turned and ducked inside.

Our family had gone up in the world just a bit since those very early days in the Fifties. My father had worked for the Prudential Insurance Company since he left the army, and had been promoted a number of times, from an agent who went door to door collecting premiums, to a deputy manager counting the money collected by the agents, and eventually to district manager, which seemed ever so exalted. A framed photograph on the mantelpiece showed him receiving an award of a gold watch for long or dedicated service, and as I write these words today that very same watch is fastened to my left wrist, a daily reminder of my link to the past. I glance at it just as my dad used to glance at it, adjust it and wind it as he used to, a passport across the decades of our fleeting lives.

The upshot was that in recent years our house had received something of a makeover. This included the replacement of the rickety old garden shed which Roger and I had used as a den, and which had housed his early interest in the insect farm. The new shed was made of planks of varnished wood, fixed together in a horizontal pattern, and with a green sloping roof. Maybe it was large as garden sheds go – perhaps fifteen feet by eight. There was only one small window at the far end, itself overshadowed beneath the overhanging branches of an apple tree, and so we had to wait for our eyes to adjust to the darkness.

There was no point of comparison between what I had expected and the sight which met me. When I had last been here, the sum total of the equipment that Roger kept in the place was an ancient wooden barrel in which I believe he was keeping worms, and a couple of old fish tanks converted for use by ants and spiders. It wasn't much like that now. All along one wall of the shed was a series of glass screens, some of them illuminated with a dull blue glow, and each of them filled with different kinds of gravel, soil, small stones and foliage.

My first reaction was amazement at how impressive it all seemed, and then curiosity about how all this could have been made possible. My dad had made no mention of getting involved with Roger in his hobby, and there was no way to match up the construction of this amazing project with what I knew of Roger's limitations. I was about to speak when Harriet beat me to it.

"Wow, Roger. You've got an entire civilization in here. Your own world in miniature." Roger was plainly delighted, and his face beamed.

"Come and take a closer look."

Roger led the way as we shuffled slowly and carefully between the racks of shelves which displayed his various bits of apparatus. He seemed to have been experimenting with different shapes and styles of containers, and some of them were clearly work in progress. At one point we came to a glass screen, about eighteen inches square, and behind it was a maze of tunnels and shapes which had been carved out of wood. Some of the tunnels led to dead ends, but there was one main thoroughfare.

"Did Dad make that with you?" I asked. I was keen to know how it had all been possible, but also didn't want to detract from Roger's achievement.

"He got the wood for me and showed me how to use a chisel," said Roger, and then smiled proudly, "but I did all the carving. Do you like it?"

Harriet said that it looked fabulous, and asked what it was for. Roger did not hesitate.

"It's called a formicarium. It's a way of keeping and studying ants. When you first put them in you can see how they are scared and confused. They run around this way and that and seem to be in a panic. They hurry down whatever route is in front of them and bump into the ends and don't know what to do. But then gradually you see them learning about their surroundings, and after a while they know their way around, and you can see them scurrying back and forth carrying food. Before you know it they have organized themselves into their own way of doing things."

I was watching Roger carefully as he spoke, and realized, not for the first time, how little I really knew about what went on inside that strange mind of his. I had always known that he lived in a little world of his own, but the world he had constructed around him was far more elaborate and sophisticated than I ever would have thought possible.

Once again, it was Harriet who picked up the conversation. "A bit like Adam and Eve when they were first put into the Garden of Eden," she said. It was a reference Roger recognized from the times that he and I used to be sent to Sunday School as kids, and the comparison seemed to delight him. There was a brief silence as he absorbed the thought.

"Yes," he said, "exactly like that." When I looked again at him he was smiling and his face was glowing. "I am, indeed, a benevolent God."

Chapter Five

The group of teenagers who hung out together at that time came from very similar backgrounds, and no doubt we had very similar interests, tastes and idiosyncrasies. We were young and badly wanted to be different from the grown-ups who seemed to rule our lives, but few of us wanted to be different from one another. We all lived in the same neighbourhood and went to one of two or three similar schools. We all had parents who had jobs, some more exalted than others, no doubt, but none of us were likely to be short of the basics of living. Some of us were painfully thin, but none of us was especially fat. We all dressed alike and had untidy hair and affected accents which were a bit more working class than the ones we were brought up with.

We dabbled in a small way with marijuana, some took a few French blues or purple hearts, but none was into anything harder. Like most kids of that age, from time to time we all drank a bit too much beer or wine, and I worked out quite early that I seemed to lack the off switch in my brain which told most of my friends that they had consumed enough.

Among this otherwise rather homogeneous group was the man who was eventually going to change all of our lives for ever. He was called Brendan Harcourt, and from the very first he was not quite like the rest of us.

When most of us were keen, within limits, to conform within our group, Brendan did not seem to care. If we all wore denims, he wore cords. If we were wearing T-shirts and granddad vests, he wore a polo shirt. We all wore scruffy-looking walking shoes known as desert boots, and Brendan would think nothing of turning up in a pair of business shoes that even my dad would have thought were a bit old-fashioned. While most of the kids with a talent for music were trying their best to play Bob Dylan songs on the guitar, we heard that Brendan was learning to play the cello.

I have saved to the last the main differentiating factor which made Brendan Harcourt so different from everyone else in our group. While most of us had brown hair or black hair, and one or two had blond hair, Brendan's hair was red. I don't mean just auburn in the run-of-the-mill kind of way. Brendan's was bright red, the sort of colour that if you saw it in a TV advertisement for hair dye you'd say it looked obviously artificial. It seemed implausible that it had occurred in nature, and yet it had. I never liked Brendan too much from the beginning, and no doubt this was partly due to the fact that he did not seem to care much about fitting in. However, I should admit straight away that much more of it was because Brendan fancied Harriet. Even that might have been OK – others in our group fancied her too – but the problem with Brendan was that he made no secret of the fact, even after the point where it was clear and public that she and I were an item.

If a group of us were hanging together drinking espresso in the Prompt Corner coffee bar on Croydon High Street and Harriet walked in, Brendan would be the first to stand up and offer her his chair. If she wore a new shirt or shawl that she had found in one of her favourite vintage-clothes shops, he was always the one to notice and compliment her on her originality. Any time I arrived late to a gathering, I would find that he had taken the seat beside her and showed no inclination to allow me to sit next to my girlfriend.

"You should take it as a compliment," I can remember Harriet saying to me.

"A compliment? How the hell am I supposed to do that?"

"Because if other blokes fancy me, it's because they find me attractive, and the fact that I choose you over them means that you are the best of the bunch."

"Isn't that what is known as 'damning with faint praise'?"

"What?"

"'The best of the bunch'. It sounds very much like 'not great, but at least better than all that lot'."

"If you are determined to turn something nice into something horrible, no doubt you can find a way to do so," she said. "I was just trying to make you feel good about yourself."

It was so effective a put-down that I'd have preferred to have received a slap in the face. As it was, it felt like one.

"OK, OK, I know I'm acting like a schmuck, but I thought you'd want to know how I feel about it."

"I do know what you feel about it. You make it so obvious that I would imagine that most of south London knows how you feel about it. Which means that Brendan also knows how you feel about it, which has probably made his day."

It seems obvious in hindsight that part of my special sensitivity to what might otherwise have been written off as a bit of harmless flirting was the realization that both Brendan and Harriet were, in their own ways, outsiders. Neither seemed to feel any obligation to follow the trends adopted by just about everyone else of our age. I, on the other hand, was acutely aware that any style I might have was entirely interchangeable with everyone else's. I guess I just lacked the self-assurance which was no doubt essential in anyone who dared to make a statement of individuality.

Meanwhile Harriet seemed at ease with herself and her surroundings in a way that I could only envy. She showed no signs of the teenage angst that everyone else seemed to have about adolescent spots or an inch more or less on her waist size. She did not get freaked out over studying for exams, or interviewing for university. She did not make a big deal of overreacting to stories in the world news that others seemed to find unduly shocking, as if the starving of Biafra were somehow doing it just to upset the teenage girls of south London.

So despite what must have seemed to much of the rest of the world to be something of a mismatch, when we sat down to discuss how we would approach the question of further education, I was delighted to learn that she was taking it for granted that she and I would apply for the same universities. She planned to study Music while I did Politics, so we carefully went through every prospectus to find places which could cater for both of us. One day Harriet and I were sitting on the floor of the living room in Croydon, surrounded by brochures, when my father came in and began thumbing through one of them.

"So are you two determined to go to the same city to study even if the courses aren't exactly what you want?"

Until that point my dad had never taken much interest in the subject, and so I was surprised by the question, and all the more so since it seemed to imply some reservation. Harriet started to reply, but I interrupted her.

"That's the plan," I said. "Any reason it shouldn't be?"

"No, not really," he said. "It's just that I would have given my eyeteeth for this kind of opportunity at your age, and I suppose my instinct would be to go for whichever is the best course, come what may."

"We plan to do that, Mr Maguire," said Harriet, "but Jonathan and I want to be together, and I'm sure we can find a way to achieve both things."

Harriet had a way of just coming out with stuff that other people might have been shy about, and I absolutely loved to hear her say what she said. My dad grunted, neither agreeing nor disagreeing, and I didn't feel like pursuing the matter right then. Later though, when Harriet was reading a book in the garden, I found my mother alone in the kitchen.

"Is there any reason why Dad might disapprove of Harriet and me being together?" I asked her.

"I don't think so." She had not had to pause to consider before replying, which made me think that it was not a new idea. "It's just that you are both very young, and he doesn't want you to make a mistake. He only wants what's best for you." She paused. "And then of course there's always Roger to think about."

"How so?" I was confused. "What's any of that got to do with him?"

"Nothing directly," she said. "It's just that your brother has probably always thought of himself and you as inseparable, and it wouldn't be all that surprising if he felt just a little bit jealous of you and Harriet."

It was a new thought for me, and my face showed it. "Really? Has he said anything to suggest that?"

"It's not anything he has said. More that he gets these moods. Nothing to worry about, I'm sure, but you know what we're like. No doubt your dad and I are destined to worry about Roger till the day we die."

* * *

Our first choice of university was Newcastle-upon-Tyne, and we were lucky to be accepted onto our chosen courses. The letters dropped on both of our doormats on the same morning, and reinforced our feelings of what increasingly seemed to be our destiny.

It was the start of Freshers' week, and the train going north was packed with kids making what felt at the time to be the important transition from being pupils to being students. We were "undergraduates", and it seemed and sounded so grown-up. For me, though not of course for Harriet, this was my first time to be living away from home. My departure from the house in Croydon had been awkward. I had waited at the window, suitcases packed, for a taxi to come to take me to the station. I was due to meet Harriet on the train. When the car arrived, we all ran around as though there was an emergency; we were not a "keep the taxi waiting" kind of family. Out on the front porch my father and I faced each other clumsily. Neither of us, it seemed, were quite sure what was the appropriate procedure for such an occasion, and certainly we were not going to hug. For what I feel sure was the first time in our lives, my dad gripped my forearm with his left hand and brought it level, so that we clamped our right hands together in a manly grip. Later I could not get the feel of that handshake, and the look in his slightly watery grey eyes, out of my mind.

My mother also made an effort at restraint, but was less successful than my dad. I could smell her make-up as she pressed her cheek against mine and embraced me, her arms tight and urgent. I think I felt embarrassed by the duration of the hug, but did not want to seem to be first to pull away. As we did so I could see the tears trickling down her face.

"Don't forget to phone as soon as you get there," she said. Suddenly I felt once again like the tiny cub going off to camp, and a rush of memories filled my head. They reminded me that my brother Roger was nowhere to be seen, but the driver was waiting, and I could almost feel the tension rising in concert with the meter indicating the increasing fare.

"Does Roger know I'm heading off this morning?"

My parents exchanged a glance before my dad spoke. "I have told him a few times – just to get him used to the idea, so that not having you around won't be too big a shock. But who knows what goes on? Last I saw of him was a couple of hours ago, heading for the shed."

"I need to go to see him," I said. "I can't go away for months on end without saying goodbye."

I turned towards the cab driver and held up my fingers to indicate five minutes, and was about to go back towards the house when my father took me by the arm.

"Don't do that, son." There was a further moment of awkwardness, as though he was trying to find the best way to explain what was going through his mind. "There's no time to talk about it now. The taxi is waiting. Just take it from me that it would be best if you leave it to us to let him know you have gone."

Still I didn't really understand, but there was no time for discussion. I had a train to catch and a new life to begin.

"Tell him I said goodbye then. I will phone when I get there and write as soon as I've got my bearings."

Harriet had brought no food for the journey, and we had shared the cheese-and-pickle sandwiches which my mother had made before we got halfway. There was nothing further to eat on the train, so that by the time we arrived at Newcastle both of us were famished. We went to the station buffet, but did not recognize the shapes of the bread or the names against them. "Stotty" and "barm cake" and "bap" clogged the tongue like the floury-white dough they were made of.

Everything at the railway station seemed monumental and uninviting, and we had no idea how to transport all the baggage to the halls of residence where we had both been allocated rooms. Each of us had a trunk and suitcases which were too heavy to carry, and there was no sign of any porters.

"You wait with the luggage and I'll go and see if I can find a trolley." A chill wind took my breath away as I rounded the corner and into an arch that led to a main street. A few yards farther on I saw a man in British Rail uniform who spoke some words to me in an accent which I was at a loss to decode, but more helpfully pointed to the place where I could see a line of trolleys stacked together. It was with some difficulty that I freed one from a tangle of twisted metal and set off to return to where I had left Harriet.

I turned the corner and scanned the concourse, expecting her to be standing alone with our luggage. Instead I was surprised to see a group of three people in the place where she had been. Harriet was helping a station porter to manhandle our trunks and cases onto a heavy-duty trolley. Standing on the other side, and lifting a large case I recognized as my own was another figure, and it took a few moments for me to compute that the shape was familiar. I felt as though someone had kicked me in the stomach. It was Brendan Harcourt.

I had made it my business in recent months to have as little to do with Brendan as I could, and indeed had no idea even that he was attending a university at all. This, then, was a complete and unwelcome surprise. The prospect of having him near to me and, more importantly, near to Harriet, for the next three years, left me reeling. I closed the last few yards and caught the end of what he was saying.

"…and so my dad has arranged for a local driver to collect me. He has a minibus so I'd be glad to offer you both a lift." Of course it was the effect of my prejudice distorting the moment in retrospect, but did the tip of his tongue in that split second end in just a hint of a fork? Such a silly notion. Nor did the bright red hair and matching eyebrows evoke any spectre from the underworld in any reality beyond that inhabited by my screwed-up brain. I was about to refuse his offer, but Harriet had the advantage of me and responded before I could collect my wits.

"That would be lovely. Thanks, Brendan." She seemed far less surprised by his presence than I was. "Are you going to Havelock Hall?" He was. We all were. Our destiny was unfolding.

* * *

Harriet and I were both housed conveniently close to each other on different wings of halls of residence situated on the Town Moor close to the centre of the city. Havelock Hall was a purpose-built block, maybe only three or four years old at that time, about a mile from the university. Each student had a small room with a single bed, a desk, a lamp and a tiny cubicle at one end where there was a wardrobe and drawers, and a small sink and mirror. There were a dozen rooms on a corridor with a kitchen and shower at the end of each one. Three different halls of residence on one site, each accommodating about 330 students, making just short of one thousand in total.

Notwithstanding the strictures on free circulation on the girls' corridors, this was the first time in our young lives that we had been able to make love at more or less any time of the day or night, and to be together every night if we wanted to. The restriction of a single bed, if it interrupted our sleep, was a small price to pay for such freedom. We felt lucky to be born into these times, in this age, with these privileges and this amount of adventure still ahead of us. Like the pictures from my parents' photo album, the snapshots from the time suggest no cloud anywhere on our horizons.

Even in paradise, however, there can be wisps which temporarily obscure the warmth of the sun, and I, as I have already confessed, was prone to jealousy. Sometimes Harriet and I would arrange to meet in between lectures, and when I arrived at our rendezvous I would find her chatting to a group of mates from her department. Though I could never identify anything specifically untoward, frequently I felt a sense of discomfort. Maybe it was because it seemed that all of the new friends she was making were men, and I thought back to earlier times and realized that her circle always seemed to be made up of male friends rather than women.

When, from a short distance, I saw her laugh her uninhibited laugh, I felt a twinge of anxiety that it was possible for her to laugh so easily without me being close by. How stupid that must seem. No doubt it was possible to interpret her demeanour simply as friendly, open and outgoing. What I saw, however, or thought I saw, seemed rather more like flirting. There was never anything serious or overt, but perhaps just a level of intimacy which made me uncomfortable. Maybe it was just the realization that not everything in Harriet's life revolved one hundred per cent around me.

I do not wish to leave the impression that at this time I was consumed by jealousy. Not at all. It's only that as I look back from my current vantage point at the progression of events that led to what lay ahead, I must identify those days as a significant part of the process.

There was, to take one example, Jed. Tall, slim, good-looking, black hair and a perpetual three days' growth of beard. I remember the beard – so obviously far more full and coarse than the barely post-adolescent fluff which sprouted unevenly on my chin. These things seemed to matter, to me at least, but I never had the insight or wit to learn whether they mattered a hoot to Harriet. There was another one called Martin, the same sort of thing actually. I had seen them together in a group, walking along a corridor way ahead of me, probably not actually touching, but with hands by their sides so that a smallest twist of the wrist would spell the difference between innocence and agony. Just two inches of empty space separated an innocuous exchange from the end of my world. The smallest touch, maybe accidental, would make my house of cards come tumbling down.

Perhaps it was the common bond they found in their adherence to music that brought them together. While Jed rather unexpectedly majored in violin, Martin's instrument was the viola. I recall the day that Harriet first told me that she had agreed to become part of a small collective of students who would play regularly together. They were encouraged to do so by the course tutors, and probably they could earn a bit of spare money. Naturally I was horrified.

"Who else will be in your collection?" – as though I didn't already know the answer.

"Martin and Jed. We're still looking for a fourth."

"Any chance that could be another woman?" I heard myself saying. "That way you'll make a lovely foursome."

I remember it so well because for a long time I had been trying to remain silent on the subject of my feelings of jealousy, and this was the first occasion in a while that I had

53

broken my resolve. Also, I still have within my mental hard drive a precise snapshot of the expression on Harriet's face: a perfect mix of surprise and disbelief, with the slightest hint of indignation thrown in. The indignation, however, was growing by the second.

"What?" There was no doubting that she was genuinely amazed. "What on earth are you talking about? You don't?…" I could see that she was working hard in trying to process the thought, and seemed undecided whether to laugh or to cry.

"I'm just saying that you already seem to spend a lot of time with these guys, and this'll mean spending a whole lot more."

She was still struggling with what seemed to be the totally new thought that she had given me any reason to be jealous, and that I was plainly feeling so.

"But what the fuck are you saying?…" Clearly the "laugh" option was receding. "I've never given you the slightest reason. After all, you fuck me just about every night of the week. What on earth are you talking about?"

The word "fuck" did not pop up frequently in Harriet's usual vocabulary, and so now I knew I had to try to put the genie back into the bottle, but there was nowhere to retreat to. As I looked at her I could see the heat of her incandescence increasing.

"I'm not saying anything. Obviously I'm talking bollocks, but surely you can understand. I love you so much and I guess it's hard for me to see you so close to guys who obviously fancy you so much."

"Neither Martin nor Jed fancy me. And it wouldn't make any difference if they did, because I am committed to you, for all the difference it seems to make to you."

"Obviously I don't mistrust you, and I know you are committed and I love that you are. But please don't tell me that Martin and Jed don't fancy you. It couldn't be any more obvious if they stood under your balcony and sang sonnets to music."

"What... the hell... are you *on*?" I don't think I had ever heard Harriet's voice go above an everyday volume before this, and it made me feel nervous to see her losing control. I could feel my own pulse quickening as I wondered whether to escalate or defuse. Something about Harriet's demeanour – evidently simmering just short of total explosion – told me that defusing was the better option.

"I'm not on anything. Or if I am on anything, I'm on you. And maybe my addiction to you has made me a bit deranged, but nothing is going to convince me that these guys don't fancy you. They're blokes, for fuck's sake, and if they've got red blood in their veins, they fancy you." I paused for a second to let the compliment seep in. "So possibly you have sent out signals to them that they haven't got a hope, but that won't stop most blokes from trying – it wouldn't stop me from trying if I didn't have you already – and it won't stop them."

"So I guess that all you've got to do is to trust me."

"It is. That's right, it's all I have to do, and I do. Of course I do. But what you've got to realize is that I am so exposed with you: I love you so much and I'm so vulnerable that you've got to make allowances for a little bit of occasional lunacy. Because I am lunatic about you. Fucking potty about you, and so I am deranged. I just am and that's that. You are going to have to try to find a way to get used to it. "

You know that moment when things have been headed in either one direction or the other, either towards thermonuclear or back from the brink, and you see a turning point and realize it's all going to be OK? That's what it was like. As I spoke these words I could see the tension draining from Harriet's face and almost feel the temperature dropping in the room. Her expression morphed before my eyes from one of tempestuous and righteous indignation to what I choose to believe was a wave of love. She came towards me and took my right hand in hers. "So what's the bottom line on this musical group then?"

"What do you mean, what's the bottom line? You're doing it, obviously, and I had better get used to the idea."

"No, I'm not. Not if you don't want me to."

And just like that, she had turned the tables on me and I was the one who was cornered. As if there was any way I could stop her now – but I had achieved most of what I wanted.

"So you're saying that if I don't want you to do it, you won't do it." I said, unable to resist the temptation.

"Yes that is what I'm saying," she responded without hesitation. "I have to form a quartet for my course, but if you are unhappy about me hooking up with Jed and Martin, then I'll try to find some other women and get together with them. I'm sure it will be possible."

"OK, so I'd have to be some kind of an arse to insist on that, but thank you for offering it. I appreciate that. I really do. But no, you go ahead... and I'll just get used to the idea of these guys drooling over you."

"That's right. You can think of them getting to drool over me, while you get to take me home every night and make love to me. If you can get your head around it, that should feel rather good to you."

"I can see its merits, certainly," I said. "On which topic..."

We made love, and for that time, she and I were alone in the world. She was me, and I was her, and I would have staked my life that we would never part.

Chapter Six

For all this time, still there was Roger. Roger Roger Roger. Still living at home with my parents, of course, but now attending full-time at an adult centre of some sort and staying home at evenings and weekends. I don't think I ever knew exactly what he did there. All I knew was that each day Mum used to walk with him to the end of the road where a mini-bus would stop at 8.30 a.m. and pick him up. Then she would be at the same spot at 6 p.m. that evening to bring him home.

I spent that first summer vacation from Newcastle back at my parents' house, and a few times I walked with Roger to the bus. The first time I did it, I recall that I walked down the road with Roger but that I hadn't given much thought to what his day would be like. I remember that the van pulled alongside us at the pavement and I looked through the windows at the other passengers.

Maybe half of the fifteen or so seats in the bus were occupied. A couple of the people in them had Down syndrome – one of them was apparently about fourteen years old and the other maybe twice that age. I remember seeing the younger kid laughing and giggling with apparently untarnished delight when he saw Roger, greeting him like a great old friend he hadn't seen for six months, when in fact they had of course been together just the previous day. A couple of people were bent and twisting in their seats and making involuntary movements, jerky and uncontrolled.

I found myself looking hard at one man in particular. From the neck upwards he could have been a bank clerk or a stockbroker – groomed hair, smooth skin, passive face. However from the neck down he seemed to be nothing less than a person possessed, apparently locked in a perpetual battle with some malevolent demon which was wrestling him from the inside out. Like an innocent man in a full-body straitjacket, struggling for freedom against ungiving leather straps. It was a shock.

Another young man sat and rocked backwards and forwards, seemingly oblivious to any adverse consequences arising from the fact that he was banging his head against the back of the seat with alarming force.

I was struck by the contrast between all these other people and the appearance and behaviour of Roger, but was brought back to reality when the bus driver opened the door and shouted what seemed to be a sincere welcome, but at the volume you usually reserve for an idiot. I found myself feeling grateful to the driver and cross with him at the same time. He nodded to me in the way that two white strangers might acknowledge each other if passing in a street in the Congo.

Roger's demeanour when he got on the bus was one of great enthusiasm, not looking back at me as he departed, and immediately he was absorbed with the undiluted joy of seeing his friends. I stood and watched as the old bus headed for the horizon, belching out black fumes as it did so. I was ready to wave goodbye to Roger, but he did not glance round.

Back at the house, I waited for a few minutes, making tea for Mum and Dad and perching on the edge of the kitchen table before I spoke.

"I was a bit amazed at the state of some of the people on the bus."

"What do you mean?"

"Well, most of them seem so much more damaged or troubled than Roger is. I know that Roger has lots of problems, but it can't be too good for him to be hanging out with people with bigger problems than he has."

My father said nothing for a little while, obviously weighing carefully how to put what he wanted to get across. When he spoke, it was with a weariness which had the instant effect of making me feel guilty for even having raised the subject.

"I think Roger is a bit more damaged, as you put it, than we think of him as being. Because he is so used to us, his behaviour when he's here can be much more predictable than when he is with people or in situations he finds unfamiliar. There have been a few problems…" I could see him hesitating, trying to work out what was the best way to express the next bit to the younger brother of the "damaged" person. "But basically we're bloody grateful for it because it gives us a bit of a break."

I don't think he intended it to cause me to experience an enormous wave of guilt, but that was what happened. I glanced at my mother, whose eyes were watering. She took a few steps to the kitchen table to tear off a piece of kitchen roll.

"What your father is saying is that neither he nor I are getting any younger. You have reservations about Roger going into a place like that, and we have reservations about it too. But Roger is Roger, and he's always going to need some support of that kind, and we aren't going to be able to provide it for him for ever."

"I know that, but obviously when that time comes, I'll take care of him."

I have no idea where the words came from. I had never really given serious thought to what I was now saying. I think I must have assumed that I would take care of Roger when my parents could not, but had never spelt it out, either to myself or to them.

"It's nice to hear you say so, Jonathan," said my dad, "but realistically you won't be able to do that."

"Why do you say that?"

"Because you won't. One way or another, looking after Roger is more or less a full-time responsibility. And you won't be able to take it on, because you'll have a full-time job yourself. With luck you'll have a wife who, heaven help her, will have enough bloody trouble looking after you, let alone your half-helpless brother."

If it was clear that I had not thought it through, it was every bit as clear that they had.

"I understand all that, but I don't agree that looking after Roger is a full-time job. Sure he's got problems, but it's not as though he's going to fall out of a window or set fire to the house, is it?"

The simple fact was that I had always been reluctant to accept that Roger was as far from normal as everyone else seemed to think he was. And obviously I now felt a strong sense of guilt that Roger had to spend his time with people in similar circumstances at all. Where was I, his only brother, when he needed me?

"What are you planning to do with these holidays?" I'm not sure even now if there was any irony intended in the juxtaposition of this question with what had just passed. If so, at the time it was lost on me.

"Oh, take some time off, do some college work, and I guess I had better get a job of some sort." I think probably I had a brief moment of clarity, because I added, "and obviously take time to do some stuff with Roger."

"You'll be lucky." Even at the time, I thought that was an odd thing to say. Though I loved Roger every bit as much as any kid would love his brother, there was no escaping the fact that spending time with him was not much like spending time with any normal person. It wasn't that I regarded doing so as an act of charity, but the idea that I'd be lucky to be able to do so was certainly an unfamiliar one to me.

"Why so?"

"Because you'll do well to tear him away from that bloody insect farm of his. He spends every spare minute he's got in the shed doing one thing or another with it."

The insect farm. I had scarcely given a thought to the insect farm since he had shown it to Harriet many months earlier.

"Why do you say 'bloody'? I'd have thought it was a perfect way for him to spend his time without having to trouble the pair of you."

"We thought so too," said my dad, "but the doctor at his day school says that he is spending too much time with it, and is becoming obsessed to the exclusion of the other things he needs to do. They say that someone like Roger needs a variety of other types of stimulation if he's to develop at all. It wouldn't matter if he spent a few hours a week with the thing, but he spends every possible moment in the shed, and when he does it's like he's in a trance. After he comes out, he sort of goes blank for a few hours, and then he just heads off to bed."

It was easy to see the logic. Roger had always responded well to new things happening in his life. For example, he would get tremendously excited whenever Dad was about to buy a new car. From the moment it was first mentioned he would become preoccupied with what kind it would be, what would be the colour, what would be the features. Sometimes when we were younger he would prevail upon my mother to send off to the manufacturer for as much information as possible. For weeks on end glossy brochures would drop through the letter box, and would become the object of complete absorption, until Roger could recite by heart every detail of the horsepower, the type and configuration of brakes, and any and all modifications to the gearbox versus the earlier model. When the new car would eventually arrive he was like a five-year-old on Christmas morning, unable to know where to put himself for his excitement. He would want to sit in the driver's seat, and then the passenger seat, and then in the rear seats. Once, memorably, he was desperately keen to remain in the boot when the lid closed, simply to ensure that the interior light went out.

These were some of the fun times we all had with Roger, and was part of what marked him out as the unique individual that he was. They were the best of times for him. The idea that he was now becoming so immersed in one subject, albeit something as apparently harmless as his insect farm, felt wrong.

"Have you tried restricting the times he can be down there?"

My father said that they had, and at first had prevented him from going down there for more than an hour in the early mornings and half an hour in the evenings.

"Well, what happened?" I asked.

"What happened was that he would do as he was told, of course, but he would just spend the rest of the time sitting next to the kitchen window and staring down the garden at the outside of the shed. It didn't matter what we did, all he was doing was passing the time until he was allowed back there. In the end it just seemed cruel to keep him away from it, and so we let him go back. At least he was doing something, rather than just staring out of the window."

"But what does he do down there for such a long time?" I asked. "There must be a limit to what you can do? It's only a heap of soil and some bugs, for Christ's sake."

"That's what you think."

Dad opened the door from the kitchen leading to the back garden and headed off down the path. I stepped out into the sunshine and fell in behind him, noticing for the first time that my father had begun to adopt a trace of the shuffling gait of an older man. I watched as his bumpy fingers fumbled with the keys in the padlock. He was only in his mid-fifties at that time, but I knew that he had been suffering from progressive arthritis for some years. Only now did I notice that his knuckles were swollen and his fingers were distorted out of shape, and as I watched him it seemed to me that his hand was shaking.

"Are you OK, Dad?"

"Yes," he said, turning to face me. "Why do you ask?"

"No reason. I thought that maybe your hand was shaking a bit."

My dad laughed, apparently carelessly, and turned back to the task. "Too much coffee I expect. Since your mother got that new percolator I think I must be suffering from a caffeine addiction." I looked at his profile as his frustration mounted, and once again he seemed to be a much older man than the one I thought of as my father. "Bloody thing," he said, "it gets stiff after the rain." I was on the brink of offering to help when the lock snapped open, and I realized that it would have been an error to have intervened.

He pulled open the door and his hand fumbled against the inside wall as he sought the switch. A series of strip lights had been mounted on the walls and on the ceiling, and for a few seconds it seemed like the first flickering hint of an electrical storm. Moments later the blackness inside was illuminated by a strange blue half-light, more in keeping with the interior of a spacecraft than a garden shed.

"Bloody hell, Dad. What on earth has been going on here?"

You know what it's like when your mind thinks it knows what it expects to see, but then what happens next is completely different? It takes a while to become reorientated. That's what happened here. I had a mental image from the last time I had been in there with Harriet, when the contents of the shed had been a series of glass-fronted display-cases, stacked up against the wall one on top of another. What I now saw looked more like the inside of one of those animal-experimentation laboratories you read about in the Sunday supplements.

Not that there was anything recognizable as an animal. No ugly experiments going on involving chemicals or electrodes, but all of the walls were now obscured by glass-fronted cases of various shapes and sizes, and all of the containers held different materials of every texture and colour. Some seemed to be nothing more than deep-brown soil or mud, while others consisted of bigger grains and sometimes pale blue, sometimes pale green gravel or tiny stones.

At first glance, and with my eyes still adjusting, it was not possible to detect much movement or anything of great interest. Only if you concentrated on one tank, in one spot, and focused in tight close-up, could you begin to make out the interconnecting highways and tunnels which made up the networks of these communities. The first one I looked at, close to the door and benefiting from some extra light from outside, contained what seemed like ordinary soil. I recognized it as the project Roger had been working on when I first brought Harriet to meet him. Looking closer at it now, I could make out the grooves which had been excavated next to the glass, enabling tens and then hundreds of oversized ants to tumble over each other, darting this way and that, apparently indiscriminately.

"Dad," I said, "what on earth is in all of these?"

"God knows. I lost track of them months ago. Worms, beetles, butterflies, locusts, spiders – you name it, he is collecting it."

My attention shifted further into the shed, where I could see some glass tanks which were not filled with soil, but instead were more like very narrow aquariums – with bits of stick and leaves where you might expect to see weeds and a sunken shipwreck. At first glance there seemed to be nothing moving, but then my dad pointed out the shape of a huge moth, its wings more or less indistinguishable from its surroundings, sitting motionless on a fragment of twig. "I believe they're from South America," said my dad, "very rare apparently."

"Astonishing. Does he send for them, or what?"

"Some he does. He spends everything he earns – from whatever bits of work he does at the day centre and anything your mum and I give him – on mail order, and so there's a constant stream of parcels arriving at the door." He gestured towards the wall at the back of the shed, which was piled high with cardboard boxes, most of them small and square. I walked across to look more closely and examined the labels.

"*Lep-tin-o-tarsa decem-lineata.*" The words were entirely unfamiliar and I pronounced each syllable slowly and separately, and then again, trying to get a flow. "I wonder what that is in English." I picked up several others and squinted at the names through the half-light. *Timarcha tenebricosa. Dorcus parallelipipedus. Sinodendron cylindricum.* I tried another one aloud: "*Xestobium rufovillosum.* Are all these inside these tanks and starting up their own colonies?"

"That's one of the few names I recognize," said Dad. "It's the deathwatch beetle. Over here." I walked across to where he was standing and he indicated one of the tanks which, like most of the others, seemed to contain only decaying twigs and leaves. Once again I had to wait for my eyes to adjust to be able to make out the tiny creatures. "Press your ear to the glass," said my dad. I did so, and after a few moments I could hear a faint clicking sound. "That's a mating call which they make when they are boring holes in your floorboards. I told Roger to make sure they are secure, because they'll eat the bloody house if you give them the chance."

"You see, that's extraordinary," I said, "and illustrates what I was saying earlier. You can't see anyone else on that bus being capable of even embarking on something like this. We all know that Roger has his problems, but you've got to have grasped a huge amount of stuff to be able to put all this together."

"All I can tell you is that his doctors and carers say he is too obsessed by it. After all," my dad's tone of voice changed a bit, as if he was reverting to a matter of greater gravity, "after all, by the time your mum and I can't look after him any more, Roger is going to have to be as independent as he can be. He needs to be able to do some kind of work which will pay a few bills and keep him occupied, but he will need extra support as well as that – and will have to find a way to pay for it. And I don't think the insect farm is going to do it."

The subject had gone away, but now, in the absence of my mother, it had come back again. At eighteen or nineteen, you still assume that your parents are going to live for ever. They seem to have been put on the earth to serve you and your needs, and the idea that that may one day stop is far off your horizon. Obviously at that time I had no way of knowing that the life-changing decisions which were going to be necessary were in fact coming up quite so soon.

Chapter Seven

Life at university gave Harriet the freedom to develop her individuality even further than before, and wherever she went and whatever we were doing, she could always be relied upon to stand out. At college discos, when most students cultivated studied neglect, she might wow the crowds by dressing as a Spanish flamenco dancer, complete with corsets, cleavage and roses in her hair. Often the men found it impossible to disguise the effect she had on them, and I would catch a glimpse of some of the girls who made little effort to hide their disapproval. One day I was struggling to finish an essay when she burst into my room bubbling over with the news that the quartet had been booked to play at a dinner and award ceremony for the Royal Television Society at the Grosvenor House Hotel in London. There would be TV producers and even some celebrities there, and who knew what might follow from such a gig? It was their first really grown-up and professional engagement, and they had been told that they would have to wear formal dress.

I hadn't ever seen Harriet wearing a ball gown before, and it's not within my powers of vocabulary to express the effect it had on me. She looked absolutely fabulous, quite literally breathtaking and, as far as I was concerned, about ten years older than her twenty years. Suddenly she was a proper adult, doing something properly grown up, in the real world, and getting paid real money for her efforts. It was a shock.

The quartet had been hired to provide background music while everyone gathered to drink champagne and get a bit oiled up before their dinner and the prizes. She had managed to wangle a job for me at the same event, walking around with trays of canapés, and as I look back on it I realize that she had probably done so because of the risk that otherwise I might actually be physically consumed by my own jealousy. After our falling-out on the subject, I obviously had to withdraw my objections to her teaming up with Martin and Jed, but my initial reservations were nothing compared to what I had felt a few weeks later when she came home and told me the proposed fourth member of the quartet.

"Brendan Harcourt? You have got to be fucking kidding me. "

"Why have I got to be kidding you?"

"Because, for one thing, fucking Brendan isn't even in the fucking music department. And that's before I get on to the 2.4 million other reasons why I don't believe it."

"Brendan's major is Economics, but his minor subject is Music. But the most important thing is that he plays the cello, and everyone else in the department who plays the cello has already joined another group, so we didn't have a lot of choice."

The long and the short of it was that Brendan Harcourt was there that night, playing in a quartet with Martin and Jed and

Harriet, and I loved one of them and hated the other three. More accurately, I loved one of them, disliked two and hated the fourth, and now I also hated all these blokes dressed up like penguins who had no reason or occasion to disguise their lust for my girlfriend, while I had little choice but to listen quietly as more and more drunken jackasses made less and less subtle remarks about what they would like to do with her.

"Have you seen that fabulous bird in the quartet?" The speaker was an overweight ex-public-school boy who looked like a refugee from the Billy Bunter books, and this was the way over-educated hooligans talked to each other in those days. "What I wouldn't do to her given half a chance."

"I'm sure it would make her night to hear that, Roderick," said his friend. "Shall I ask her if she'd like your telephone number?"

The leer on Bunter's face turned quickly to pain as I walked past with my tray of drinks and the heel of my left shoe accidentally trampled his right foot.

"Oh I say, steady," he squealed, and began to hop on one leg.

"I'm so very sorry," I said, but it had been my single moment of pleasure of the entire event.

All things taken together, in fact, it was one of the worst evenings of my life, maybe actually the worst up until that point. Serving drinks and snacks, clearing huge stacks of empty glasses from tables, trying to stay calm and casual as these stuffed shirts got themselves more drunk and ill-mannered. Had the evening gone on for another half an hour,

I guess I would have ended up decking one of them and being thrown out, or worse. As it was, after five hours it was all over and Harriet and I were sitting on the train on the way home to my parents' house in Croydon, where she and I were both staying. Neither of us had spoken since leaving the hotel.

"Well, that went well, I thought."

"What went well?"

"Jonathan," she said, clearly exasperated, "this was our first proper gig. It was important to me that it went well. I felt it did. I'm sorry that I have to ask you what you thought."

It is part of the folly of youth that we think that every event is all about ourselves, and instantly I realized that I'd been a total fool in failing to see and respond to the significance of the thing for Harriet.

"Oh God, Harriet, I am so sorry." I knew I had screwed up badly and it was too late to row back, but also that I had to try. "It was great. By which I mean that you were great. You looked great, you sounded great and you all went for it as though you'd been playing performances like that for years. You were fabulous."

It was late but it was working, and instantly I could see her indignation beginning to melt away. Of course she wanted more.

"People seemed to enjoy it," she said. "We got loads of people asking for contact details at the end of the evening."

"I'll bet," I said, then, making my next mistake of the night, asked, "Did any of them also want to get in touch with the guys?"

It took Harriet a second to understand what I was talking about, but when she did, the blow across my arm from the case containing her flute nearly obliged me to divert to the nearest hospital.

"Whoa, Harriet! Be careful with that. You could do some serious damage." She didn't reply. "Listen, I'm not saying that people didn't appreciate the music. Of course they did. You sounded great, but so do loads of other quartets, several others of which were there tonight." I was nursing my arm. "Let's face it, you look bloody lovely, and even you cannot have failed to notice the army of gibbons lusting after you half the night. I nearly had to call the keeper once or twice." Her silence confirmed that what I had said was undeniable, and her slight smile indicated that she did not mind at all.

Harriet's parents were still living abroad, but by now her father had retired from his job with the government. As far as I could tell, he was now some sort of go-between on behalf of Arabs who wanted to sell oil and newly emerging nations which wanted to buy it. The point was that she had nowhere to live out of university term time. My parents were happy for her to stay at our house, but were not sufficiently enlightened to allow us to sleep together, and so during the holidays I slept on a made-up campbed in the corner of Roger's bedroom, while Harriet took the single bed in my old room.

On this night, however, I would have given anything to be able to do with Harriet exactly what all those morons at the awards ceremony had fantasized about. I put my hands on her hips as she walked ahead of me up the stairs, and when she turned towards me she was smiling.

"Jonathan, I don't think so," she whispered. "It would wake your parents."

I was disappointed, but knew she was probably right. By now it was the early hours of the morning, and there was complete silence in the house. "Anyway, to be honest, I'm shattered." She bent down from her exalted position on the stair ahead of me and kissed me on the forehead. "Maybe tomorrow?"

I put a brave face on the inevitable and managed a half-hearted smile.

"Yes, tomorrow."

Despite the very long day and emotional exhaustion, I found sleeping on an air mattress in Roger's room a challenge. I closed my eyes and tried to empty my head of all the unwelcome thoughts which had filled it during the evening. My best efforts were to little avail, and my mind was invaded by images of this exquisitely beautiful creature surrounded by ever more grotesque and multiplying caricatures of sweating and salivating men. No matter how determined I was to convince myself that my anxieties were unfounded, somehow I was simply unable to accept that Harriet was entirely mine, and that niggling sharp edge of doubt was enough to drive me to distraction.

It was already getting light before I dozed off, and when I woke four hours later, everyone was up and about, and I was glad to see Harriet and my parents chatting over breakfast in the kitchen. I asked where Roger was.

"See if you can guess," said my dad. I opened the back door into the garden and walked down the path to see him. For some reason it seemed appropriate that I should knock on the door of the shed – the insect farm felt like his exclusive domain. Hearing no response, I turned the handle carefully and stepped into the gloom.

"Hi, Roger. How did you sleep?"

My brother turned to look up from the workbench and smiled at me but, as quite often happened, he did not feel it necessary to answer my question. I walked towards him and stood by his shoulder. Lying flat on the surface in front of him on the desktop was a perspex sheet, covering what looked like an aerial view of a huge and busy metropolis. As usual I needed time for my eyes to adjust to the light, and as they did I could see thousands upon thousands of oversized ants, some larger than others, some with red markings and others with black markings, scurrying around as if in the Tokyo rush hour.

"Wow, Roger," I said. "This is great. What's going on here?" Clearly he was delighted to be asked.

"These are my new red tropical fire ants," he announced proudly. "They come from Western Australia. I sent for them. They are as old as the dinosaurs, and they have an advanced social system where they look after the young and the old, and all of them take care of their queen."

Neither of us spoke for a while as I looked more closely at the apparently frantic activity going on beneath me. I noticed a piece of polythene tubing extending from a hole which had been drilled in the perspex. Just at the open end of the tube, lying on the bench, lay the half-decomposed carcass of a caterpillar. Perhaps three hundred ants were clambering all over it, nudging and prodding and nibbling.

"Some of the soldier ants stand guard while the others feed – but the ones climbing all over it don't actually eat what they are consuming. They take it into what's called their 'social stomach'. When they have had their fill, they return to the nest, and regurgitate the food to their young and the old."

"That's cute," I said. "How do they do that?"

Again Roger did not hesitate. "Through kissing," he said. "They clamp their mouths together and transfer it, and when the younger and older ants have had enough to eat, the soldier ants digest what's left for themselves."

"And they all take care of the queen?"

"Yes," he said, "that seems to be the purpose of their lives. To look after the queen."

"A feeling I know well," I said. Roger looked sideways at me, not quite understanding what I was talking about. After a moment that seemed not to matter, and next time I glanced at him he was absorbed once more in his project, apparently unaware that I was even present alongside him.

Chapter Eight

Two weeks later Harriet and I were back in Newcastle for the new term. It was 3 a.m. and she and I were asleep in my single bed when I became aware of a soft but determined knock on the door. The previous night there had been a discotheque in the halls of residence and we had gone to bed late, our sleep deepened by an excess of alcohol. Only gradually did the sound permeate my consciousness. I mumbled something which would have been incomprehensible even had anyone else been awake to hear it, and swung my legs out of bed, searching for my underpants among the detritus of student life. I'm not sure if I even dozed off again in the process, because half a minute later I heard the same knocking, as if to nudge me.

When whatever will be the modern equivalent of the Gestapo eventually comes for me, 3 a.m. would be the best time to do it. I felt totally disorientated, with no more idea of what could be causing this interruption than I had any sense of my surroundings or time of day. "Just a second. Just a second. I'll be there," I called out, pulling on the T-shirt I had discarded a few hours earlier.

Eventually I was able to pull open the door a few inches, and I squinted into the corridor, which was barely illuminated by emergency night lights. I found myself trying to focus on the face of Mr Stroud, who was the hall warden. Behind him I could see the uniformed shape of Wilf, the hall porter who did double shifts as the nightwatchman.

"Sorry to disturb you, Jonathan," said the warden. "Are you alone?"

I wasn't immediately clear about the reason for asking and considered lying, but even in my confused state, I soon realized that this would be a pointless deception. "No, Warden, I have my girlfriend with me. We were just—"

"That doesn't matter." I was clearly on the wrong track. "Would you mind just popping on your dressing gown and coming down to the Lodge for a moment? I need a quick word with you."

Something about his manner prevented me from saying "at three in the morning?", because my brain was gradually beginning to sharpen up, and even I could work out that he would know what time it was.

"Sure thing, give me a couple of minutes. But what is it about?"

"Just pop a few clothes on and come down," he said. "Better to speak downstairs."

Harriet was resting on her elbows when I came back into the room and I should be ashamed to admit that it crossed my mind how that position made her breasts stick up in a way which made me want to climb back into bed with her.

"What's happening?"

I told her that I had no idea, but that the warden needed to have a word with me downstairs in his residence. Even slower to become alert than I was, Harriet asked the question I had resisted.

"At three a.m.?"

"Evidently."

"I can't be about me being here, can it?"

"No, I don't think so." Even then, it still hadn't really occurred to me that this was something serious. "I'll come straight back up when I've spoken to him."

I walked through the silent corridors, my mind searching for the possible explanation but failing to reach any conclusions. The door to the warden's residence was ajar when I got there, but I tapped on it anyway. "Come on in, Jonathan," I heard him say. I had been in his sitting room months before, at a reception for Freshers. It was altogether like an upgraded version of the junior common room, except that there were books everywhere. The pictures on the walls looked as though they had been bought at the local department store and had been purchased to be innocuous rather than arresting. My confusion increased when I saw that he was there with his wife, who was wearing her dressing gown, her hair still dishevelled.

"Can I get you some tea, Jonathan?"

I declined, still more confused than anxious to find out what was going on. The warden asked me to sit down and I did.

"Jonathan, I'm afraid I have some bad news for you." Looking back on it, I can see that he knew what he was going to say, but was measuring the pace at which to say it. Just as, when you are imparting words of great import, you need to ensure that each one is going in before moving on to the next, and you don't want to cause confusion by getting ahead of yourself. His words came out one at a time, with no joins between them, all carefully enunciated. Exactly, in fact, as though he was talking to an idiot.

"Jonathan, there has been an accident at your parents' house," he said, and waited for that thought to sink in. "There has been a fire." He paused again. One step at a time, making sure it was all computing before proceeding. "I'm afraid that there has been some serious damage and that your parents have been badly hurt." Another pause. "They were both taken to hospital." One, two, three seconds. "But I'm afraid that they seem to have suffered from smoke inhalation." One, two, three more seconds. "And Jonathan," beat, beat, beat, "I cannot tell you how sorry I am to have to say that both are in a critical condition, and are being treated in intensive care."

God knows what I was thinking. I was aware of the warden's wife planting herself on the sofa beside me and taking one of my hands in both of hers. The face of the warden was a mix of sadness and apprehension, like someone standing at the bedside of a dying man, expecting at any moment for them to expire. But he was waiting, waiting for just a few more seconds. "Jonathan," he said at last, "I am so so sorry."

I can still vividly recall the feeling that the electronics of my brain were exploding, as thoughts and shock waves burst down the nerves, scrambling anything that got in their way. Even now I don't know why this was the first more or less coherent thought that came into my mind.

"What about Roger?"

"I'm sorry?"

"Who's Roger?" It was the first time the warden's wife had spoken since the offer of tea. I looked at her as though the answer to her question was too obvious to justify a response.

"Roger. My brother Roger. He will have been in the house too." I think the volume of my voice was increasing with the intensity of my panic. "What has happened to Roger?"

Now the warden was confused and obviously at a loss. "I'm so sorry, Jonathan. I am just passing on what we have been told."

"By who?"

The warden stood up and went towards the window, pulling back the curtains. I could see that outside there was a police car. A uniformed officer was standing beside the car, apparently waiting for this signal, and another officer was sitting in the driver's seat. The warden beckoned, and I saw the policeman walk around towards the front entrance to the halls.

I sat with my head in my hands, my fingers digging painfully into my scalp, and was only aware of the warden standing just inside the outer door, conferring in muted words with the policeman. After a few moments I could see the officer step back into the hallway and bring his two-way radio to his lips. In a blur, through the maelstrom of thoughts in my head, I could just make out the odd word here and there.

"Brother... Roger... Yes, in the house apparently."

There was a further conference between the policeman and Mr Stroud before the latter came back and knelt down in front of me. I remember thinking it was not a stance in which he could have been comfortable, and wanting to assure him that I had not suddenly become an invalid.

"The officer says they have no information that there was anyone else in the house. The fire brigade are still out there, and he has asked them to conduct a full search to be sure." Now I wondered if Mr Stroud knew about Roger, because he added, "Could he have been out on his own?"

"No, he couldn't." It came in a louder volume than might have been appropriate, but I don't think I was being rude, maybe just abrupt, the result of anxiety rather than of impatience. "Roger has a handicap. He is twenty-five, but he isn't able to be out of the house at night on his own. He must be there; in the back bedroom. Tell them to look in the back bedroom."

The warden's wife went to speak to the police officer once more. I could half-hear snatches of the conversation in the hallway, but their words were interrupted by the crackle of life from the policeman's hand-held radio. More muffled voices, and after a moment I heard Mrs Stroud suggest that maybe the officer should come in to speak to me himself.

He was a police sergeant, a big presence suddenly filling the room, the blue uniform and brass buttons bringing a new dimension to the occasion. Now it was official; now it was real.

As he entered the room, the officer took off his peaked cap, the first of many prescribed gestures of sympathy which were to characterize the coming weeks. Mrs Stroud was still in the hallway when there was another tapping on the door. She opened it to find Harriet standing outside. Instantly I could see the look of alarm on her face as she registered the warden, his wife and a bloody big policeman. Later she told me she thought it was about the little bit of pot we had been using, a thought which was banished by her first glimpse of the expression on the face of the officer. I got up and walked towards her, now concerned about what would be her reaction to the appalling news.

"Harriet," I took her by the arm and led her to the sofa, urging her to sit. "The warden has had to tell me that there has been a fire at my parents' house. It seems that they were both in the house and have suffered from smoke inhalation." I found that I was doing with Harriet exactly what, just a few minutes earlier, the warden had been trying to do with me. "They've been taken to hospital, but it seems that both are very badly hurt. The warden says they are in a critical condition." The next cliché in the series would no doubt have been "and are not expected to live", but that was not for now.

It was the first time in my life that I had spoken any version of these words, and they seemed to me like a new and bitter taste in my mouth. I felt a wave of nausea run through me and in that instant thought surely that I would vomit. Then I caught sight of Harriet's face, still not comprehending what she had heard, and struggling to take it on board. When finally she did, I was amazed by what she said.

"What about Roger?"

Now the policeman, who had been just about to speak when Harriet arrived, resumed what he had been saying.

"It seems that the first reports were correct, and that there was no sign of any third person on the premises." He had lapsed into the mode which is usually reserved for giving evidence in court, choosing his words carefully and instinctively protecting and justifying the actions of the force. "However, one of my colleagues has subsequently carried out a full search of the whole premises, and he found a young man in his early twenties, apparently hiding in a shed at the bottom of the garden."

My mind whirled with questions, and foremost among them was what on earth was Roger doing in the shed at that time of the night.

"That will be Roger. Is he OK? Is my brother all right?"

"We believe he is, sir, yes. He seems confused and is probably in shock."

"He'll be traumatized." I turned to the warden. "Roger has a mental handicap. He'll be terrified. He won't know what the hell is happening. I have to get there as fast as possible."

"And to the hospital before there are any further develop-ments with your parents." The words from Mrs Stroud were out before she could catch the look of disapproval on her husband's face. "Not that I mean…" – but it was too late, and no one was in any doubt what she meant.

It seemed that the warden and the police had already had the discussion. There were no trains or planes for several hours, so the police car outside was waiting to take me on the three-hundred-mile journey south "blues and twos".

"What does that mean?" asked Harriet.

"It means that he'll get there in a hurry," said the officer. I could tell it was a question they loved to be asked.

"I want to come with you," said Harriet instantly, and I was about to demur, but decided against it. "Let's go."

Chapter Nine

It was January and a thin layer of snow covered the fields alongside the motorway as we blasted through County Durham and on our way south. I never did ask any questions on the journey. Probably it was because I did not want to know the answers, but I think I also knew that the two silent officers in the front seat would not tell me even if they had anything new. Several times they took calls on their comms system, but I could not make out the import of the muffled words and did not strain to do so. I feared my own misinterpretation of any slight shake of the head, and also any confirmation it might bring me.

It was light and the rush hour was in full swing when finally we reached Croydon Hospital. In spite of the time of day, we had made the journey in just over four hours, so it was about 8.30 when the car stopped outside of the A-and-E department. The expert drivers had played their allocated roles, and I felt that my part in the unfolding drama was to leap out of the door and rush inside, screaming to be directed towards my parents. But I found that I could not do it, much as though my mind and body were reluctant to embrace what was destined to unfold. If I failed to move, failed to enquire, failed to absorb what was coming next, maybe none of it would be true. At last I became aware of the officer who had been driving standing beside me with the door open. By my side, Harriet whispered, "Better go in."

Once inside the reception area, it was clear that we were expected. The glow from our blue light continued to flicker rhythmically onto the glass doors, half reflecting and half penetrating inside. I saw the young man behind the desk reach for the telephone, and he had finished his conversation before Harriet and I reached the counter.

"Mr Maguire?"

"No, that's my dad." It wasn't intended to be flippant; it just came out and the poor bloke was thrown into a little panic.

"Oh yes, sorry," he said. "But you are Jonathan Maguire?" I confirmed that I was. "And your parents are Mr and Mrs George and Judith Maguire?" Hearing their names from the mouth of this stranger stung me, and I felt one side of my face go into an involuntary twitch, as though I was flinching in response to a threatened slap. I nodded. "Will you just wait here a moment? Someone from the ward is coming down to see you."

That was all I needed to know. I could feel the primal scream of the newly orphaned welling up inside of me, and I had to place my hand over my mouth and seem to cough hard in order to suppress the sound. Why did I feel the need to suppress it? Even then, the requirements of convention held sway. I did not wish to make a scene.

We waited, we sat, I paced a bit and then we paced together. It probably wasn't as much as three minutes, but it's funny what goes through your head. What was the point of that mad and dangerous overnight dash if we are now going to have to wait in an antiseptic foyer? We could have waited at that stop sign that we ran through. How do they dare to fritter away the seconds that we had gone to so much effort to save?

I struggle to recall the immediacy of that moment, the turmoil of interacting thoughts buzzing backwards and forwards across the synapses of my brain. What I do remember as clearly today as I saw it then is the expression on the face of the nurse who approached along the corridor a few moments later. The look of someone whose next words were going to change for ever the life of a person they had never met.

"Are you Jonathan Maguire?" You cannot be too careful. You don't want to tell the wrong person that his parents are dead.

I confirmed that I was. She took me by the arm and steered me towards a little alcove off the main foyer – a space with six hard chairs tucked away, just a little aside from the bustle of activity. I had time to register a poster warning against the dangers of drugs, and also indicating where to go to get counselling for obesity. Something in their exhortation rang a bell from a long time ago.

"Would you mind sitting down?"

I had time to wonder how many people had been told this kind of news when standing up and had instantly fallen over. Harriet was alongside of me, and I remember detecting a barely audible whimper as she put her hand on my arm. Oddly enough, it was her distress that sent a pang through me, bringing the tears to the edge of my eyes.

The nurse started to speak, but her words did not compute. I could see her lips moving, but suddenly I could not focus on their meaning, and the only thing I could think about was Roger. Where was Roger? I realized that I hadn't thought about Roger at all for all these last hours, not since asking the question in Newcastle. How weird that now seemed. Ordinarily he would be among my first concerns, yet for all that time I had been thinking about my parents and about myself, about what had happened to them and what was happening to me.

I could make out a few phrases such as "did what we could", and "hung on for as long as possible", but the bottom line was that they were no more. They had not been burnt; the nurse was at pains that I should know that. They had died in their beds from the effects of smoke inhalation. The fire brigade had managed to get into the house to bring them out, before the rest of it was destroyed. They probably had not even been aware that anything was amiss. No doubt the police or the fire officers could answer any further questions I might have.

"What about Roger?" It seemed to be the only question I was capable of asking since being woken in the small hours of the morning. "Where is Roger?"

My question threw everyone into another panic. I explained to the nurse who Roger was, and she was visibly dismayed that she had no idea of the answer. She looked across at the receptionist as if to seek information, but did not find any. She turned around and made a facial enquiry of the officers who had driven us from Newcastle. The response was the same.

"Please wait just a minute, Mr Maguire."

It was some time before the nurse was able to ascertain that Roger had indeed been brought to this hospital, and another few minutes before she was able to determine that he was currently being taken care of in a small side ward just off the main area of the Accident and Emergency Department, just a few steps away. I had the feeling that someone somewhere was going to have to explain why she had not known that there had been another relative in the house, but for the moment that was the least of my concerns.

I was shown to a side room with a small hospital bed on wheels, a steel-framed chair, a sink and a locked cabinet with glass windows full of pharmaceuticals. Sitting upright on the chair, way over in the corner of the room and facing the blank wall, was Roger.

He did not raise his head as I entered the room, and was apparently unaware of my presence as I looked at him. I was about to speak his name, but instead I stood silently for a few moments and watched as he picked up a stethoscope from the table and carefully fitted the earpieces into his ears, and then took the chest piece and pressed it against his heart. I watched as he breathed in, held his breath for a few seconds and then breathed out. Then he gently shook his head, as though preparing to give the patient some bad news. This was my older brother Roger, shortly after his experience of a fire which had killed our parents, almost literally inhabiting a world all his own.

Only then, when gazing across this tiny space at this lost and lonely soul in the corner, did the full weight of what had happened flood into my brain. Like a tap that turned suddenly from a trickle to a torrent, I looked at Roger and felt a deluge of distress filling my head, welling up inside me so that suddenly the tears were pouring down my face in a joined-up stream. Amazingly so, at a rate which I would not have thought possible, it was as though my head was an empty vessel filling up with water which had at that moment reached the overflow and was now pouring out. I could feel the dripping on my shirt, and the snot running from my nose. Despite even all that, something within me was able to suppress the audible sound of the sob which I knew must equally overflow from me. I turned away and back out of the room, quickly identified the route to the exit and ran towards it, just as though I was trying to avoid vomiting in someone's living room.

Harriet was at my side, but I shrugged her away and leant against the wall, instantly bent over as if to throw up. I wasn't going to do so, but I could feel my stomach and chest straining in a physical reaction to the stress.

Harriet, poor Harriet, had no idea what to say; how could anyone know what to say? At that moment I think she was probably more concerned that I might faint than about my emotional state. I saw her glancing around, plainly wondering whether to call for help. But what help could there be? Suddenly the framework of my world had collapsed. The structure upon which rested my equilibrium had been swept away. Where once there had been stability and support, now there was a vacuum. Our family had been halved in an instant, and now it was just me and my older brother Roger. And in so many ways that simply meant that it was just me.

Chapter Ten

No one was able to say for certain what had been the cause of the fire. The forensic people from the fire brigade established that it had started in the kitchen, but such had been the ferocity of the inferno that any evidence that might ever have existed at what they referred to as "the seat of the blaze" had been obliterated.

I went to see the ruins of the house. I don't know why I did, because I had been warned that there was nothing left. The police decided that I should be accompanied by a policewoman when I went along. Again, I'm not sure why – perhaps they thought I would break down among the ashes of my early life. There was, indeed, nothing left other than the charred and blackened shell of what had once been our home. Curiously, the adjoining houses on either side of ours had remained more or less undamaged. I learnt that the neighbours on one side had been away on holiday at the time, and on the other side the family had quickly been evacuated.

The wooden rafters which had supported the roof had burnt, and now protruded through what was left of the plaster like the ground-down stubs of bad teeth. All that remained was the bare brick walls, with nothing which would even indicate where one floor had finished and another had begun. No staircase, not a picture, not a piece of furniture, nothing had been spared. Ironically of course, the only things on the property which remained intact were the garage at the far end of the garden and the garden shed.

"Is it OK for me to go in?" The policewoman thought that it was. I unfastened the catch and entered, and was immediately struck by the fact that nothing in here gave any hint of the mayhem that had occurred just a few yards away. All of Roger's glass tanks, stacked one upon the next, remained undamaged, and if I half-closed my eyes in the gloom I could see his little creatures hurrying and scurrying across their own little landscapes. Hundreds of pairs of eyes, thousands of tiny legs, all going about their business as though nothing untoward had happened. Of course they were just going about their business. Why wouldn't they? The tragedy that had unfolded next door was nothing whatsoever to do with them.

"Will these be all right until someone can work out what to do with them?" It was the voice of the policewoman who was now standing in the doorway. I didn't know for sure, but assumed so.

"I'll ask Roger. I have no idea what care they need, if any."

Having urged me not to visit the house, I at first found it surprising that the police encouraged me to view the bodies of my dead parents. Their rationale was that, after a fire, the bereaved are often left with a dreadful mental image of their loved ones as charred cadavers. In a case like this one, where they had died of smoke inhalation rather than in the flames, they believed that it might be a relief to me to find that they looked peaceful.

It was. They did look peaceful. They also looked far younger than their years. Somehow in death the skin on my father's face seemed to have stretched, smoothing out the worry lines. My mother's face was covered with far more make-up than she would ever have permitted in life, and I remembered the perfume of the powder she was wearing as she hugged me when I left home for university. The police were right to advise me to see them. Now, my last memory of my mum and dad was of them lying alongside each other, not touching but as close as could be, leaving this world together, just as they had lived in it.

My most urgent concern was where Roger was going to live and, for that matter, how and where I was going to live myself. Most of my clothes, books and essential stuff were away with me at university. I had no passport, no birth certificate, no family photographs, no pots, pans, plates, towels, anything. Until I could find time to go back to Newcastle to collect a few items, all I had was more or less what I was wearing.

Recognizing my predicament, a doctor at the hospital arranged that Roger would remain there for a week while I worked out what to do. The assumption being made by everyone around me seemed to be that Roger would be taken into the care of the social services, at least for a period, while I returned to university to finish my degree. That would give everyone enough time to see how he settled in to a new institutional environment. After that, I was assured, we would all be in a better position to decide on a plan for the longer term. I was told that something called a "case conference" would take place at the hospital in two days, when everyone involved in Roger's welfare would be invited to give their views.

"It'll be attended by at least one or two senior members of the staff from the day centre, where they know Roger well." All this was being explained to me by a very good-hearted woman from the local social-services department called Mrs Willis. "There will be a clinical psychologist from the hospital where he is being looked after now, I will be there, and of course there needs to be someone from the family. I presume that's you?" I confirmed that it would be.

"What about Roger?" I asked. Mrs Willis looked surprised. "I was wondering whether Roger himself would be at the case conference? He's not totally incapable and he's not a mute. I think he should be there while a whole lot of people he hardly knows decide his future. Don't you?"

After some hurried phone calls and whispered discussions in corridors, I was informed that, though it was very unusual, Roger would be invited to his own case conference.

I did not get a chance before the meeting to speak to my older brother about what was going to happen, and half a dozen people were already present when I turned up at the appointed time at a glass-walled meeting room at the hospital. Mrs Willis was going to be chairing the discussion, and invited me to sit next to her. Everyone took their places around a large table and started to introduce themselves. I was about to ask about Roger when, through the window into the corridor, I saw a porter pushing a wheelchair in our direction. I was momentarily confused, and then horrified, to see that the forlorn figure apparently slumped in the chair and staring fixedly ahead of him was my brother. I leapt to my feet and went to hold open the door.

"Hi, Roger." I spoke in as cheerful a voice as I could manage and placed my hand on his shoulder. "Quite an entrance. You OK? What's with the wheelchair?" Roger seemed not to have heard my greeting and showed no sign of responding. It was something he did from time to time, and was one of his habits which left people unsure of how to react. Mrs Willis explained to me that it was a hospital rule that patients were not allowed to walk unaided through corridors for fear of accidents. "But Roger isn't a patient, is he? There's nothing wrong with him. They're just looking after him for a few days while we decide what to do?" I was quick enough to see the exchanged glances between the case workers around the table. Roger's wheelchair was positioned in the only available space, more or less opposite me and just set back slightly from the rest of us.

When medical and social workers speak about a disabled person, they often find it necessary to adopt a particular tone of voice that is never used for anything else. An odd lilt, rather like someone reciting poetry or delivering a sermon, which I assume is intended to suggest care and compassion, but to me only ever sounds sanctimonious. On that day and in that room, that special tone was all I could hear; no individual words, but the bounce of joined-up syllables recited as if by rote. Only the odd term such as "management" and "supervision" and "monitoring" dented the barrier being erected in my mind by the echoes of recent conversations with my parents.

"Roger is Roger, and he's always going to need some support," my mother was saying, "and we aren't going to be able to provide it for him for ever."

Obviously none of us had expected anything to happen so soon, but my own breezy reassurances came back uninvited into my head.

"I know that, but obviously, when that time comes, I'll take care of him."

"I'm sorry for wasting everyone's time." The people around the table stopped speaking. I had said it out loud, and heard myself continuing. "I will be looking after Roger. Full time. He will live with me. If you would be kind enough to keep him here for just a few more days while I collect my belongings and find a place to live, I will take responsibility for him from next week." I glanced across the table and saw my brother Roger's impassive face illuminate into a beam which penetrated like a rainbow through the storm clouds. His joy seemed to be unbounded; but what was it in his expression which made me wonder if this was the outcome he had expected all along?

* * *

I more or less sleepwalked through most of the next few days, but Mrs Willis, it should be said, was terrific. By the end of that week I had found and moved into a small furnished flat on the third floor of a large Victorian house in Clapham and had gathered together some bits and pieces of essentials. I was able to obtain from the charity shop enough clothes to tide over the pair of us. Roger would continue to attend his day centre, it was agreed, and we would meet with social workers and psychologists from time to time to keep an eye on his welfare and progress.

With every piece of paper in the house burnt to a cinder, I had no idea of the status of my father's insurance, or even if the house had a mortgage on it. I think I must have waded through the swamp of bureaucracy with the help of the solicitor who had been recommended by the local authority. My memory of it is hazy because of what I suppose must have been my confused mental state, and anyway it all feels like a very long time ago.

There was no clarity before the funeral, which was another thing that seemed to happen more or less on autopilot; only later did I learn that Harriet and her parents had made most of the arrangements. I had never met Harriet's mother and father before this, and I recall that it was a revelation to me to learn on the day before the funeral that they had returned from Singapore, where her dad had recently taken up another new job with the embassy. There seemed at the time to be nothing memorable about them, or perhaps they simply faded into the background of the fog I was groping my way through. I had no reason to believe that I would get to know them both so much more fully later on. When in the following weeks it occurred to me to ask questions such as "Who chose the coffins?" the answer was invariably "You did" – but I can say with certainty that I had and still have no recall of having done so.

My memory of the funeral feels exactly as it would if I had seen it in a film rather than attended it myself. I have a series of ill-defined images of haggard-looking people traipsing past me, all of their faces a slight variation on a theme. I saw the many anxious glances in the direction of Roger. People are afraid of the unknown and, as no one was fully aware of the extent and type of the problem with Roger, no one knew quite what to expect of him on an occasion such as this. Did he "get it"? Did he know what was going on? Would he embarrass us all at the service itself?

My dad had one brother, Uncle Jim, and my mum had one sister, Margaret, neither of whom had been around Roger and me much for our entire lives, and both of whom attended the funeral with their spouses. Both Uncle Jim and Aunt Margaret did the "anything we can do" routine, but in a manner which positively pleaded for there to be nothing.

I must have been responsible for choosing the music, because the order of service lists a lot of my parents' favourite pieces. All this was long before the days when anything goes at funerals, but I had asked Roger if there was a particular tune which he would like to have played as we said goodbye to the people who had brought us up and taken care of us for all these years. He thought for a moment and then said "What about 'I Do Like to Be beside the Seaside'?" My reaction was to smile, and I was about the find a kindly way to say that that wouldn't be appropriate, when Harriet interrupted.

"What a lovely idea," she said, and reminded me that I had told her it was a song we had sung in the back of the car when, as kids, we used to head off to the coast on picnics. "It's a lovely way to remember some of the happy times that you and Roger had with them." And so it was that, after a couple of mawkish pieces by Mozart and Handel, the tiny chapel was filled to the rafters with the uninhibited sound of Reginald Dixon on the mighty Wurlitzer. After some audible gasps of surprise from the mourners, traces of smiles began to spread across hitherto grim faces, and the simple significance of the song lightened the load.

"Well done, Roger," I said, and put my arm around him. Roger shrugged his shoulders but smiled anyway. The poor fucker didn't have a clue what I was getting sentimental about.

The police had the sensitivity to wait until a few days after the funeral before the questioning began. Two detectives, both men, came to the flat while Roger was away at the day centre. One was a "DS", who introduced himself as Detective Sergeant Peter Wallace. The other a "DC", Detective

Constable Steve Pascoe. They explained that in a case such as this one, where the cause of the fire was undetermined, they were obliged to make enquiries. I made tea in the tiny kitchen which was set to one side of the living area, and we sat around a Formica-topped table which I had acquired courtesy of the Salvation Army. DC Pascoe took out his notebook and prepared to write, while the older man asked his questions.

Did my parents have any enemies that I knew of? Of course not, my dad was an insurance salesman, the most innocuous character anyone could wish to meet. Did anyone in the house have any hobbies which involved flammable liquids, or candles – anything like that? I didn't think so. Did either of my parents smoke? No, they did not. My dad used to smoke twenty Capstan full-strength per day, but had given up altogether about five years earlier. Did any regular visitor to the house smoke cigarettes? I could not be sure, and anyway, I didn't think I knew of any regular visitors.

Then they began to get to what turned out to be the point. Did I know that six months earlier my father had increased the insurance on his own life and that of my mother? No, I did not know that. I had no idea. How could I know?

"He had never discussed it with you?" asked Wallace.

"No, he had not, but my father spent his entire life selling insurance. He was a very prudent man," I said. As I began to think about it, for the very first time, it was obvious to me that my dad would always have been concerned about the expense of taking care of Roger after he and my mum had passed away. But quite why he had chosen this time to increase his insurance was a mystery to me. Both of them were in their mid-fifties, and I was aware of no reason why they would have begun to contemplate their own mortality.

It turned out that my father had been paying into what at the time was an enormous policy which would pay out £10,000 on his death through illness or accident, and that the unusually large sum was the reason that the police were making enquiries. I can honestly say that I still had not given more than a passing thought to what our financial situation would likely be, and this new information took a while to sink in. As they continued with their questions, I began for the first time to be grateful that I had been three hundred miles away at the time of the fire. By the time the question came, I was half expecting it.

"Would your brother be capable of lighting a fire?" asked DS Wallace.

"What on earth do you mean? Are you asking if he is able to strike a match?"

No, that wasn't what they were asking. They were asking if I thought there were any circumstances in which Roger could have started the fire that burnt down our house and killed our parents. I was about to speak when my mind was suddenly filled by a vivid image of my older brother squatting in the corner of a cold dark shed, the palms of his hands clamped over his ears and face, to try to keep out the sound and smell of a fire raging in the house just a few yards away.

Roger would have had no idea what was going on, and no idea what to do about it. I shuddered to think of what must have been going through his brain when, sometime later, the firemen came in and found him. The whole scenario made me angry about the detectives' line of questioning.

"No, there aren't." I immediately wondered if my extreme vehemence would seem inappropriate, but then realized that I didn't care what they thought. They were suggesting that my older brother had torched our house and murdered our parents, and that didn't seem like a subject to be neutral about. "Roger has some learning difficulties, all right? But he has never hurt a fly in his entire life. Never done anything that would get him into trouble. Never so much as taken a sweet from a bowl without asking permission."

"So you are saying that he does know right from wrong?" said Wallace.

"Of course he does," I said, becoming even more angry. "He's not a bloody half-wit." And I knew as soon as I said it that in fact Roger was indeed a half-wit.

The two detectives looked at each other, as if trying to decide whether to proceed with something. The DC continued writing and the DS continued talking.

"Were you aware that your parents had told Roger that they were going to dismantle his insect farm?"

"What?"

"Were you aware of that?

"No, I wasn't. And what's more, I don't think it's true."

"Why do you say that?" asked Pascoe.

"Because I think they would have told me." And the thought occurred to me that perhaps these officers had spoken to Roger separately – maybe at his day centre – and no one had informed me. "Anyway, how do you know?"

"We were given the information by one of the members of staff at the day centre."

"Has he told you this himself? Has he said anything about this to anyone else?"

"No, we haven't interviewed him yet; but I wondered if you would mind if we did?"

"Yes, I do mind." My response was instant. "Roger would be utterly confused and would be just as likely to give you wrong and self-incriminating answers if he thought that's what you wanted to hear. Roger didn't do anything relating to the fire – I would stake my life on it – and, if you don't mind me saying so, it's a bit of a cheap and easy answer to suggest that he did, just because he cannot properly account for himself and no one has a better idea."

* * *

Days followed days, and gradually Roger and I emerged into some kind of routine. The two detectives came back after about three weeks to tell me that they were "keeping the file open", but that their investigations had produced nothing tangible. I knew that they still harboured their doubts about Roger, but I was relieved that they did not articulate them.

Eventually the insurance money came through, and I did the mental arithmetic. By the time I'd found and bought a suitable place for Roger and me to live in, bought some decent furniture, clothes and everything we needed to start a new household, we'd still have more than half of the original £10,000 left over. I would need to put that away somewhere safe just in case – in case anything happened to me before it happened to Roger.

The flat we had found gradually became our home, and I set in motion the process of buying it from the landlord. The place had been fitted out with a fairly decent range of furniture – none of it of any particular note except perhaps for a rather grand but worn and battered maroon leather chesterfield sofa. The owner was happy to include it all, along with the other fixtures and fittings, in the purchase price.

We were even adopted by a cat. The woman in the flat downstairs had lived there for twenty years, and her pet Siamese called Olly had obviously decided that our flat was as much his home as the one below. Mrs Chambers explained to us that when she had first moved into the building, her husband was still alive and she had two children. At that time they had occupied the top two floors, but when her husband died and the children left home, she had given up the upper floor. However, her cat Olly probably still believed that he owned the place.

For the time being I was allowed to take Roger over to the old house a couple of times a week to check on his precious insects. Roger showed absolutely no concern about having to pick his way through the debris of our former lives to access the back garden and the garden shed. To him it was as though none of it had ever existed, and once or twice I found myself envying his dislocation. I knew we would have to find an alternative arrangement for the insect farm once the builders started clearing the site, but it looked as though it would be a while before that happened.

It was several weeks before our lives got back into anything like a routine, but eventually Harriet and I found an opportunity to sit down together to discuss the future.

"I could decide not to go back. I could get a job – I'm sure I could get a job as a session musician or in a BBC orchestra with my education so far."

"You could," I said, "but you're not going to. Bad enough that all this has screwed up my education, without it doing the same for yours."

"Don't you want me to stay with you? I thought you'd want us to be together."

"That's a cheap shot," I said. "You know I do" – and I did – "and we will be together. I'm letting you go back to Newcastle to finish what you started, but you're going to come down to see me every three or four weeks, and by next May you'll be finished."

"And what then?"

"What do you mean?"

"I'll be finished at university. So what then?"

"Then you'll come back to me."

"As what?"

"As what? As my girlfriend? My lover? My partner? What were you thinking?"

"I was thinking as your wife."

Which is how Harriet and I came to be married, with about twenty of our friends in attendance, and with Roger as my best man, on 7th September 1972.

I recall feeling that Harriet's parents seemed to be mildly irritated to have to return to London so quickly after the funeral, almost as though we should have made up our minds to get married sooner in order to spare them the inconvenience. Maybe we had even done it precisely to cause them maximum trouble. Our marriage took place in Lewisham Register Office, which is an entirely unprepossessing public building right next door to the library where I was about to begin work as a clerical assistant. Mr and Mrs Chalfont left us to make all the arrangements for the marriage of their only daughter, merely undertaking to contribute the sum of £400 to the costs of the occasion. Actually, in those days that was more than enough to fund the modest luncheon party for forty that we hosted in an upstairs room at the unlikely named Waggoner's Arms in Catford. I think we even had some change left over with which to buy a set of saucepans.

Harriet's father's speech might as well have been taken verbatim from a reference book under the section "the father of the bride", perhaps only omitting the part where he was supposed to welcome his new son-in-law into the family.

None of this offended me, however, and it became a constant source of amusement between Harriet and me to recall how they had struggled to remember their manners when they walked into the Waggoner's and been shown to the upstairs room. What I found far less amusing was the supercilious attitude they always took towards Roger. Perhaps it's easy to understand why any parents might have reservations about their daughter marrying someone whose family included any kind of handicap, but I inferred that it was more a question of what people would think. They came from a background in which the family idiot had traditionally been locked away in a wing of the country home and conveniently forgotten, so no doubt Roger was a bit too much in evidence for their comfort.

"Jonathan," I heard Roger say. It was the morning after the wedding and Harriet was sleeping late while I made breakfast for Roger. "Do you mind if I ask you a question?"

"Of course not, Roger. You can always ask me anything."

"What does 'for ever' mean?"

"For ever?" I repeated. "That's a funny question to ask. What's put that in your mind?"

"It was what you said yesterday: you and Harriet. You both said that you promised to love each other for ever." Roger had his own particular way of turning things over in his mind, and it was often fun to see how they would emerge.

"That's right, Roger," I said. "Harriet and I are in love, and we know that we are going to love each other for ever."

"But what does 'for ever' mean?"

"It means for the rest of time. Never stopping. It means always."

"But how long is it?"

"I don't know what you mean Roger," I said. "It means what I said. It means never stopping. 'For ever' means never stopping. Not ever."

Roger stopped speaking and I could almost hear the cogs inside his brain turning and grinding. It was a full minute before he spoke again.

"But you aren't going to live for ever," he said.

"No, of course not. When two people in love talk about 'for ever' they're talking about all of their lives."

"So it's a lie, then."

"It's not a lie exactly," I said, "but it's not one hundred per cent accurate. The other person knows that when their lover says 'for ever', it means all of their lives. Harriet knows that I will love her until the day I die, just as I know that she will love me." I felt a bit foolish saying it like that to my brother, but this was just how it was coming out.

"Until one of you dies," he corrected me.

"Yes, I guess so," I said, and suddenly felt sad. It was not a thought I had spent any time on.

"Or until one of you meets someone else you fall more in love with."

"That's not going to happen," I was relieved to be back on territory I felt confident about. "We are both certain that we

111

will love each other for all of our lives." I had been about to say "for ever", but had been duly put right.

"But it does happen though, doesn't it?"

"Yes, it does, all too often, I'm afraid. But it's not going to happen to us."

Once again Roger was silent for a while before he spoke again.

"So when two people in love say they will love each other for ever, they don't actually have a clue what they are talking about, do they?"

I thought more about what Roger had said, and how odd is the lover's "for ever". It's like the greengrocer's apostrophe – in there because we feel it should be, but most of those who use it are not quite sure what it means or where to put it. We say "for ever" at a time of our lives when we have not the smallest idea of what that means in reality. Yet when we say it, we mean it, and would vehemently defend the sincerity of our intentions. As far as Harriet and I were concerned just then, any idea that our union was less than permanent was inconceivable, because now we felt ourselves to be inseparable.

On the Monday following the wedding, however, Harriet returned to Newcastle to finish her degree course, and I started work in Lewisham Public Library – the main attraction of which was that I could work what later came to be known as flexi-time, thereby enabling me to drop off and collect Roger at the bus stop every day. It was a pattern which was to serve us all well in the months to come.

Chapter Eleven

Sometimes in the early mornings I would sit and watch Roger for a few minutes before waking him. It was at those times that he seemed at his most vulnerable and, perhaps, at his most pathetic. Here he was, a man in his mid-twenties, with firm dark overnight stubble on his chin, but occupying the world of an eight-year-old. Anyone coming upon him while asleep, with no prior knowledge, would expect him to wake as a fully grown man, perhaps with sour breath, having overindulged in alcohol or reminiscing about some sexual conquest from the previous night.

Instead of this, Roger woke up like a small child, blinking his way back into cognizance of a world which required constant explanation and held unknown mysteries. Often when I would go to wake him in the mornings, I would find Roger looking like a victim of a long-term coma, his face squashed into the pillow and with little traces of saliva caked on his cheek and dampening the sheets. His sleep was apparently entirely untroubled by the cares that come with being an adult.

I envied Roger his ability to sleep the sleep of the inno-cent, and apparently to remain peacefully in another world until roused into this one. All evidence suggested that his sleep remained undisturbed by dreams or concerns, and any enquiry on the matter was always met with an entirely non-committal reply, much as if he didn't know what he was being asked, as most probably he did not.

"Do you ever think about our parents, Roger?" I asked him. It was a Sunday afternoon and Harriet had been visiting for the weekend. We had just returned from King's Cross, where we had seen her off on the train back to Newcastle. I had opened a bottle of beer, as I frequently did on these occasions, but had made a mental note to stop after just one. These were the times when I was most vulnerable to my circumstances, and on more than one occasion after Harriet had gone for the train a single beer had turned into a few more than I had planned to have.

"No," he said, as though he had been expecting the question, "do you?"

I thought for a moment. "No, not much," I said. "But I do sometimes find myself wondering how the fire started."

Roger seemed to consider. His mouth drooped down at the corners and his brow furrowed, as if someone had asked an eight-year-old who had left a scratch on the piano. I thought he might be about to say something which would make me wish I hadn't asked the question, but after a few seconds he said: "I don't know." Then a moment later: "Good job it didn't affect the insect farm."

If Roger had not mentioned the insect farm at that moment, the question would probably have fizzled out into something else. But he had planted a seed in my mind, and so I asked him: "Is it true that Dad had suggested that you would have to get rid of the insect farm?"

Sometimes, when something happened to Roger that he didn't expect or understand, he would react by involuntarily hitting himself on the head with the inside of his wrist. It was an alarming gesture which he had made occasionally from quite early in childhood. Maybe it arose out of the frustration he felt at not being able to get an idea into his head, or perhaps he was punishing his head for not being up to what he required of it. Whatever and whenever, it always took me by surprise when it occurred, and that's what happened now.

"What?" he said. I had no doubt that his alarm was real. "Get rid of the insect farm? You don't mean it?"

"I don't mean now, Roger. No one is suggesting that now. I just wondered if Dad had ever suggested it before they…" I let the sentence peter out.

"Why would he do that? It's not hurting anything!" Once again he used his wrist to bang on his forehead, as though physically trying to force information into his brain that he could not otherwise compute.

"Don't worry, Roger. As I said, no one is suggesting that now. Nothing is going to happen to the insect farm. It is safe and you are safe."

I wondered whether I should tell Roger what the police had suggested, and then I realized that there was no point in doing so. Already he was confused by what I was saying, and I could see that to go into the reason I was asking would only make matters worse. However, I did wonder: if the thought hadn't come from Roger, where had it come from?

"Bad enough to have had to move it" – as so often, his train of thought was now fixed in one direction and ploughing forward – "let alone the idea of getting rid of it altogether. That would be over my dead body, that would. That would be the end of the world."

"Don't worry about it, Roger. No one is going to scrap the insect farm. In fact," I said, "let's go and have a look at it this afternoon."

* * *

After weeks of searching for a suitable place, we had eventually alighted on the perfect location for Roger's pride and joy, on a patch of allotments not more than about two hundred yards along the road from our flat. I had used some of the money we inherited from Dad to buy a new shed, bigger and better than the one it had previously been housed in, and probably only just a bit smaller than a standard single garage. With a bit of help from me and from a kindly older bloke who worked on the allotments, Roger had filled it with new shelving, and we had carefully transported his prized possession to its new home.

"I hope you aren't breeding anything in there that's going to eat my bloody cabbages," said Mr Bolton, as he and I manhandled one of Roger's larger glass tanks from the back of a hired Ford Transit into the shed.

"No," said Roger, and pointed to a mangy Labrador that never seemed to wander farther than three feet from its master's side. "But we do have a few that would be very happy to come and eat that dog of yours." He giggled and put his hand across his mouth, as though unsure whether or not he had gone too far. Old Mr Bolton looked puzzled until I put on a convincing laugh and finally he got the joke.

"I can see I am going to have to keep an eye on you," he said.

Roger and I did a lot of work together in the new shed, and you could say that immersing ourselves in it helped to heal some of the wounds we each were nursing in our own ways. We constructed a whole series of different containers of every shape and size to accommodate his worms and insects. Some had glass sides; others were wooden tubs or boxes. We had access to a tap and there was even a mains electricity supply provided through the goodwill of the headmaster of the primary school which was situated next door to the allotment site. The expanded space in the garage made Roger ambitious, and over the coming months he developed all sorts of plans to keep and to breed a still-greater range of exotic varieties.

On evenings when we did not visit the farm, Roger would sit at our kitchen table and pore through magazines and catalogues containing a whole world of information about bugs and beetles and flies and worms from all parts of the globe. He would spend hours studying the appearance and behaviour of this or that newly discovered genus, and tell me in the greatest of detail what made each one of them unique. He would meticulously complete order forms and then queue up at the post-office counter to send off for some new addition to his collection, and then spend more hours planning how it would be housed, fed and temperature-controlled. From time to time we would receive through the post a sturdy cardboard box containing a selection of leaves and twigs and, on closer inspection, a little colony of bugs of one kind or another. Even someone with no interest at all would have to admit that Roger's collection of worm and insect habitats was impressive.

"Why do you keep all these different species in different containers?" I asked him. "Don't they all have to live together when they are out in their natural habitats?" I was peering through the semi-darkness into the glass tanks that were lined up in rows at eye level. Some were filled with soil and others with bits of trees and other vegetation arranged on gravel.

"They do, but if you leave them to themselves, they fight." Roger was doing his favourite thing, which was pottering about, placing his fingertips against the cages and his eyes as close to the glass as he could get. Left to himself, Roger could and would spend every hour of the day and night doing just that, watching his creation.

"But isn't that the natural order of things? If some of them die, that's their natural state."

"It is, but I love them, so why wouldn't I try to do what's best for them?"

"That's good, Roger," I said, "Truly you are a good shepherd to your flock."

Roger gave me the look he adopted when he passed over the barrier between what he understood and what he did not, but it was a smile which sometimes left me with an impression that he knew so much more than I did. About everything.

Chapter Twelve

Harriet used to come to see us in London as often as she reasonably could, and I tried not to underestimate how difficult that was for her. She was studying hard and also she was obliged to accept as many offers as she could get for her quartet to play at functions. She and her group had become personal favourites of the Vice-Chancellor, and so he tended to invite them to play at any social gathering organized by the university. These events were not especially well paid, but often they would involve the bigwigs from the city and the local council, just exactly the sort of people who organized similar functions, and so the reputation of the quartet might spread.

Quite a few of these engagements fell on weekdays, but others were at weekends, so although gigs helped us to be able to afford her visits to London, they also sometimes got in the way of her having the time to make the journey. And of course with Roger to think about, there was no real possibility that I could visit her.

It was not often that we would quarrel or even disagree. For the most part we were both content to know that the other was as keen for us to be together as we were ourselves, and that the only barriers were practical. There was no lack of will on either side. Still it would be foolish to deny that I felt the occasional knot of resentment. This happened most often when we had a provisional arrangement for her to travel, but then a reasonably paid opportunity to perform came up at the last minute and she had to cancel. On these occasions, when I had looked forward to seeing her and had built myself up for the joy of it, the disappointment could be acute. Our conversations at these times would be agonizing.

"Jonathan."

"Yes."

"About this weekend…"

That was all she needed to say, and I could feel my stomach tightening. And the worst of it was that, while I would know that she was every bit as unhappy about it as I was, and that she would have been dreading raising the subject, still – and this says something unattractive about the human condition – still, I could not stop myself from being grumpy about it.

"What about this weekend?" As if I didn't know.

"We've been asked to play a gig at short notice for the VC's conference, and the others can make it…"

"Yes. But obviously you can't make it, because we have a long-standing plan for you to come here this weekend. I've made arrangements. I've bought extra food. We are expecting you."

A pause.

"Don't worry. I'll tell them that I can't do it." Another pause. "Jonathan?"

"What?"

"I said I'll tell them I can't do it."

My indignation was a pendulum in full swing, accelerating downwards and then meeting the resistant gravity of the guilt I instantly felt about having given her a hard time. This would send the thing with equal and opposing velocity in the other direction, propelled on the wave of shame and regret that I had been less understanding and supportive than I should have been. At about the midway point on my journey back to reason I would begin to reverse.

"Obviously I am not saying that."

"What are you saying then?"

"I'm saying that of course you have to accept. You'd be letting the others down."

"And so you are implying that I would rather let you down than to let Brendan and the others down?" Harriet's response was as quick as a flash. "You know that's not what it's about. It's about the money. If we start to turn down gigs like this, they'll find someone else to play, and then we might not get the chances in the future."

"I hadn't mentioned Brendan. And why is it more about letting him down than it is about letting down Martin and Jed?"

"Only because he was the one who got us this particular gig. It's not about Brendan more than it's about anyone else. You know that. Don't be stupid."

I did know that in my head, and that I was indeed being stupid, but somehow I had never got around to knowing it in my stomach. So every mention of Brendan carried with it a nasty little twinge of pain in my guts, like a corkscrew being inserted and then twisted in my flesh.

"OK, OK, uncle," I said. At last the swingometer had reached its final extreme. I was conquered. "It'll just mean a few extra helpings of pepperoni pizza for Roger and me, and while you are slaving over a hot flute on Saturday, Roger will be enjoying a very nice bottle of cola, and I will be enjoying a very nice bottle of claret."

"My loss then," she said, and we were friends again.

On average I reckon that Harriet and I saw each other one weekend a month during term time, and then obviously we were together all during the end-of-term vacations. The quartet did one or two London-based performances during holidays, and at Easter Brendan arranged for them to play in the market at Covent Garden. The four of them set up their music stands in one of the lower tiers of shops, where the sound they made could bounce off sharp corners and around the colonnades, echoing in and out of doorways and walkways and market stalls and café furniture. The effect was wonderful, and Roger and I went along to ambush the foreign tourists who may have thought they were getting a free concert, but who looked appropriately embarrassed when asked for a contribution. It was a great success – so much so that we ended up staying far longer than we had originally intended.

"I'll get some coffee," I said, and Roger came with me as I headed off towards the greasy spoon inside the covered market which still catered for the traders. On the way there I counted the money and reckoned that we had earned enough to justify a small celebration. "Go back and ask them if they want anything to eat," I told Roger. He did, but I think he must have got lost on the way, because it took him all of ten minutes to return. When he finally turned up he seemed a bit confused and disorientated, and all he could tell me was that everyone seemed to have everything they needed.

Having Roger collecting money on such occasions was a gas – basically because very few of the people he tapped up for a donation could work out whether he was acting or was not quite all there. We raised £28 that day – minus £4 between us for coffee and doughnuts – split four ways, this was a very good take for the times.

Weekends with Harriet were usually wonderful, and were marred only by the fact that we always knew that our time together was limited and therefore we needed it to be perfect. We didn't have enough of it to do a lot of the routine stuff that is as much a part of a decent marriage as the highlights. The grocery shopping, the going to the launderette, the hanging out. Because our hours together were so limited, we seemed to feel that we had to pack them with pleasurable things, and that would sometimes cause a strain.

One thing we never disagreed about was having Roger around. He used to go to the day centre on Saturday mornings until noon, which meant that Harriet and I could have some time to ourselves. I would walk with him down to the bus, and then come back to the flat with only the now constant presence of Olly the Siamese cat competing for attention. I'd make tea and bring it to bed, and then Harriet and I would spend a couple of hours making love and catching up with each other's lives.

Those times were among the most wonderful I have ever known in my life. In some ways I knew her so well, and yet in others she was a stranger to me. We had the comfort of familiarity, but also the joy of rediscovery. So much was happening to her – she was learning so much, experiencing new stuff, but little of it was very relevant to me. She was growing in her own world. The result was that in small ways she was a slightly different person every time I met her. She had learnt more, discovered more, while my routine was more or less static. Yet when we made love there was none of the hesitation or trepidation which goes with a new romance. We were instantly utterly at home, with no inhibitions, no holding back. I felt like a man crawling through the desert towards an oasis, but when I got there, the oasis was not a mirage, but a wonderful, absorbing, revitalizing, regenerative immersion.

After kissing and drinking tea and lovemaking and more tea and then some more lovemaking, it would be lunchtime and one or other of us would take the short walk to meet the bus which dropped Roger off. He would always be delighted to see Harriet, they would kiss and embrace, and then we would all have some food together, and as quickly as possible he would want to head off down to the allotments to check up on the insect farm. Either Harriet or I would usually walk down there with him; we knew that he was safe and absorbed when he was there, and so it gave us the chance to do as much of the ordinary stuff as we could do in the time. Harriet would bring me up to date with her news, which inevitably would centre around the stresses and pressures of studying.

"They expect us to do three essays a week," she said, "and then one of us has to read out their work in the seminar and all the others pick it to pieces right there in front of you."

I would be treated to a blow-by-blow account of the projects she was being set, the essays she had to write, the seminars she had to lead, the assessments she had to endure and the exams she had to prepare for. To listen to Harriet, you would easily gain the impression that every waking hour was spent with her books and with music practice. However, I knew enough from my own experience in Newcastle that, even for the most conscientious of students, it really wasn't possible to work the whole time, and there was plenty of it left over for socializing. At those times my mind would inevitably go back to those few weeks of our first term when both of us were students, and the stings of pain I would experience when I used to see Harriet surrounded by admirers. I remembered once again thinking that she seemed to have few if any female friends, and that she was just one of those women who enjoyed the company of men so much more. No sooner would such thoughts come into my mind than I had to shoo them out, for fear that they would sting me all over again, and I knew myself well enough to know that that way lay madness.

I guessed that Harriet was choosing not to talk about how she spent her free time, in order to avoid giving me any reason to become concerned. My idiotic expressions of jealousy over the years had left her in no doubt that I was capable of being totally unreasonable. Hardly surprising, then, that she would exercise the discretion of brevity or omission rather than take a risk that I would start up again.

By and large I had managed to control, if not totally to conquer the most negative of those feelings. There can be no doubt that in those days I was drinking far too much, and when I did so on my own, I had a tendency to become depressed. However it never got out of control, and I was always aware of the need to stay the right side of a line. I worked out that, as our choices had made it inevitable that we were going to be apart for so much time, if I wanted to stand any chance at all of retaining my sanity, I would simply have to find a way to deal with it.

I had made my choices, and by and large I was content with them. Roger was my priority and no one needed to remind me of that. Nonetheless, knowing what your responsibilities are and being happy to live up to them is not the same as being blind to what might have been. I think I would have been less than human if, on hearing Harriet's tales of university life, I had not experienced the occasional pang. Of course I did, but I became very good at keeping it all bottled up, because Harriet never seemed to notice. When she had finished her breathless account I would bring her up to date with mine, all of which was inevitably less interesting.

"We set up the mobile library on one of the dodgy estates up in Deptford on Wednesday," I told her. "Then they left me on my own all afternoon. It was like the siege of the bloody Alamo. Dozens of kids throwing handfuls of gravel at the caravan, so that at one time it sounded like it was raining hailstones. I thought I'd have to call the police when one kid tried to release the handbrake."

I'd tell her how Paddy the delivery driver had been told off by the branch librarian Mr Waddington, and how the Irishman had told the boss to go and fuck himself. Mr Waddington had been to see the town clerk to try to get Paddy fired, but the unions were so strong that no one could be dismissed for something as trivial as insubordination.

"And how about Roger?" she would ask. "How's he getting on, do you think? Is he happy?"

That would be my cue to run though some of the funny things that had happened to us, usually involving the reaction of some unsuspecting bystander to the realization that Roger was not all he seemed.

On one visit, not long after the Easter concert, I told Harriet about my conversation with Roger on the subject of the insect farm. About how I had asked him whether our dad had ever suggested that he would have to get rid of it, and how he had reacted with alarm but had given no indication that the incident had ever happened. Harriet hadn't remembered, or maybe I hadn't told her, that the police had raised the question when they were investigating the cause of the fire.

"You don't think it's possible, do you?"

"What, that Roger started the fire that killed our parents?"

I had said it. The thought that had remained unexpressed to anyone; suddenly it was out there as an idea, floating around in the airwaves.

"Yes," said Harriet, "I suppose that's exactly what I'm asking."

My instinct was to answer unequivocally, but the directness of the question caused me to crystallize the niggling thoughts which must have been stored away in the corners of my mind. Suddenly I had an image of Roger crouching in the darkness of the insect farm, while the orange glow of flames cast flickering light against the window panes. I saw again the lonely figure sitting in the side ward of the hospital and playing with the stethoscope while our parents lay dead just a short distance away. And then, just as quickly, I remembered that this was Roger, and nothing that Roger did could be judged by the standards of normal behaviour. My moment of doubt had gone as quickly as it had arrived.

"No, I don't. You know what he was like on that morning after the fire, waiting for me in the hospital casualty department. He was sitting there in a world all of his own, completely oblivious to anything that had happened in the previous few hours. No doubt Roger is capable of some weird stuff, but never anything as weird as that."

I saw Harriet looking beyond me, focusing on the middle distance, and after a moment I saw that she was gently nodding her head in agreement.

"Yes," she said, "I see that. Obviously I don't know him anything like the way that you know him, but I would swear on a stack of Bibles that he wouldn't be capable of doing something like that. He is just so innocent; I don't think he has the kind of mind it would take to carry it off."

We sipped our tea and paddled around in our own thoughts, occasionally murmuring our continuing assent.

"Mind you," I said, "if Roger was ever going to do anything drastic, it would be that bloody insect farm which would cause it. He's obsessed by it, which is great for me because it gives him something absorbing to do where I know he is completely content. Whether it's good for him or not, I don't know."

"It must be good for him," said Harriet, "sorting it all out and having to organize it to make sure all his tiny creatures are fed and looked after has been incredibly stretching for him." She seemed to think for a moment or two. "But you are wrong about one thing."

"And what's that?"

"If Roger was ever going to do something drastic to protect something he treasured, it would be to protect the thing he cares about more than anything else." I looked at Harriet, wondering what she was going to say, my eyebrows raising the question. "That's you," she said. "And, by the way" – she leant towards me and took my hand in hers – "the same goes for me too."

Chapter Thirteen

It was in the summer holidays before Harriet's final year in Newcastle. I had taken off my whole holiday allocation from the job at the library to spend as much time as possible with her. Harriet would need to do quite a lot of studying, but one way or another we would have a fair amount of spare time to hang out and do the things that normal people do. To be like a married couple.

The quartet had been booked to play at one or two summer parties, and one I remember in particular was to be held in an enclosed garden in a square in a very smart area of Chelsea. The booking had come through an agency, and at first there was some secrecy about the identity of the host. Then one day Harriet took a phone call from Brendan, who told her that the event was the annual party of the TV presenter David Frost.

I was no more interested then than I am now in the world of celebrities, but even for casual observers such as myself, David Frost's annual garden party was a well-known part of the social calendar. His was a very unusual world which took in politicians, statesmen, musicians, actors and comedians, and so a party that brought them all together was bound to be an experience.

When Harriet and I went to have a look at the venue a few days in advance, the organizers were busy erecting a marquee in case of rain. The garden was surrounded on three sides by large fine houses of red brick. Access was through a locked gate, and the whole area was bordered by shrubbery and then railings which came up to shoulder height. In the course of chatting to the caterers, I got myself hired as a waiter for the evening.

Occasions like this left us in a slight dilemma about what to do with Roger. Not that there was any problem in leaving him on his own. Roger's disability did not make him a danger to himself or to others, and he was usually perfectly content to be left for hours at a time at the insect farm, and was happy to walk the couple of hundred yards back to the flat when he was ready. It was no real problem to leave him in the flat either, though I was never certain how he spent his time when we were away. I know that he used to sit and watch the same programmes over and over again on children's television; sometimes when he would be viewing in the other room I could hear him laughing and speaking back to the TV presenter. I'd go in and find him sitting on the sofa, stroking Olly the cat, and watching something I knew he had seen many times before.

On the occasion I'm thinking about now, however, Roger was a bit fractious. It worried me, partly because it was a rare thing. He didn't actually complain, but seemed more disappointed than usual when I said that Harriet and I would both be going out for the evening.

"Where are you going?"

"Harriet and the quartet have a booking in Chelsea and I'm serving drinks. It's an open-air thing in a square. Lots of posh people. Maybe even some celebrities." Roger shrugged his shoulders. He was one of the few people who were even less likely to be impressed by the idea of celebrities than I was. "Maybe there will be some TV producers there and they'll want to put Harriet on the telly." I don't know why I said it, but I thought the idea would amuse Roger. It did.

"Yes, let's get Harriet on the telly. She'd be wonderful." His lighter moment was short-lived and quickly Roger's smile faded from his face.

"What's the matter, Roger? Won't you want to spend the time down at the insect farm?"

Roger shrugged his shoulders. Suddenly he seemed like the eight-year-old boy that he was in his head, just fed up without any obvious reason.

"Maybe he could come with us?" It was Harriet. She had overheard our conversation. At first I didn't quite understand what she was talking about.

"How?"

"Well, there's no reason why not. Lots of musical groups have their own road manager. Roger can help to carry our instruments and put up our stuff. It'll make us look more professional."

Whatever were the possible consequences of taking Roger to the garden party, making the quartet seem more professional was unlikely to be one of them. However, as I reflected on it, I couldn't think of any serious reason why Roger shouldn't be able to go along as a helper of sorts. Undoubtedly there would be a whole range of flunkies of one kind or another, and it seemed perfectly plausible that he could come in with us and remain unnoticed.

Roger was delighted by the idea; indeed, he was a little bit too delighted, to an extent that quickly made me worry about whether we had made the right decision. I have said before that one of the big things about Roger was that he looked perfectly normal, and you could easily think he *was* perfectly normal until you spoke to him. Even then, on his best days it might take a few minutes to realize. However, if he was nervous or overexcited, and especially when his usual routine was thrown too far out of the norm, he could easily get a bit overwhelmed.

A little while later I heard Harriet speaking on the phone to the others to let them know what we planned. The conversations with Martin and Jed – both of whom were at Martin's parents' house in Pimlico – seemed to be fairly uncontroversial. I wondered if it was significant that Harriet left telling Brendan until last, and I thought I detected some nervousness in her when she was about to make the call. She stood for a moment with her hand on the receiver and took a few deep breaths. As she dialled the number, I asked her if she was all right. She nodded without pausing, as if now psyched up for the conversation and not wanting to be diverted.

I couldn't hear much of the dialogue, but I could tell that Harriet's voice was more strained than it had been when she spoke to the others. The discussion took longer, and it was clear that Harriet was getting some resistance. Most of her conversation was muffled and indistinct, but there was no mistaking her closing words before she hung up the phone: "If he isn't allowed to come, I won't be coming either." She returned to the living room and sat down hard on the sofa. "Sometimes that Brendan can be a total tosser," she said.

Of the two of us, it was unusual for Harriet to be the one who was irritated by Brendan, so my mind started working overtime to think how to perpetuate her mood. If I joined in, I suspected that she would soon move to his defence.

"Well, maybe he's got a point. It's an exclusive party full of politicians and rock stars. They've probably got all the halfwits they need already."

Harriet's expression could have frozen me to the spot. "It's not funny, Jonathan. Sometimes that Brendan gets right up my nose. He's such an arse."

I loved it when Harriet used words like "arse". Bad language came so unnaturally to her that it sounded as though she was dealing with a sour taste in her mouth.

"I've been telling you that for years." I saw in her expression the realization that she was getting on to, and potentially feeding, one of my pet subjects. Suddenly the conversation was at an end.

The weather was a bit growly and overcast all day, and we wondered whether we would be playing inside or outside of the marquee. By late afternoon though, the skies had started to clear and it looked as though the rain would stay away.

We were due to arrive an hour or so ahead of the guests in order to set up the seats and music stands, and so there was no special security on the gate when we went in. I had borrowed a Ford Transit from my mate Paddy at the library, and probably we looked a bit incongruous turning up in a van with London Borough of Lewisham Library Service emblazoned in bold letters on the side. Half a dozen photographers from newspapers and society magazines were already in position at the north end of the square, but they took no notice of us as we unloaded music stands and instruments. To give him something to do, and to avoid awkward questions, we told Roger to take one end of the cello, and once he was in, he was in.

It took only a few minutes for us to get set up, and the plan was to leave Roger with Harriet until there were enough people milling around for him to seem less conspicuous. I was due to report to the catering tent half an hour before 6 p.m., when the first guests were expected to begin arriving.

At about 5.15, we could see David Frost himself appear at the top of the garden square and begin to make his way in our general direction. He seemed to be full of very natural bonhomie, and greeted everyone he saw with a smile and a handshake. I could hear his familiar nasal tones as he spoke and the big laugh seemed very genuine. You could tell that all the waiters and waitresses were thrilled to meet him.

This was the first TV personality I had ever seen in real life and, to my own surprise, I could feel a growing sense of excitement and anticipation. Eventually he arrived next to us, and I was irritated to see Brendan take charge of the introductions, almost as though he was in some way the leader of the quartet. Up close David Frost seemed smaller than he did on TV, but he had one of those smiles which, when he flashed it at you, made you think you were the only interesting person in the world.

I stood to one side as Brendan introduced Harriet, and Frost took her hand and kissed it. Harriet's face reflected her delight. I think she even blushed.

"This is Jonathan, who is Harriet's partner and is also helping with the catering this evening," Brendan said, turning to me.

"Lucky man," said Frost. He shook my hand vigorously as though he had just been introduced to the new President of the United States. "And I don't mean lucky to be serving vol-au-vents at my humble gathering, obviously…" We all laughed and he laughed loudest of all of us. Just behind me stood Roger, and Frost's eyes and attention naturally went to him. "And this is?"

"This is Roger." I took over and for a moment considered lying. "Roger is my older brother. He helps us to carry the instruments and music stands, and he also helps us to collect money when we are busking."

Frost saw the opening and was quick to fill it. "Well, I don't suppose you'll get much tonight," he said, shaking Roger's hand and lowering his voice as if in conspiracy, "all my guests are a lot of miserly old bastards." I watched Roger's face carefully as the rest of us broke up in uproarious laughter, and I think his uncomprehending smile went unnoticed in the general hilarity. Seconds later, Frost was off to the next group of people, making their day and passing along.

Now I was late and had to report quickly to the catering tent.

"Now, Roger," I said, "remember what I told you. Stick close to Harriet, but don't get in anyone's way. Don't open up a conversation with anyone, but if anyone speaks to you, just say you are working and walk away." I figured that if anyone did speak to Roger, they would soon work out what was going on, and would be likely to move on quickly anyway. That was what usually happened. Roger nodded to indicate that he understood, and if anything he seemed excited and keen for me to leave him.

The invitations said that the party would last from six until eight, but we were told that we would need to go on serving until 9.30 at least. The first guests began to arrive very promptly, and I went into action with trays of champagne.

I think the cliché for describing these occasions is "glittering", and as the mêlée of guests gathered, I began to see why. There were famous actors and actresses. Anthony Andrews and Sarah Miles. Claire Bloom and Bob Hoskins. Also among the early guests whom I knew instantly were Ronnie Corbett and Ronnie Barker, both dressed in candy-striped blazers and obviously having fun. I reckon that there must have been a lot of people there whom everyone else recognized apart from me.

The main challenge for me was to manoeuvre my way through the crowd, preferably without spilling champagne on any passing royalty. The best way to avoid accidents seemed to be simply to follow natural instincts, heading for any opening in the crowd and meandering at will. One tray of drinks lasted just a few minutes as people exchanged their empty glasses for full ones. There was Willie Whitelaw talking to Neil Kinnock. Over there Jimmy Tarbuck was entertaining Uri Geller.

As things turned out, for most of the evening my wanderings kept me on the other side of the garden from where the quartet was playing. Of course I could hear their music, and once or twice I heard someone saying how delightful they sounded.

A busy hour had passed by when it occurred to me that I hadn't thought or heard about Roger. I felt a twinge of concern as the consideration dawned. A moment later I realized that, if anything had been amiss, I would have heard or seen something. The gathering was not so large that any significant incident could go unnoticed.

I began to move more purposefully among the crowd, still holding my tray, but perhaps giving people less time to think about whether they wanted to swap an empty glass for a full one. I skirted the edges of the gathering, glancing outwards into the trees that marked the boundaries of the garden. There was Bruce Forsyth accompanied by a fabulous-looking blonde woman with the shape and proportions of a Barbie doll. Maybe she was the hostess from some game show he was presenting at the time. There was Edward Heath, wearing a white dinner jacket with a red carnation in his buttonhole, surrounded by a group of what looked like equally chinless wonders.

But there was no sign of Roger.

Eventually, and now with a rising sense of concern, I abandoned the drinks tray behind a bush and headed towards the area where Harriet and the quartet were playing. People were standing in tight groups, entirely absorbed in their conversations, and oblivious to any need for passage between them. Almost all of the men wore suits, and most of the women looked attractive in their summer evening gowns. I struggled in the general direction of the music, and when I reached the corner of the garden where they were playing, the quartet was in the middle of performing that lovely piece by Pachelbel and all in all it made for a perfect English scene.

I guess my fast approach must have caught their attention, because I saw Harriet's eyes glance towards me. She was producing magical sounds from her flute, but still she must instantly have seen the look of anxiety on my face because, scarcely moving her head and with her lips still pursed in that tight pucker which I always found irresistible, her eyes indicated for me to look behind her, towards the trees. I kept on walking past her and quickly saw a little clearing, and in it there was a group of ten or twelve people, all apparently standing around and listening to a single person whose shape I could just make out, perched on the low-hanging branch of a tree. I could hardly sort out my amazement from my concern when I realized that the person at the centre of the group was Roger.

I was on the brink of walking straight into the group, taking Roger by the arm, and marching him away. The word "surreal" is entirely overused, but that's exactly what this felt like. My concern was no doubt heightened by the fact that Roger did not even have an invitation to the party, let alone to provide his own little entertainment. Yet there he was, in the middle of a group of celebrities, holding forth about heaven knew what. What was even more amazing was that this was obviously a party where people were keen to see and to be seen, but this group has chosen to hide themselves away under the trees to listen to my older brother. Yes, and I admit that I thought it then as I think it now: my "idiot" older brother.

The quartet was only a few yards behind me, so I struggled to make out what it was that Roger was talking about. I edged up behind the group, anxious not to be seen by him before deciding what to do, and eventually could hear a little of what he was saying. His words followed one upon the other slowly and very deliberately, and there was an odd calmness in his tone which seemed to invite attention.

"You have to imagine that you have caught a beautiful but fragile butterfly in the cup of your hands." In the gaps between the arms and shoulders of his audience I could see that Roger was holding his cupped hands together, as though keeping safe a tiny creature. "If you hold it too loosely, the butterfly may fly away or fall to the ground and immediately come to harm." He moved his hands apart as though to allow the butterfly to fall. He spoke softly and looked at the ground, as if in mock dismay at the damaged creature. "On the other hand, if you hold it too tightly," and now he cupped his hands back together again, but closer than before, "you risk crushing the life and the beauty out of it."

One of the men had only just joined the group, obviously to see what everyone was listening to. He asked the woman next to him what was going on.

"I don't know," she said. "It's this bloke. As far as I can make out, he's talking about looking after little creatures."

"Is he supposed to be a comedian or something?"

"No, I don't think so," the girl said. "If he is, he's not very funny. But there is something…" Her voice trailed away because Roger was speaking again, and the odd thing was that he didn't sound quite like Roger. His words were enunciated individually, as though one word had no relationship with the one before it or with the one that followed it. Like the speaking clock, where individual elements are inserted electronically to make up a coherent sentence.

"So you have to look after them closely and tightly enough to keep them from doing too much harm to themselves or to others, but loosely enough so that you don't stop them from being creative, and able to follow their natural instincts." Roger seemed to address each member of his audience individually, momentarily catching the eye of every one of them before addressing the next in line. "You could control everything that they do, and everything about their lives if you wanted to," he was saying, "but where would be the fun or the interest in that? If you let them do what comes naturally to them, sometimes they will harm or even kill each other, but that's just a part of their nature. Most of the time they will lead wonderful and inspirational lives."

I looked around and saw heads nodding and heard the soft murmur of people agreeing. For all the world it was as though these people had found some mystical guru dispensing wisdom. Except that this wasn't some mystical guru: it was my mentally challenged brother Roger, who went to a school for people with special needs and giggled incessantly at kids' cartoons.

"Who is this guy?" I heard a man in a white dinner jacket say to his girlfriend. And for the first time in my life, I really wondered.

* * *

144

"So what the fuck was all that about?"

Two hours later, I was driving the Transit, Roger was in the passenger seat beside me and the other four were in the back. Harriet was immediately behind me, with Martin next to her and Brendan in the seat by the sliding door. Jed crouched among the gear in the row at the back. By the time we had packed up, had been profusely thanked by our very elegant host and were on our way, it was ten o'clock.

It was, of course, Brendan who had spoken. I had not had either time or opportunity to talk to Harriet about what had happened, and I could sense that she was waiting to know what to say. Obviously she wanted to be supportive, but I think she genuinely had no idea what had taken place. Her curiosity was probably as intense as everyone else's.

I could easily have been conciliatory and, had it been anyone other than Brendan who had asked the question, I probably would have been. But it had been a long day and I myself was a bit discombobulated by the turn of events.

"Actually, Brendan," I said, "whatever happened is nothing whatever to do with you, so why don't you keep the fuck out of it and mind your own fucking business?"

"Actually, I think it is my business," he was saying. "This was a very important booking for us, and if it isn't enough that we have to take your brother with us for some reason that the rest of us can only guess at, he then starts to act like he's the bloody Maharishi Mahesh Yogi."

I hated it when people talked about Roger as though he wasn't there, and this was made worse by the fact that Roger was also behaving as though he wasn't there. During all this he was just gazing out of the window, apparently entirely unperturbed, and watching the crowded streets of Chelsea turn into the less crowded streets of the suburbs.

"First of all, Brendan" – the temperature was rising and the others were keeping quiet – "you wouldn't know a wise man if he came up and dropped an ice cube down your neck. And second of all, Roger did no harm to you, to the quartet or to anyone else."

"But what on earth was he talking about?" The bastard was making things even worse by remaining calm as I was beginning to lose control.

"Like I said, Brendan" – now I was shouting, every word just a little louder than the one preceding it – "what happened here with Roger is none of your fucking business. And if I knew myself, I probably wouldn't tell you. So why don't you just keep quiet?"

Harriet put her hand gently on my shoulder, and I knew I had to try to calm down, but in spite of my best efforts, I could feel my pulse racing. Brendan remained silent for a few moments, and I thought it might be the end of the matter, but then he muttered a few words which he may have thought were under his breath.

"The bloke's a fucking nutter. Shouldn't be allowed out."

I felt an immediate and involuntary surge of blood rush to my face, and I knew I was teetering on the very edge of control. I tried taking a deep breath, but then suddenly any opportunity to go back had passed. I swung the steering wheel hard to the left and the van swerved sharply as I jammed on the brakes. There was the sound of a blast on a horn from the car behind, but I did not wait to check passing traffic as I threw open the driver's door and ran around the front of the vehicle onto the pavement. I had a momentary impression of the look of alarm on Brendan's face as I grabbed the handle and yanked it backwards. Rusty bearings squealed against the slide, and the door came to an abrupt halt as it crashed against its own buffers. No rational thoughts were going through my head as I leant into the van and grabbed Brendan by the lapels, unclear even in my own mind whether I was pushing him backwards or dragging him outside, the effect of which was to rattle him back and forth like a marionette. I was using all my strength to shake him, and then I let go with my right hand and drew it back in a fist.

"Jonathan!" The sound came not from Brendan but from Harriet, who was jammed behind the driver's seat on the other side of the vehicle, with Martin between her and the fight. "Stop it. Stop it. For heaven's sake!" I looked across at her, expecting to see surprise or shock on her face, but what I saw was instantly recognizable as fear. It was an expression I had never seen before and it stopped me a split second before my punch would have crashed into Brendan's face.

Brendan himself had made no attempt to resist or to fight back, and the moment I loosened my grip he slumped back in his seat. Immediately his hand went to his collar, pulling at the place where the pressure had been. Already a red line was visible on his neck. We all remained where we were for a few moments, and gradually I felt control beginning to return. I was shocked by the violence of my own reaction, but even more so at the look of horror I had seen from Harriet. A second later and my thoughts returned to Roger and whether he would be freaked out by the incident. I took a step to my left so that I would be able to see him through the window of the passenger door. In total contrast to Harriet and the rest of us, his face and demeanour indicated nothing amiss. He seemed to be completely unperturbed, or even unaware of what had happened.

Straight away I knew that I should apologize, and that probably I eventually would, but at the moment I was unable to calm down sufficiently to do so. I reached for the handle, and was about to slide the door closed, when I caught a split second flash of an expression on Brendan's face which I had not expected: maybe it was one of triumph. Quickly he looked away, and I pushed the door closed, walking very slowly around the back of the van as I struggled to collect myself. Harriet did not look at me as I passed her window and got back into the driver's seat. I started the engine and drove two or three miles in silence before anyone spoke.

"I don't know, Jonathan." Martin's words were spoken in the most conciliatory tone he could summon. He and I were closer to being mates than I would or could ever be with Brendan, so telling him to fuck off and punching his lights out wasn't such a tempting option. "However you look at it, it was a bit weird." Obviously he was trying to work this out as he spoke. "I'm not worried about us or whether anyone had any kind of an issue with the quartet. Just curious, really. It was like he was giving the Sermon on the Mount... what do you think he was talking about?"

"Well, we could always ask him." It was Harriet speaking, and I was immensely relieved that she had calmed down sufficiently to resume the conversation. "In case none of you has noticed, Roger is sitting right there in front of us."

"So how about it, Roger?" I half-turned to him as I continued to drive through the city. My brother was looking out of the window to his left, showing no sign of being aware of the conversation or that it had anything to do with him. Sometimes he was like this, mostly when he was tired. He just sort of checked out, much as I sometimes do myself, but in a way which seemed more impenetrable. Usually I would be content to leave him alone, but I had more or less calmed down by now, and the truth is that I was only a little less curious than everyone else in the van. "Roger? Are you with us?"

Slowly he turned his head to me, as though waking from a light sleep.

"Oh hi, Jonathan," he said. "What's happening?"

"Are you OK?"

"Sure, yes, I'm fine thanks. Why do you ask?"

"I was just wondering if you enjoyed the party?" For a moment I thought he was going to say "What party?" – but he didn't, and I continued. "You seemed to be having a great time. You seem to have made yourself the centre of everyone's attention."

Roger looked back at me with one of those looks of his which I knew well. His face was completely passive, giving no trace or hint of what he was thinking. It was one of the many features of Roger's condition which no doctor had ever been able to explain: an apparent capacity completely to blank out incidents he did not wish to remember. They did not need to be anything traumatic, but could include relatively benign occurrences such as what had happened at the party. In such cases, his reaction to questions would be just exactly as though they had not been asked, so that it was impossible to tell whether he had completely failed to comprehend, or was simply choosing not to reply. This seemed to be just one of those occasions.

I turned to look at him again and saw his face glowing against the yellow light from the streetlamps. I noticed a little cobweb of wrinkles around the corners of his eyes, the very early signs of loss of the elasticity of youthful skin. Suddenly he seemed much older to me. An odd look in his eyes, or something in his expression, suggested that he had learnt something, or had acquired some wisdom which was unavailable to the rest of us.

My imagination was going into overdrive, but I also knew that I was not going to be able to get Roger to open up any more. All I wanted to do was to drop everyone off and get home. No one mentioned my loss of temper, and nothing more was said other than the routine stuff which is necessary at times like these: "You played well", "So did you", "David Frost was nice, wasn't he?" When the door slammed and Roger, Harriet and I were left alone, we were all too tired to pick up the threads.

Later that evening I went into Roger's bedroom as usual to say goodnight to him. He was in bed with his head sideways on the pillow and the bedclothes tucked up tightly under his chin. Any sign of growing maturity had vanished in the half-light, and his eyes were drooping like a kid struggling but losing the battle to stay awake. These were the times when I loved Roger the most. I didn't usually do this, but on that evening for some reason I kissed him on the forehead and said goodnight.

"Jonathan," he murmured as I was about to close the door.

"Yes, Roger, what is it?"

"How old was Dad when he died?"

The question came from so far out of the blue that I had to think for a minute before answering.

"I think he was fifty-seven, Roger. Why do you ask?"

"And how old are you now?"

"I'm twenty-two, Roger. But why are you asking?"

"OK," he said, "that's fine then. We've still got plenty of time."

"Time for what?" I asked him, but when I looked again he had gone to sleep.

I was never able to get anything resembling an answer from Roger about what he meant. Indeed, by the following morning, after a night in which I had little sleep as I turned the matter over in my mind, Roger didn't even seem to remember it. When I asked him, he gave me one of that same repertoire of blank looks. The one that seems to imply that I am just a little bit crazy.

Chapter Fourteen

We were all still very young in those days, and were changing fast, just as the world was changing around us. Where once I had seen her every day and slept with her every night, I felt in some ways that I was losing track of the person Harriet was and was becoming. She had always dressed to surprise, for example, but these days when I saw her for the first time after a period of absence, the surprise was not always what I might have hoped.

Her outfits, which had once been entirely carefree and looked as though they had been compiled with abandon and *joie de vivre*, now seemed to have been put together with more studied eccentricity. One weekend she arrived off the train wearing a man's suit – the real thing, which she had actually bought from a men's outfitters. The jacket was chalk-striped and double-breasted: the trousers seemed too big and were tied tightly with a belt, with turn-ups spilling over brown-and-white brogues. I had not known what to say, and she struggled to suppress her irritation that I could not immediately enthuse.

We had a slightly stilted version of our usual first evening together, and on the following day we were sitting at the table having eaten lunch. I had made my special dish of lamb chops with lots of mint sauce out of a jar, peas out of a tin and mashed potatoes. Tinned peas were just inside what would have been acceptable in my mother's household, but if I had made instant mashed potatoes I would have been able to hear and feel the sound of her turning in her grave. We had opened a bottle of wine, but I noticed that Harriet seemed to be drinking far less than I was. Possibly I was just a little bit drunk.

"When will you start looking for a job for after graduation?"

"The careers advisers are saying that the BBC does an annual trawl to recruit for its orchestras," Harriet said. She was putting away the cutlery into a drawer lined with gingham Fablon. "I think that starts early in the new year, and they say that maybe I've got an outside chance of getting that, which would be great. And as soon as I know a precise date when the exams finish and I can be back in London, I will be in with a better chance of getting some session work. Playing background music for feature films or on recordings, that sort of stuff."

"That sounds fantastic. Really fun." I had to take a moment to measure my tone when I spoke the words I wanted to say next. I know that by now I was feeling the effects of the wine, and so I probably got it wrong. "So you don't see any future for the quartet then?"

"Why do you say that?" Her reaction was of someone being accused of something.

"No reason. It's just that you listed a few options, and continuing in the quartet wasn't one of them."

"Well, it wasn't one of them because I can't easily see how we can make a full-time living playing Vivaldi at twenty-first birthdays and weddings. But I feel fairly certain that all of us would want to supplement what we can earn during the day with whatever gigs we can get in the evenings."

Strange how sometimes we can feel ourselves wading into ever-deeper water, but instead of making for higher ground, we continue until we are up to our necks.

"So you've discussed it then?"

"Discussed what?"

"With Martin and Jed and Brendan. You've had a talk together and made your plans for the future of the quartet after you all graduate."

Whatever else she was, Harriet wasn't stupid. She could see where this was going, and her sigh of impatience was overlaid with a tinge of anger which should have sent the danger signs. Indeed, I think they did send the danger signs, but at that moment I was wearing eyeshades.

"So you are getting ready to be offended that I have talked about the future with them before I have talked about the future with you. Is that it?"

"I didn't say that. But since you mention it…"

Harriet threw down the damp tea towel, intending it to land on the edge of the draining board, but instead it fell to the floor, further adding to her irritation. Ignoring it, she perched her lovely bottom on the edge of the kitchen table and folded her arms.

"We haven't sat down and planned the future. In the normal course of conversation, when everyone has talked about what they want to do next, it's natural that people have said whether they think they would be available if the quartet were to continue. If one of us was going abroad, or going into a different line of work altogether, the other three would have to give up, or try to find a replacement. It's just chat, that's all."

"Thank you for explaining." I picked up the tea towel and threw it in the corner where the laundry basket should have been. "It's good to know. And so do I assume that all of them are coming back to live in London, and that all of them anticipate being available on evenings and weekends for bar mitzvahs and funerals?"

"Yes," she said, still not moving and more or less challenging me to a "What do you want to make of it?"

"Excellent." I was like a blind man stumbling through a minefield. I took a long drink from my wineglass and then refilled it. "So we're going to have the marvellous red-headed wonder as part of the next phase of our lives as well. Having endured the last five years in which Brendan fucking Harcourt has lusted after you like a puppy on heat, I'll have many more years to look forward to evenings where you are out late, wearing sexy outfits, with two blokes who fancy you and one who has never made any secret that he has the total hots for you. And I'll sit at home like a good wife waiting for you to turn the key in the latch."

The look on Harriet's face suggested that she was struggling for the right way of expressing what she had in her mind, but after a few seconds she definitely found it.

"Fuck you."

I don't know what had come over me, and I guess that Harriet's response was exactly what I could have anticipated and probably deserved. By now the water was lapping around my chin, but I was still wading in.

"Why so? What is it about what I have said that doesn't ring true?"

"Because, you fucking idiot," she said, or rather she didn't say, because by now she was shouting at close to the capacity of her lungs, "because I am the total ass who heads off home when everyone else is going for a nightcap. I am the idiot who says no every time someone asks me to go for a drink after the gig. I am the complete fool who has remained faithful to you, in mind, body and spirit, in sickness and in health, ever since we met as relatively young kids. And all I get is suspicion, bollocks and patronizing and snide remarks for my trouble. So" – and now she stood up straight and headed for the door, only looking over her shoulder as she disappeared – "fuck you, fuck you, and one more thing," she said, tossing her hair dramatically. "Fuck you."

The funny thing about saying something in anger is that once it has been said, it cannot be unsaid. The second it's floating in the ether, it's there for ever. Hanging there, like a sword. As soon as I saw and heard the vehemence of Harriet's

reaction to what I had said, it had the effect of instantly so-
bering me up, and I knew that I had been a complete prat.
The picture she painted of living the life of a nun among a
bunch of hedonist students had the ring of truth about it.
Knowing that I had chosen to look after my brother instead
of pursuing my education and the fun that would have accompanied it, Harriet was doing her bit by keeping to a quiet
and dignified life. In her own way, she was doing everything
possible to remain true to me. She was making a significant
personal sacrifice, which I had patently failed to appreciate
or be grateful for with my pathetic suspicions.

"Oh darling…" I said, but it was too late. The front door
slammed and she had gone.

* * *

It took a while to heal that particular rift, and it was all made
much worse because it happened so close to the time when
we would have to go back to our separate lives. She was due
to set off on the Monday morning, and by the afternoon of
the day before I think we had more or less regained our usual
harmony, but still the wounds were fresh.

"I don't suppose you know yet when you'll next be able to
come down?"

Harriet smiled half-heartedly. It was a gentle scratch on an
open wound, but she seemed keen to pour balm on it.

"I don't know yet. I'll have to see what the timetable does,
and what essay or project commitments I'll have for the next

few weeks. They've already warned us that this year is going to be the toughest so far."

I was about to remind her that the long, slow train journey provided excellent quiet time for reading and study, but thought better of it and just nodded.

"Listen," I said, "I know you'll do your best. Just remember that we are here to support you. It isn't easy for you, and the very last thing I want is to be an extra pressure on you."

"Thank you," she said. "I really appreciate that."

"I mean it. I know that I haven't properly acknowledged that this is all every bit as tough for you as it is for me. And I don't want to take for granted that you don't do everything every other student does to have a good time." Harriet smiled a lovely little half-smile that told me the frost was melting. At that moment her face seemed to me to be the loveliest thing I had ever looked at, and I stepped forward and put my arms around her waist. "It's only that I love you so much, and if anything ever happened to you I just don't know what I would do."

Instead of looking at me, Harriet pushed her face into my shoulder. After a few seconds I could feel little convulsions rippling through her body and could tell that she was crying.

"Hey," I said. "No need for tears. I just wanted to make sure you know how much you mean to me."

She didn't move, but the trembling continued. After a while I heard her voice, muffled because her face was pushed hard into my jacket.

"I do know it, Jonathan. I really do."

Chapter Fifteen

Over the next few weeks, our lives slipped back into the same familiar routine. Each morning I would wake up at around 7 a.m. and lie in bed collecting my thoughts about the day. I can't pretend that I thought anything terribly profound in these meanderings. I suppose I wondered what Harriet was doing, what time she would be waking, how she might have slept. These were days when a long-distance telephone call was an event, so it did not occur to me that I could call her to find out. Anyway, this was her final year and Harriet had moved into a university-owned house with three other girls from her department. I never had the opportunity to see it, but I knew that the shared telephone was in a public area, and so our conversations were not completely satisfactory.

After about ten minutes I would ease myself out of bed, slip on my dressing gown and pad into Roger's bedroom to wake him. In all the time I had lived with Roger, and indeed in all the years since, I don't think I ever went into his room in the morning and found him already awake. God, I envied him that. Not that my own sleep patterns were not regular and more or less satisfactory, but Roger just seemed to be able to sleep like a baby.

What's more, when gently aroused from the deepest of deep sleeps, Roger always came to life in a way you'd want to wake up yourself. It was like he felt a mix of surprise and pleasure to have woken up at all, coupled with an inbuilt joy at finding himself in such a happy place as the world. A bit like waking up in a strange bed and realizing that you are somewhere lovely on holiday and outside the bright sun is shining and the blue sea is beckoning. That's what each day seemed to be like for Roger.

There is no doubt that his generally very sunny disposition was a significant factor in helping me to keep my equilibrium through some of the difficult times. Not infrequently at the end of the day and partway through my third drink of the evening, I found that the life I had chosen would feel humdrum and routine, and the long separations from Harriet would make me feel sad and lonely. But it wasn't easy to be for long in Roger's company and remain immersed in your own depression. It was as though he was inviting you into his world, where everything was far less complicated than it was for the rest of us.

"What's for breakfast?"

Roger had the same breakfast every day of his life, and had never to my knowledge accepted any of the hundreds of offers he had had to try something different. Two pieces of brown toast with butter and Marmite, a cup of milk and a banana. That was it. It was what he had been having regularly when I took over his care from our deceased parents, and it was what I made for him every single morning.

When Harriet was at home with us, and I anticipated an extended early morning of lovemaking, I might occasionally go for the "full English". In the early days I assumed that Roger would want to participate; but no, what Roger wanted each and every day was two slices of brown toast with Marmite, a cup of milk and a banana. That didn't stop him, though, from asking the same question every morning. "What's for breakfast?"

It became one of our many standing jokes that I'd say, "I thought we might have a toasted rhinoceros today Roger" – and Roger would start to giggle – "perhaps with some prunes and a devilled kidney." It would take him a few seconds to enjoy the idea before he knew that he had his line to say:

"No, thank you, Jonathan," he always said as though it was for the first time, "I think I'll just have the toast and Marmite today."

I made it my personal challenge to describe an offering which was ever more extravagant and eccentric each day and, good old Roger, he anticipated my weak humour with the same undiluted glee, and was guaranteed to think my joke to be the funniest thing he had ever heard.

"I thought we might have a scabby tortoise today, Roger," I might say, "with a little toasted cheese on top to enhance the crust," and Roger would chortle away until he could collect himself sufficiently to come in with his line. Oh, what a double act we were.

Anyway, one way or another, every day started off with only the slightest of variations on a narrow theme. For the most part, Roger was more or less able to get himself ready for his day. Our dad had spent many hours with him in the bathroom, showing him how to wash himself in all his private places. Sometimes, when our mother was alive, he would overdo it and emerge smelling like a perfume factory. Mostly though, he was pretty good.

He shaved with an electric razor, but it was beyond the patience of my father first, and then of me, to persuade him to do the job thoroughly, so that frequently Roger would walk around with thick tufts of facial hair in clumps jutting out at odd angles, usually the prerogative of the absent-minded professor or the vagrant. Roger made a strange sight as a twenty-eight-year-old with the shaving style of an alcoholic.

More amusing, if you were in the right mood, were Roger's various attempts at getting dressed without any help. You might have expected that this, being essentially a repetitive activity, was something that Roger would be able to manage, but for some reason he had a blind spot on the subject. His ability to put on a pullover the right way round was entirely subject to the laws of chance. If there were two possibilities, he would get it right fifty per cent of the time. And once the sweater was on, even if it meant that the collar was now tight around his neck, he would never seem to be aware that there was any problem. Sometimes I would try to nudge him towards discovering the matter for himself.

"Does that feel OK round your throat, Roger?"

He would respond with more or less the same facial expression as I might have expected if I had asked him to describe the movement of the solar system.

The same went for vests, and the same went for pants. Sometimes it was not until he needed to go to the lavatory that he discovered that his pants were on back to front, which could lead to a whole world of confusion.

Socks, of course, were a particular challenge, because putting on socks involves getting a number of things right at the same time. However, it didn't seem to matter much, and I reckon that Roger went out of the house wearing odd socks rather more often than he went out wearing a matching pair.

All in all though, our routine worked well, so that by the time Roger had emerged from the bathroom, washed and dressed, I would have his Marmite toast and cup of milk ready for him, with the banana ready to go so that he could eat it on the way to the day centre.

I also tried to make sure that he and I had a few minutes together in the mornings, just so that he would have the chance to tell me anything that might be on his mind about the day ahead. I had discovered that it was an easy matter for Roger to misunderstand something, in which case it might then begin to build up and fester in his mind until it got out of all proportion, before he would tell anyone what it was. Usually it would be something fairly trivial, such as that someone had said something to him which had hurt or been misunderstood. Rarely was it something worse, like a bit of bullying.

For that reason, I knew that it was important to give Roger the chance to unload anything that might get bigger if left alone, and experience had also taught me that it was better to do this in the mornings rather than in the evenings. Maybe most minor confusions were filtered out in his apparently untroubled sleep, leaving only the more difficult matters still needing to be shared. So it became a routine that while Roger sat eating his toast and drinking his milk, I'd ask him if everything was all right.

"Yes," he'd say – then he would usually smile and shake his head, a bit like a small boy whose mum was fussing.

"And is there anything you want to talk to me about? Anything on your mind?"

To be honest, I was so programmed to hearing the answer "no" that on this particular day I was slightly taken aback when the answer was "yes". "Yes" wasn't a totally rare answer, but it was unusual for it to come right out of the blue. Usually other aspects of Roger's behaviour would have given me an inkling. If something was troubling him, there were multiple indications that it was so.

"Really?" I said, catching myself just before I revealed too much surprise. I had to take care not to discourage him. "That's good. What is it you've been thinking about?"

"Well," he said, popping the last piece of toast into his mouth and allowing me a panoramic view of it being minced between his tongue and his teeth as he spoke, "you know Harriet?"

"Yes, Roger, I know Harriet. She's my wife." This didn't sound as patronizing at the time as it reads on the page. I was just trying to put his mind at ease that I knew whom he was talking about.

"Well, I was wondering" – another agonizingly long pause as he seemed to consider the best way of expressing it. After a few moments, he did. "What I was wondering was: what does she see in that Brendan?"

Of all the things that Roger could have come out with, this was right up there in the top five things that would get my attention. I looked at him, turning down my mouth at the corners and shrugging my shoulders, in a gesture designed to indicate that he needed to say more. It didn't work, so I asked him.

"What have you got in mind, Roger? You mean Brendan who plays in the quartet with Harriet?"

"Yes," he said, as though it was obvious, which of course it was. "Brendan with the red hair."

"What do you mean, what does she see in him? Why do you think she sees anything in him?" Now I was anxious not to scare Roger off from what he was intending to say by overreacting. Still, I was more than averagely keen to know what it was he was talking about. I waited for a few seconds, and was about to give him a further prompt when the words came out. He said them in the way that a schoolboy does when he has stumbled on something he knows is naughty and doesn't know if he's allowed to talk about it. His left hand half-covered his mouth, and he broke into a little giggle as he said it.

"I saw them kissing."

* * *

Six hours later I was sitting in the kitchen, watching the hands of the clock tick around the dial at apparently about a quarter of their usual pace, waiting waiting waiting for the moment I could head off to collect Roger from the bus. With the possible exception of the day I received the news about the fire, this had been the worst day of my life thus far. I say "possible exception" because, if completely honest, I'd probably have to admit that I was more freaked out by what Roger had told me that morning than by what the nurse had told me in the foyer of the Croydon Hospital rather more than two years earlier.

When Roger said what he said, my instant reaction was to go up in the proverbial blue light. Somehow I managed to control myself, knowing that if I succumbed to my instinct Roger would be likely to retreat into his shell and to say nothing more on the subject. The idea of being the cause of dispute or disharmony would be sure to make him stay silent. Only if I managed to behave casually, as though there was nothing amiss, did I stand a chance of discovering everything there was to know about what was inside Roger's head. So it was with a supreme effort of will that I told Roger there was nothing to worry about; that he should head off for his day at the centre, and that we would talk about it again over tea this evening. This seemed to satisfy him.

"Can we have fish fingers?" he said, and of course I confirmed that he could, indeed, have fish fingers for his tea. At that moment I was so distracted that I would have acquiesced if he had asked for kippers and caviar. My mind was racing at one thousand miles an hour as I gave Roger his banana for later and we walked together to catch the bus, but I think I managed to remain apparently calm, giving little hint of the turmoil that was going on inside my head.

"Have a nice day, Roger," I said to him as he got on the bus, but already his attention had been completely absorbed by one of the kids with Down syndrome who seemed to be his particular friend. I tried to catch his attention as the bus pulled away from the pavement, but he took no notice of me, standing on the edge of the kerb, my eyes already brimming over with salty tears which flowed down freely, creating large fresh raindrops on the front of my T-shirt.

My usual routine would be to pop home quickly after taking Roger to the bus, to pick up my book and bits and pieces, and then head off for the Underground on my way to Lewisham. As I waved goodbye to Roger, I knew that there could be no work for me today; no chance of freeing up space in my head to the degree necessary to carry out even the most mundane tasks of stamping in books and stamping out books and making reservations for books and shelving books and stacking books. No free capacity to spare for anything other than my attempts to find a way to cope with the monster that had burst its way into my head through my ears and now was busily marauding around my brain and plundering my sanity.

All day I could feel the fight going on – between the beast whose weapons were images of passionate lovemaking between the woman I loved and the man I hated, and the defenders who said that of course Roger had obviously misinterpreted something trivial and that it was all a misunderstanding. A case of mistaken identity, or more probably he had mistaken a peck on the cheek for something more.

Yes, as likely as not that would be it. A goodbye kiss on the cheek, maybe last Christmas. Maybe at another time? Maybe at Frost's? That might be it: perhaps Brendan and the others had kissed Harriet as they left the Transit after the garden party. I tried to remember. I revisited the scene in my mind. Did they? Had they? And if they had, had Roger turned around at that moment and seen them? Could he have caught sight of something in a mirror? And if so, was it something innocent? Or had he inadvertently witnessed a secret moment?

Mangling and torturing these thoughts over and over in my mind through the day, I completely lost sight of whether they were likely scenarios, or whether I was grasping at straws. I honestly did not have a clue. One minute the green-eyed monster was ripping out my intestines with imagined scenes of kissing and sweating and fucking and betrayal. The next minute I was casting my mind over the wonderful words of reassurance spoken by Harriet before the start of the new term, and was sure that it was all a mistake. She could not have been more open, more honest, more sincere. She could not have seemed to be more full of love for me. It was simply not possible that she could have said those things, and yet secretly be deceiving me. No, not possible. Surely.

Tick tock, tick tock. It was twenty past three and still an hour and a half to go before I could head out to meet the bus which might bring me the answer I so desperately needed.

I considered calling Harriet, but then even if I was able to locate her, what would I say? I never called her during the day, and would only ever have done so in an emergency. What was my emergency? "Hello, Harriet, Roger tells me that you are having an affair with Brendan, and I just wanted to ask you about it," I would say. "Yes, Jonathan, I am. I've wanted to tell you for ages," she might respond, one possibility that felt like the emotional equivalent of a knife through the heart. "Jonathan, are you bloody mad?" she might say instead. "Are you really going to get yourself stressed out and even take a day off work because of something Roger has obviously completely misunderstood?"

No, clearly I had to try to discover from Roger what was going on before I decided what to do next, and if I was to be able to do that, I knew that I would have to handle things carefully. If it had been a struggle to suppress my instincts this morning, how much harder would it be now that I had experienced this day of mental torture? Every bit of me wanted to grab Roger by the arms, shake him hard and yell "what did you see? what did you see?" into his face. Yet if I gave in to that urge, or to anything approaching it, I could be certain never to learn anything further.

I persuaded myself that the ten-minute walk to meet the bus actually took twenty minutes, and ended up getting there even faster than usual, with the result that I was waiting on the pavement with a good ten minutes to spare. Usually I had it all timed to perfection, so that I hardly had to pause in my step as I arrived at the stop at the same time as the bus, put my arm briefly around Roger's shoulders in greeting, and then marched back home. Today I remembered why.

I'm not proud of this, but to be completely honest I never liked small-talking with the relatives or carers of other people with problems comparable to Roger's. I suppose it was because I never really accepted that their problems were similar to his.

"You're Roger's brother aren't you?" In this case, the man speaking to me was the father of the Down-syndrome kid with whom I knew Roger was great mates. Looking at him, I reckon he was about seventy-five years of age, which meant that he would have been sixty when his son had been born. I often wondered whether people in that situation blamed themselves, which in turn made me blame myself for being such a complete arse.

"Yes, I am," I said tersely. Then that feeling of being an arse took a lunge at me. "And sorry, I don't know your son's name, but he's a friend of Roger's, isn't he?"

The old man confirmed that he was, and that, indeed, Roger and his son Terry were the very best of mates. He was probably used to the idea that his son's name didn't matter – that to so many people like me he was just "the Down-syndrome kid".

"Once or twice I've suggested that Roger might want to come back to tea with us," he said. "Terry would like that. Maybe he could even stay the night. It would give you a break and I could pop him back to get picked up here in the morning?"

There were so many aspects of this idea that I didn't like that I had difficulty in immediately choosing one. Anyway, my mind was far too full of other stuff to allow me to give it proper consideration.

"Actually, Roger and I both really like our routine," I told him. "Neither of us is very good at having it changed or interrupted." I should have said more, about what a kind thought it was, and how otherwise we would have been delighted, but the truth is that I just didn't feel like it. I was so preoccupied with getting Roger home and finding out what I needed to know that I could barely remain civil.

Thankfully, just at that moment the bus appeared at the corner of the street and I could begin to seem distracted away from the conversation. I don't know if he tried to start it up again, because as soon as the side windows came into view I was waving and shouting like a madman welcoming home a triumphant football team. When Roger's face came into focus he first of all looked startled, and then overjoyed by my apparent enthusiasm to see him. Careful, I told myself. Keep calm or you'll worry him.

It took all my restraint to keep the conversation light and general on the way back to the flat. To my consternation, Roger repeated the invitation I had just heard from Terry's father that he should go to eat with them and maybe stay the night. Obviously the suggestion had been the subject of wider discussion before being broached with me. I tried never to imply that I made all of his decisions for him, so I told Roger that we should both think about it and decide whether it was a good idea or not. Obviously I was hoping that it would go away.

Roger was always ravenously hungry when he got home, and so I had everything ready to stick his fish fingers under the grill. I used to make sure he also had some vegetables, so we had a can of peas and some tomatoes which we both liked to have grilled. Today though, I was about to turn on the oven when Roger said he thought he would like to go to check on the insect farm before we sat down to eat. I was dismayed.

"I was hoping we would eat first and have a chat, then if you like I'll go down there with you and you can show me some of your latest stuff."

That was a treat for Roger, because usually I would walk down to the allotments with him and leave him

173

on his own while I came back and tidied up. He loved showing me around, even though I had seen the vast majority of it all a hundred times at least. He agreed, and while I got on with cooking the food, I asked him about his day.

"Miss Tresize brought in her parrot today," he told me. "You should have seen it. Great big blue-and-green thing. I taught it to speak."

"Really?" I said. "What did you teach it to say?" Once again, Roger dissolved into the same mini-fit of giggles which had overcome him this morning, covering his mouth and looking away. It was all I could do to remain calm. "Seriously, Roger, what did you teach the parrot to say?"

It took him a few more seconds to get sufficiently over the hilarity of the situation so that he was able to get the words out, and when he did so it was like a five-year-old trying out a mild swear word in front of his parents.

"I love you," he said at last.

"Well, that's a nice thing to teach it, Roger," I said. "Now whenever anyone speaks to the parrot, it'll say 'I love you', and that will give everyone a good laugh."

"I love you," he said again, as though, having said it and not got into trouble, he now wanted to see how the words felt on his tongue. "I love you. I love you."

"Yes, thanks, Roger," I said. "You are beginning to sound like the parrot. I think the novelty might wear out quite quickly." But he was still going on.

"I love you. I love you. I love you." And then it was as though, having pushed his luck thus far, he was pausing to wonder whether to push it just a little bit further. Then he did.

"I love you, Harriet. I love you, Harriet. I love you, Harriet."

The grill tray hit the floor with the sound of a thunder-clap, and Roger's hand went instantly to his mouth, this time covering it. When I turned round to face him, I could see that his eyes were wide and pleading with me to tell him that everything was all right. It took me a second or two of struggling to regain self-control, but I managed to do so.

"It's OK, Roger," I said. "It was just an accident. The handle was hot and it slipped out of my hand." I bent to start picking up the fragments of half-cooked fish fingers which had come apart and were spread across the kitchen floor. "That's a shame. Looks like we'll have to start again." I felt a squelch under the heel of my foot, but failed to recoil fast enough to avoid squashing a grilled tomato into the rug.

* * *

Fifteen minutes later I had cooked more fish fingers and Roger and I were sitting opposite each other at the tiny table which took up about a third of the entire space of the kitchen. It was covered with a plastic, easy-to-clean cloth which featured old-fashioned kitchen utensils against a white background. There was a mangle, and a washboard, and a smoothing iron. It had been one of the items I picked up from the charity shop when I was trying to equip the flat quickly.

"So, Roger," I said, making my very best effort to seem as calm and casual as I knew how. "You were asking me this morning about Harriet." I put another forkful of food in my mouth and chewed it for a little while, trying to give the impression of being in no hurry for the conversation to continue. "You were asking what I thought Harriet saw in… who was it… Brendan, I think you said?" I went on chewing, and then folded a piece of bread and dabbed it in the tomato ketchup which was now in place of what would have been the grilled tomatoes. "I think you said you had seen them kissing? Was that what you said?"

I glanced up from my plate towards Roger and saw that he was not sure how to respond. Plainly he wasn't entirely comfortable, but he didn't seem too ill at ease either. He nodded his head. I went back to my food, torn in two by the feeling of urgency to get to the point, but fighting against the certainty that any sign of it would have the opposite effect.

"So when was that, Roger? When did you see them kissing?" Roger was looking back at me, but was neither moving nor speaking. It was as though he was trying to weigh up what to tell me. Or maybe he was trying to weigh up exactly what it was he thought he saw. "Was it at the garden party we went to? When we dropped the other lads off?" He shook his head. No, that was very definitely not what he was thinking of. "When was it then?" I kept chewing. "Roger?" Still chewing. "When did you see Harriet and Brendan kissing?"

176

I thought I was going to burst with impatience when I could see that Roger was struggling to get his words out. Almost as though he had a stammer, which he did not. I tried hard to force myself to say nothing, to put no more pressure on him. Finally he spoke.

"At the market square."

"Oh, really?" I said. "What market square was that?

"Was it called Convent Garden?"

"Oh," I said, "Covent Garden. You mean when the quartet was playing downstairs in the piazza, and you and I were collecting money from bystanders?" He nodded his head. We had got there. This was what he meant. "And was it when we had finished? When we had all packed up and everyone was going our separate ways?" Maybe I was grasping at straws now. Maybe I was simply reluctant to go where this was going. Roger shook his head. "When was it then?" I think that my voice was still calm, but any hope I had that there was an innocent explanation was disappearing fast.

"It was when you and I went to the shops to get coffee for everyone. Martin and Jed went off to look in the museum shop, and Harriet and Brendan were on their own. You sent me back to find out if anyone wanted any biscuits, and I saw them."

At last a coherent sentence, but even now his account was short of the final coup. His words were coming our breathlessly, as if they had been a burden to him and were being offloaded in a rush. Now it was as though I didn't want to hear it. I said nothing to encourage him to continue, but having got himself into a state where he was telling it, he was going to spill it all out. He had passed the point of no return. He had lost sight of any concern about whether I was going to be happy, or sad or angry or to totally lose my fucking mind. He had crossed the Rubicon, and here it was, heading towards me, now unstoppable.

"They were standing in the corner of the square, away from everyone else. They were holding each other. He was kissing her, and it took a long time. I watched them for a minute, but I knew that I had to ask them about the sweets. I was about to ask them when I heard Brendan tell Harriet that he loved her. Just like I taught the parrot. 'I love you, Harriet,' he said. They still hadn't seen me so I came back. I said that no one wanted anything, but I hadn't really asked them."

I've heard people describe moments like this as being like going into a long tunnel, and have always thought that it was just a turn of phrase. Actually that image is about as good an expression of what was happening to me at that moment as I can think of. I had entered a long tunnel, there were no exits on either side, and all I could do was to head forward and downwards in a long, numb, desolate hollow of disbelief. As my mind wrestled with what Roger was saying, I remembered the moment. I remembered Roger shaking his head when I asked if anyone had said yes to sweets or biscuits. I wondered if I had thought anything odd about it then. Odd that no one wanted anything. Odd that Roger had just shaken his head.

Had I seen anything unusual in his expression at the time? Had he even registered properly that he had seen something amiss... something he was not supposed to see?

I knew that there was nothing else to say, and it was with the greatest difficulty imaginable that I appeared to remain calm while Roger finished his food. I felt as though someone had reached out their hand towards me, stuck it down my throat, grabbed my guts and wrenched them out and onto the floor in front of me. I felt empty and in pain. I said nothing. I could say nothing. We ate the rest of our food in silence; Roger absorbed with his fish fingers and the prospect of going to the insect farm; me utterly lost in a labyrinth of despair.

Afterwards he and I walked the few blocks towards the allotments and I, as I had promised, went through the motions of paying attention as he spoke about his ants and his sticklebacks and his stag beetles and his worms. I listened as he talked about how they gathered their food and how they organized their lives, no doubt entirely oblivious to the fact that they were part of another larger world, where other beings also lived their lives, themselves every bit as unaware of their irrelevance to the wider universe.

Chapter Sixteen

How is it possible for anyone ever to believe the idea that an emotion can be adequately conveyed by a mere combination of words? How could we ever think that anyone who hadn't experienced them could glean from words on a page even the slightest inkling of what an intensely felt passion is really like?

I describe a wall as painted red, and if you have seen the colour red before then you may have an idea of what I am talking about. Perhaps you are picturing something from the Union Jack while I am picturing something from a pillar box, but we're likely to be in the same territory. Red is red, or something close to it. I say "red" and you have in your mind's eye something similar to what I have in my mind's eye. It works.

Or I can describe a day as sunny or a surface as rough, and, as you have experienced sunny days and rough surfaces, you can get an idea of what I am talking about. The warmth of the sun on your skin, the feeling of harshness under the palm of your hand. But how can anyone describe to someone who hasn't experienced it the exquisite pain that arises from the feeling that the person with whom you are so deeply in love is in love with someone else? How can that happen?

Most of us have put our fingers momentarily into the flame of a candle. Does it give you any idea of what it is like to experience first-degree burns in a fire? Not really. You know it is unpleasant, and the merest hint of what it might be like to keep your finger in the flame makes you withdraw it with an instant and involuntary reaction. The experience of being burned is so horrendous that the body automatically recoils from getting any closer than is unavoidable to the full-blown experience.

So when someone you love has shown a moment of inappropriate affection for another person, you may have experienced a pang of jealousy. Or the kiss under the mistletoe, or under the influence, that takes just a second longer than you are comfortable about. You feel a twinge, but nothing you are likely to have experienced as a result of such a commonplace comes anywhere close to the tangible, physical, corrosive agony that accompanies full-blown jealousy. Nothing comes close.

The nearest I can get to conveying it is to think about a heavy weight in your stomach, or rather a heavy weight just above your stomach, sitting somewhere between your guts and your heart. A physical lump, with actual mass, just sitting there. It feels for all the world like a cancer, or like a tumour that you know is going to turn into a cancer in years to come. A physical trauma that will trigger something debilitating which, in its turn, will eventually kill you.

Have you heard the expression "You don't know where to put yourself"? That applies here. You don't. You walk from room to room, unable to settle in one place. You sit, and then you get up and walk around some more. Lying down, you find that the weight of it shifts onto your lungs and that you cannot get your breath. You sit up, panting, stiff, congested and unable to get the oxygen circulating properly through the bloodstream.

The images that swim around your head are all physical. His view of her as she takes off her clothes and moves towards him. His eyes perusing that beautiful lustrous body that you think of as all your own. Your property. Your domain. Other eyes admiring it. Other hands upon it.

Her view of him, up close, as she brings the lips that you have so often kissed up to kiss his neck and his chest and his mouth. Just as she has so often kissed you. His face is not your face. His neck is not your neck; she knows it and yet she kisses him as avidly as ever she has kissed you.

Then an outside view of the two of them, entwined in a tight and sweaty embrace, tongues and bodies locked together in passion. No, even though the words come nowhere near the reality, I cannot write more. Even now, so many years after the event, the pain is every bit as sharp as it was all that time ago.

I simply cannot understand or explain how I managed to survive the time before I saw Harriet again. It was three weeks before the Christmas holidays and there was no question of her being able to come down for a weekend before then, and so I had no choice but to live with my demons. Nothing to do but to wait and drink the nights away. Not only did I have to wait, but I had to remain calm. I could not afford to let Roger know what his observation had done to me. I could not allow Harriet to get a hint that I was in hell. Any hope of managing the situation lay in the possibility of remaining in control; and so I had to quell my instinctive desire to fall to my knees and release a scream of anguish, and instead to go about my usual routine just as though everything in my life was still normal.

But nothing was. It sounds now as though it must be an exaggeration, but I really don't think that I got more than an hour per night of uninterrupted sleep in the entire three weeks from the moment Roger told me his story. Each night I lay in bed, contorted with anguish at the thoughts which flooded into my head and laid siege to my sanity. Each night I turned over in my mind the various words of reassurance that Harriet had used whenever we discussed our lives apart. I recalled in precise detail the conversation we had had when I succumbed to my unwise outburst about Brendan remaining a part of our lives. Perhaps I should have realized then? Her response had been so angry, so over the top. Perhaps there was a clue that I had missed?

I thought about the reassurance her words had given me, about the regret and the anguish I had felt for being so stupid as to harbour even the smallest suspicion. I lay in bed and thought of these things, and no force on earth could prevent my mind from travelling the three hundred miles which I could not travel with my body to the little room at the top of the stairs in the house which Harriet was said to be sharing with three other girls.

There she was, right at this moment, the woman that I loved more than the moon and the stars and all the riches of the earth, embracing and kissing and fucking the man I already hated more than anyone else on the planet. Here was I, at precisely the same moment, at the other end of the country, lying in my bed, sad, alone, pathetic and weeping for the betrayal of my faith.

My mind went through the whole gamut of possibilities. Sometimes I would grasp at the idea that Roger might still have been mistaken. I was a drowning man reaching out to a lifeboat. Yes, perhaps that was possible. After all, Roger is an idiot. Yes, he is; what am I doing taking the word of an idiot above the promise from the woman I love? Have I lost my mind? All this anger and torture and despair for nothing. A misunderstanding, a case of mistaken identity – anything could be possible.

Seldom did the respite last more than just a few minutes, as I recalled the occasion that Roger had described and remembered the circumstances, and also the look on his face when he had returned from his errand. Of course, there was no mistake. I, Jonathan Maguire, had voluntarily absented myself from the side of the woman I loved, and my presence and my affections had been replaced by Brendan fucking Harcourt. What could be sadder? Or more predictable? Or more pathetic?

My preoccupation – no, my obsession with the stark realities of the situation meant that it was only in the last week before the end of the autumn term that I began to think about how I would handle the situation directly with Harriet. She had been due to come back on the following Thursday evening, but on the Monday evening she called and said that she had made better than expected progress with an essay she had been working on, and was now planning to come the following day instead.

"I've bought tickets for Thursday," she said, "and I think I will have to pay extra if I change the day I travel." She asked me what I thought. I said that she should get on the earlier train.

"Maybe the conductor won't notice the date. Or if he does, you can no doubt charm him. And if the worst comes to the worst, you can always pay the difference. It's got to be worth it for the two extra days."

So now she was coming home tomorrow and my mind went into overdrive. In those twenty-four hours I imagined every eventuality. At times I thought that perhaps I would confront her and that she would immediately offer an explanation which was comprehensive and unassailable. I would breathe a sigh of relief which could propel an ocean-going yacht, and tell her what an idiot I had been. She would laugh at my silliness, and all the suffering, so awful and unbearable for such a long time, would quickly melt away to become just a ghastly nightmare.

Those times were few and brief. At other times I imagined her stunned into silence by my revelation, and then confessing all and imploring me for forgiveness. I did not consider what I would do in such circumstances. The wound was so deep that contemplating forgiveness was impossible, and yet the notion of being without her? Equally not possible.

Lastly, and most frequently, I anticipated Harriet telling me that she was sorry that I had found out in this way, that she had intended to tell me herself, and that she was planning to leave me to go to live with Brendan. Again, in such circumstances, I had no idea how I would be able to handle the situation. The set of facts were so repugnant that my brain simply refused to engage, and I found myself staring into an abyss.

Sometimes at the end of term, and especially if she had a lot of luggage to bring down, I would go to meet Harriet at King's Cross. While secretly hating it, I always managed to appear to do so willingly. I hated it almost as bitterly as I hated going to see her off. A formerly magnificent building which had seen a glorious history now down at heel and surrounded by a seedy selection of tramps and drunks and pathetic men, heads down, darting in and out of massage parlours. The idea of staging an emotional scene in such a godforsaken hole, be it either of the pain of parting or the joy of reunion, was anathema to me, and something I would wish to avoid if at all possible. If Harriet had heavy bags to carry, then it was not possible to avoid it. On this occasion, thank heavens, it was.

I was keen that Roger should be out of the house when Harriet arrived back, because I did not trust myself to be able to act normally and to hold it together for long after her arrival. Whatever was to transpire, having Roger on the scene could only add complications. In his own very different way, Roger was probably as attached to Harriet as I was. The realization that we were quite possibly losing her, coupled as it could easily be with the revelation that he was an unwitting player in the drama, might cause unpredictable results. No, if we were losing Harriet, then I needed to be able to manage the way the news was broken to Roger.

Once again I am ashamed to admit it, but I packed a bag with some overnight things for Roger, and took it with me as I went down early to meet the bus. Terry's father was already there and waiting.

"Hello, Mr Harries," I said, "I wanted to apologize to you for my reaction to your suggestion a couple of weeks ago that Roger might come and spend the night with you and Terry. It just came a bit out of the blue, and Roger usually doesn't like to have his routines messed up." He was a very nice man and said that he understood completely. I suspected that he understood only too well, and was used to the sort of slight that I had dealt him. "Anyway, rather than let him have time to get too worked up about it, if by any chance it suited you, I thought we might try it overnight tomorrow night? If it's not convenient for you, just say. But if it does work for you, I thought you could take his overnight bag with you now, and then you could meet the bus and let him come back home with you tomorrow?"

I didn't feel too good about the fact that, for purely selfish reasons, I was accepting the offer which before I had been so keen to reject. However, if he was offended, Terry's father showed no sign of it and appeared to be very happy with the arrangement. Of course I had no sleep whatever on Monday night, and I waited until Tuesday morning to tell Roger that he would be staying overnight with his friend Terry. He seemed to be excited by the idea, so much so that I then felt guilty about not having arranged something like it sooner.

I have no clear memory of how I passed the day while I waited for Harriet. I think of it as a blur of images and emotions of a nature and intensity I had never known before. It's as close as I have ever come, thank God, to having an idea of what it must be like for a condemned man to know that he would die within a few hours. A last meal? How could anyone eat in such circumstances? Last words? What words could possibly sum up all the multitude and variety of thoughts and feelings? I padded around the flat for some hours, then decided that I might be able to get some relief from taking a bath, but in the event I found that when I immersed myself it was as though the weight of water was constricting my breathing still further. I quickly got out and gulped down air. I thought I would faint, but at last my head cleared.

I watched the clock tick around, focusing hard on the big hand, and found that I could identify all sixty of the tiny movements in the measured minute. Three hundred would take me five minutes. 3,600 would get me to an hour.

I was alone in the flat at 3 p.m. when Harriet was due to arrive. The train came in at 2 p.m., and usually it would take about half an hour or so to ride on the Tube, and then there was a short walk from Clapham North Underground. My anxiety was at fever pitch, and only increased still further as the minutes ticked by. I thought I heard a sound at the door and turned quickly, nearly tripping over Olly the cat as I did so. It was nothing, only the wind rattling the locks.

I looked out of the window at about the time that Harriet was expected, and I recall the moment that I saw her come around the corner. Despite everything else, the turmoil going on inside my crazy head, I felt a surge of pleasure at seeing the riot of brown curls which was her hairstyle and the outline of her beautiful face which I knew well and loved so helplessly.

It was cold outside, the wind blowing with a vengeance, and she was wearing a full-length Afghan coat which she had bought at the Quayside Market in Newcastle, and which I always joked made her smell like a bear. I felt no amusement as I watched her walk the last hundred yards from the corner to the gate of the tiny garden, and then lost sight of her as she covered the last few steps to the front door two floors below. I remember feeling my heart pounding and walking from room to room, unable to decide where I wanted to be when she came into the flat. On the few occasions when she had come back alone from the station, I would certainly be at the street door to meet her. At the very least I would have been halfway down the stairs to grab her bags and pat her on the bum for the last few steps home.

I didn't know whether to be in the hallway just inside the door, or at the window looking out, or at the kitchen sink apparently preoccupied with washing dishes. I think I tried all of them in the few seconds in which I could hear her footsteps on the stairs. As it was I was halfway between the window and the kitchen when the door opened and I saw her suitcase being lifted through the gap, and then her leather boot, and then her knee – and then Harriet emerged fully into view.

Instantly she took my breath away. She was beautiful.

Harriet knew that something was wrong from the moment she arrived. How could she not? Ordinarily in circumstances like these I was of course desperate to see her, overcome with joy and emotion and utterly unguarded in my enthusiasm. Usually we would take the very first opportunity to embrace, and then remain holding each other for many minutes, whispering endearments and reassurances until we could bring ourselves to pull our faces far enough back to be able to kiss.

Given the torture and trauma that I had gone through in the previous three weeks, it had been all I could do to act naturally when speaking on the telephone. The fact that at her end she was speaking in a public place made it less obvious that we were avoiding the intimacies which otherwise might have been expected. Even then, I sensed that she knew there was something wrong. Several times she had asked me:

is everything all right? I assured her that it was, and that it was simply that I was missing her.

Oh my God. What is it about seeing someone you love for the first time in a long time? No matter what the anticipation does to you, the reality is so much more powerful. It felt so long since I had looked at Harriet's beautiful face, and in that time I had conjured her in every mood, guise, aspect and expression. I had pictured her in the distance, up close, kissing me and kissing my body. But also I had pictured her face pressed up against the face of Brendan Harcourt, kissing him with all the passion and the ardour with which she kissed me. God help me, I had pictured her face as he made love to her; I had pictured her face as he entered her, but now here she was, in the flesh, every bit as lovely as all my fantasies had ever envisaged, and much more so.

At first sight of each other, Harriet and I both seemed to be frozen. I could do nothing but stand and face her; she halfway through the door and struggling with her keys and the lock and her bags and her coat, me halfway through my perambulation through the flat, unable to decide where to be and what to be doing.

Instantly I could see the look of uncertainty and apparent confusion on her face. A faint knot of lines on her forehead, and a small downturn of the corners of her lovely mouth, said "there is something wrong and I don't know what it is" as eloquently as the words might have conveyed it. But when she did speak, there was no sign of anything other than genuine confusion.

"Hi, Jonathan," she said. "What's going on?"

I gazed for a moment at this wonderful woman who was standing in front of me, suddenly seeming so frail and small, but whose life and existence played so overwhelming an influence on my own life and well-being. She had lost weight since the last time I had seen her, and her skin was pale, as if she had been for too long out of the sun.

"Hi, Harriet," I said. It was as though a hypnotist had snapped his fingers in front of my eyes, and instantly I was able to collect myself. "So sorry. I just got behind and lost track of the time. I was trying to make sure the place was tidy in time for you getting here." I managed to get my limbs moving and walked the few paces towards her, reaching for her suitcase. She handed it to me, but again, now up close, I could see the look of confusion on her face. She shook her head, clearly indicating how obvious it was that my explanation was not complete. However, at the same moment, I could see that she had decided not to make an issue of it, but just to see where all this was going. Certainly nothing in her face or demeanour suggested guilt or any inkling of knowledge of what might be the problem. She handed her suitcase to me.

"Actually, for once I think I am a bit early. The train arrived on time and the connections were fairly straightforward."

She wasn't early, but I did not feel like contradicting her. I put down her bag, and we stood looking at each other for a moment, as if both searching the other for some truth. Then I put my arms around her and pulled her towards me with a longing and desperation which I would not have thought it possible to survive. I clung to her, wishing as I had never wished for anything that what I knew was true would not be true. I was wishing that it could always be like this; that things would never become more complicated than Harriet and I in each other's arms, embracing at the door. My head was buried in her neck, my eyes held tightly closed and, heaven help me, I could feel my body involuntarily convulse in a violent sob, and the tears running down my cheeks fell liberally onto Harriet's collar and neck. I felt her tighten her hold on me and whisper in my ear.

"It's all right, my darling. It's OK. I'm here now. It's all OK. It's been so long, but now I am back with you, my love."

What was it like to hear the very words that I so badly wanted to hear from Harriet – "It's all going to be all right" – but at the same time knowing in my heart and soul that it was not going to be all right? At that moment, I thought that my head would come apart from the anguish. The woman I wanted so much was here in my arms, telling me that everything was going to be all right. At the same time, a thousand images of her in the arms of someone else swarmed around me like a plague of locusts, biting and stinging and eating into my flesh.

I managed to pull myself together sufficiently to be able to carry off Harriet's assumption that my aberrant behaviour was a function of missing her rather than of anything else. She asked me if I wanted to go to bed straight away and at first I said that I did not. Then she looked disappointed and gave me a child-like expression of sadness which sent a wave of affection through me.

Our lovemaking on that afternoon was like nothing I had ever known before and nothing I have ever known since. Without speaking, and without embracing or kissing, we removed each other's clothes item by item and lay them on the end of the bed. When she was naked, I stood back from her just to be able to look at her body.

I have said before that Harriet was not beautiful in the same way that many girls of her age were beautiful. She did not have the stick-thin figure which was fashionable at the time, but rather her breasts were fuller, and her hips were wider. Her long, flowing brown curls fell onto her freckled shoulders, and my eyes followed a few wisps of hair down to her lovely breasts and the soft pale-brown nipples. She smiled a broad smile at me, loving the fact that I was in awe of her, and slowly turned around so that I could enjoy every inch of her. The line of her neck as it met her shoulders, the soft ridges of her collar bone just below her skin, the shape of her shoulder blades, slightly protruding, and then dipping back into her spine and down to that spot where the bottom of her back met the top of her bum. It was my favourite place, there and around the side of her, where the trim valley of her ribs and waist travelled outwards to her hips. That lovely ridge, the softest of most soft skin, the slightest hint of downy hair, and on down to the breathtaking loveliness of her.

She was still facing the other way, when I at last closed up to meet her, and put my arms around her waist to pull her towards me.. I could feel myself responding to the sensation of her flesh against me, and her head half-turned so that her lips touched mine. Then all of a sudden I was on her, in her, over her, oblivious to the pain and the anguish and the nightmares. My mind and thoughts melted away in the exquisite pleasure of her, and I was possessing her as if to make her completely my own once again.

I wonder how it is possible for the mind to continue to function when it is being bombarded at the same moment by so many concurrent thoughts, by recalled feelings and moments from the memory, by recent nightmares and by the traffic jam of sensual thrills being transported up the nervous system to end their journey by exploding into the brain. The combination of physical sensation with mental anguish, of the delirium of lovemaking with the trauma of knowing what I knew, threatened my sanity.

Not that I am getting ready for a plea, mind you. That's not the case I am making here. It is simply that I want to try to get this down on paper, maybe just so that I may be able to understand it myself, just to know something of what was going on in those few hours.

After we had made love and Harriet was lying in my arms, I remember once again the turmoil of confusion overwhelming me, and I felt unable to breathe. I sat up in bed, swinging my legs around so that my feet were on the floor, and put my head in my hands. So strong and urgent were the emotions welling up and swirling around inside me that I had to work hard to control the uprising of another convulsive sob, and I swallowed hard in an attempt to suppress the cauldron inside of me. I felt her hand upon my back as she lifted herself onto her elbow, and when she spoke, Harriet's words were soft and full of love.

"Are you all right, my darling?" she asked, concerned and yet also apparently understanding. "Is there anything I can do for you? To make you feel better?" I said nothing. She continued. "It's all right now. You've been through a horrible time, but I am back with you, and am here to make everything good for you. We'll have a lovely time together. You'll see."

And once again I felt my mind rotate from agony to joy as I believed that everything I had dreaded and feared must be wrong. It was not possible that Harriet could be saying this to me if she was also in love with someone else. Not possible.

We took a shower, not together, because the shower was in the bath and I feared an accident. However, we were naked in the bathroom, and I admit to taking every opportunity to look at her – her shape reflected in the mirror as she bent down, her breasts falling forward as they did when she sat astride me. It was as though I wanted to drink her in, to commit every inch of her to memory. Almost as though I knew what was going to happen, which I most assuredly did not.

Chapter Seventeen

An hour later and Harriet was wearing a white cotton robe and towel-drying her hair, while I pulled a string of spaghetti out of the bubbling saucepan and flung it against the wall to see if it would stick. There was a starchy smear on the tiles where the same operation had been performed a hundred times before. I had poured two fresh glasses of red, which were the end of the bottle I had opened ahead of her arrival. I was feeling the first effects of intoxication.

Did I mention that Harriet had lovely hands? Probably not – so much about her body delighted me that there is no reason to pick them out in particular. I have a strong mental image of admiring them as she twisted her fork around to gather the first mouthful of spaghetti. Her long fingers that would stretch across the keys of her flute to produce the magical music that had the power of trans-portation. Now, as she put the spaghetti into her mouth, the inevitable few strands failed to comply and I saw her make the shape which I loved so much as she sucked the remnants in between her lips.

"Delicious," she said, and put out her other hand to cover mine. Her unaffected smile radiated a warmth which instantly penetrated my aching body. "You have surpassed yourself."

There were some moments in which neither of us spoke and I was aware of Harriet glancing at me, as though to check whether our silence was serene or a signal of something else. Olly the cat jumped up on the table, keen to join in the meal, but I pushed him back onto the floor. Nothing further had been said about the odd way in which I had greeted her.

The seconds ticked past with neither of us saying anything. I was about to speak when the silence was broken by the sound of the telephone ringing in the hallway. Neither of us rushed to pick it up, and after three rings I could hear the answering machine click in and play my recorded message. The voice which followed it was one I did not immediately recognize.

"Jonathan? This is Mr Harries. Terry's dad. You know, the one... well, you know, Roger is staying with us. I just wanted to let you know that there is nothing to worry about. Roger is just a little bit unsettled – probably with his change of routine. Half an hour ago he wanted to come home, but he seems OK now. Just wanted to reassure you. I don't think we have any problem. Just wanted to keep you in the picture. All things being well, I'll see you at teatime tomorrow when they come back from the centre."

Then there was a click.

It's funny how when you look back on the big things that have happened in your life you realize that there were small things you might have done which would completely have changed the course of events. This was one of those moments, which I have gone over and over in my mind. Ninety-nine times out of a hundred on hearing a message like that, I would have taken the call, or would have called back immediately and asked Terry's dad to bring Roger home. Hell, ninety-nine times out of one hundred I would not have allowed Roger to stay away overnight in the first place. But this was the one hundredth time. I feared and believed that my wife was sleeping with another man, and I was preoccupied with my need to get the matter resolved one way or another. I had endured weeks of torture which was going to be either acquitted or dissolved tonight, and my usual judgement was so distorted that I could not hear the klaxon sound of the alarm ringing in my head.

"Are you OK with that?" Harriet asked. She knew it was way out of character for me to be apparently unconcerned after a message such as the one we had just heard. Perhaps not even so much what he said, but the sound of uncertainty in his voice when he said it. It was a tone you could interpret whichever way suited you: as the kind of nervousness that some people have just because they are speaking on the tele-phone, or more serious concern disguised as reassurance. My mood and priorities dictated that I decided to infer the former. Obviously Harriet was not so sure. "He sounded a bit on edge, I thought. Like he didn't want to worry you but he did want to worry you."

"I'm sure he's OK. Roger has been away before, and he knows that if he wants to he can ask to come back."

"He hasn't been away overnight since your parents died, has he?"

"No, Harriet, he hasn't. But he wanted to go, and it's good for him. Why are you so keen for him to come back?"

Now she looked surprised. "I'm not. Why would you say that? I am just worried about him; as you usually are. I can't work out why you don't seem so concerned as you usually would."

"Because you and I need to talk."

Speaking of moments, there are other moments when the die is cast in a particular direction, and then there is no going back. This was one of them. In those days the expression "we need to talk" did not have the connotations it has today; a euphemism for "I want to break up with you". It meant what it said.

One bottle between the two of us was always more than enough, but by now the second bottle of red wine was empty. Nonetheless I went to find another one and laboriously took out the cork while Harriet said nothing and waited for what was to follow. I imagine that at this point she must have known what was coming. Maybe it was a relief for her. Possibly she had spent many hours mentally rehearsing the scene that was about to unfold. A sort of calm settled over her, possibly one of resignation. She was sitting in a car on the roller-coaster and the ride was about to begin.

"Roger has told me about you and Brendan."

Harriet looked at me, and for all the world it was impossible to read what was going on behind her eyes. I would have defied the greatest mind-reader to predict whether she was about to protest, to ask questions, to go crazy or to confess. Her gaze was steady, her eyelids hardly blinking, so that in the end it was I who had to look away. I poured more red wine into the glasses, took a long swallow and waited.

"Has told you what?" Her voice was entirely impassive. Not angry, not indignant, not even especially curious. Just words. If there had been any going back, I might have gone back, but the wheels were turning, the car was rolling and it was bound to reach the end of its journey and land somewhere.

"That when we were out busking in Covent Garden, I went to get the coffee while Martin and Jed went shopping. Roger came back to ask if you guys wanted anything else, and he saw the two of you kissing." And all the time I was speaking, I was searching Harriet's face for an instant-by-instant reaction to what I was saying. Was she surprised? Alarmed? Angry? I simply could not tell. As I looked at her I felt one of those surges of balance and consciousness which goes with inebriation; I had drunk far more wine than I usually would, and the effects were getting in the way. "And he thinks he also heard Brendan telling you that he loves you."

For a few more moments Harriet sat still, not looking undecided about how to act, but almost as though she was waiting in the wings. While she was undoubtedly calm, I sensed that perhaps her breathing was quickening, as though psyching herself up for the performance. Finally she stood away from the table and pushed back her chair. She picked up a box of matches from the table and lit three candles, then walked to the door and switched off the lights. Still looking at me, she returned to the table and held out her hand for me to take. I put my hand in hers, she took it, and then turned to guide me towards the sofa. Once there, still saying nothing, she indicated that I should sit at one end. I did so, seating myself on the edge, unable to feel sufficiently relaxed to sit back. She echoed me and perched on the edge of the cushion, perhaps two feet away from me. Now she was ready.

"Jonathan," she said, and all of this I can report with complete confidence as to its accuracy. I fear that nothing that was said will stop reverberating around my head until the day I die. "Jonathan. Do you know that I love you?"

"I believe I do. Of course I do. What is your point?"

"Let me get to that. I want to explain everything to you. But first, let me ask you another question."

"Go ahead." By now I was drinking the wine like it was water and the swerving of my vision felt undermining as I leant to put the glass on the table, and already it was a battle to remain in full control.

"What is your favourite type of music?"

"What?" I was as much confused as I was frustrated. "What's this got to do with what I am asking you? Harriet? What the fuck?..."

She reached across and put her hand on the side of my face, briefly caressing my cheek, as if to calm me.

"Jonathan. Bear with me for just a moment. I am telling you everything. I just want to try to make you understand something first. The way that I understand it. What is your favourite type of music?"

"You know the answer to that" – my impatience was mounting – "it's the blues. Clapton. John Mayall. Peter Green. B.B. King. The stuff I always listen to. But what's this got to do with what we're talking about?…"

"I know. You love the blues. You adore it, and you get enormous pleasure out of it. And if you could only listen to one kind of music for the whole of the rest of your life, that's what it would be, wouldn't it? The blues." I was still entirely dazed, but I nodded my agreement. She continued. "But you also like listening to opera, don't you?"

By now the messages being perceived by my ears were being distorted before they reached my brain, and I began to feel disorientated by the disconnect between what I thought we were talking about, and the words being exchanged. Perhaps the stress of what I had been through in recent weeks and the excess of alcohol were working strange tricks.

"Yes, sometimes I do. I love the blues, but sometimes I like listening to opera. Please just tell me what is your point?"

"And sometimes you like listening to jazz?"

"Yes I do. I like blues most. But I also like opera and jazz. What of it?"

"So let me ask you something else." She seemed unconcerned by my increasing inability to remain in control. Perhaps it was not visible to her; I have no way to know. All I
knew then was that my brain felt it was going into overload
and was in danger of closing down at any moment. God
help me if I didn't bang my forearm against my head, just
exactly as Roger used to do when something he was trying
to compute just would not go into his brain. When I looked
back at her, Harriet was still talking, although the movement
of her mouth appeared not to match the sound coming out
of it – like when the film slips away from the soundtrack.

"Your first love is the blues. If you could only ever listen
to one type of music for the whole of the rest of your life,
this would be it. Right?" I must have nodded, because she
continued as though I had acquiesced. "But it isn't the only
type of music you can ever hear, is it? There are other types.
Not as fulfilling or transporting or wonderful to you, but
still enjoyable for what they are." I must have nodded again.
"So let me ask you one more question, and then I will stop."
She paused, and in that moment I had a tiny flash of recall
of a conversation which Harriet and I had maybe four or
five years ago, on the night we had met. About music, and
about drugs, and about lovemaking. Momentarily I struggled
to remember more clearly, but she was continuing. "When
you go to see and enjoy some jazz, do you feel any sense of
betrayal of the music you like best? The blues?" She answered
for me. "Of course you don't. You don't feel any sense of

betrayal because listening to jazz has nothing to do with listening to the blues. They're different experiences. You can enjoy one in one sort of way, but you would always go back to your greatest love."

I struggle to describe what was going on in my mind while Harriet was speaking these words. I guess the nearest way to characterize it is that I had some sort of brainstorm. It was as if I was sitting in a car when a stone hit the corner of the windscreen, and I could do nothing as it divided into a hundred thousand little cubes of glass, obscuring my vision and throwing me further and further into a panic. I was entering that same long black tunnel, one that now felt familiar to me, with no exits or junctions, but just a sensation of falling headlong. I felt my limbs go weak, floundering in mid-air. If there was any sound in my head, the nearest I can come to describing it is that it was a mix of shattering glass and a howling storm. Little things stick in my head about that moment. I'd been reaching for the bottle to top up our glasses and then froze. There had been some noise on the stairs, but all the time the tiny fraction of whatever was left of my powers of perception were trying to process Harriet's words to me. A torrent of thoughts and images rained down, and suddenly the fragments of glass which had exploded in my head each echoed one of the nightmares of scenes I had imagined over recent weeks. Square, round, triangular shards of reflection, each one a picture of the woman I loved kissing, licking, sucking, making love with someone who was not me.

And now – what was she saying? Was she saying what she seemed to be saying?

I thought that my head would burst under the pressure of what was going on inside, and I was screaming from the pain of it. Not screaming like a man falling from a building, but the moment remains in my memory as an involuntary wail of agony, like the desolate cry from a mother whose child has died in her arms.

Is it from actual recall or did I imagine an image of Roger's face superimposed on one of the patterns of glass which shattered across my vision? One of my hands had gone to cover my face, maybe to hide the tears, or maybe to keep my brain from bursting through it, and the other was still around the neck of the bottle. Was there a second when I could have altered the chain of events which then unfolded? Or any time at all when I could have found a way to halt the roller-coaster at the top of the slope before it plummeted into free fall, left the rails and came crashing to the ground? All I can know for sure is that my next instance of consciousness was when I felt myself coming around, regaining a sense of place, my head still swimming.

* * *

I could not tell whether I had been out of my mind for a few seconds or several hours. My eyes hurt as though from some caustic substance, and I blinked several times and squeezed my eyelids tightly closed in an attempt to clear my vision. I could make out no sign of Harriet and no sound from anything around me. The candles had burnt down and out, and I was peering through semi-blackness. There was only the faintest of faint glows of yellow light from the streetlamps outside. I was half sitting, half lying on the floor, my head jammed up against the maroon leather sofa, and as I looked down at my hands I saw that the neck of the bottle was still within my grip, but that it ended with sharp jagged edges where the bottom had broken away.

I looked down at my clothes and it was then that I first saw the dark stain. A deep coloured mark, feeling wet and sticky on my jeans. I touched it with the tips of my fingers and felt that it was warm and clammy. I looked again at the open palm of my hand and for a moment it appeared like an unfamiliar object, as though it was appended to someone else. Something alien – a "feeler" – and there came a further layer of confusion as I tried to decipher its shape and nature. My hand was covered in the same colour as my jeans. Deep red, an unmistakable colour, even for those unfamiliar with it. Primordial.

I know that there were a few seconds where I assumed that I had cut my hands with the broken bottle, and I looked for the gash in my flesh but could see nothing through the congealing blood. I felt a sharp pain in my elbow as I moved, just as though I had been in one position for too long and had cramped. I held on to it with my hand and started to move to raise myself to my knees. Through the gloom I could just make out the shape of Olly the cat, apparently untroubled and fast asleep in another chair in the corner. The bedside clock, whose painful progress I had witnessed so closely just a few hours ago, was on our mantelpiece, and its luminous dials indicated two thirty. I must have been out of consciousness for at least two or three hours.

With difficulty, gently unfolding the stiffness which had permeated my body, I raised myself to my feet and was immediately in danger of stumbling. My arms were stretched forward as I shuffled along, like a blind man wary of meeting a raised step. I edged towards the door to the hallway and it was then that I saw Roger's coat hanging on the peg.

I turned and tiptoed as lightly as I could down the corridor to my brother's bedroom. The door was ajar, but it was too dark to see inside. I pushed it open gently, wishing only to see whether he was there. Even now I fully expected to find his room and bed empty. I went in and had to wait to allow my eyes to adjust to the gloom, but eventually, silhouetted against the streetlight outside which left a faint glow on the blinds, I felt that I could see the shape of Roger in his bed.

"Roger." I spoke loudly enough for him to hear if he was awake, but not so loudly as to wake him if asleep. I felt a sudden need to cough, which I suppressed, and swallowed hard as I looked around for the glass of water that I usually left beside his bed. I could not see it. There was no response from Roger and I stepped into the room and walked around the bed, just far enough to be able to get a glimpse of his face.

The soft creaking sound from a loose floorboard made me pause, but after a few steps the light from the lamp outside fell onto his face, and I could see in his expression nothing to cause concern. Close up, I could tell that he was breathing deeply, apparently without a care.

Now my concern shifted to Harriet. My mind was still swimming with momentary flashbacks of recalled images as I walked back down the corridor towards the living room. I felt I was wading through the shattered fragments that had exploded in my mind. I had come across no sign of her, and when my hands touched the walls inside the door, feeling for the switch, I found it and flicked it on. The electric light was dim, but instantly I could see that my fingers had left traces of blood on the wall. I looked again at my hands, turning them over to try to find the wound, but could not do so.

My eyelids felt heavy and my head ached, but with difficulty I raised my eyes to scan the room. Immediately I saw her, and from that first moment I had no doubt. I have no idea why it should have been so. It was not that she was lying in a contorted shape; there was nothing obviously broken, no instant sign of violence or of flowing blood. There was just something in her stillness, the artificial stillness of her, which left no room for error. Harriet, my sweet Harriet, the first and last love of my short life, was lying on the floor in front of me, quite lifeless, her soul having fled from her body.

There was a vacuum inside of me, as though someone had taken a suction pump and attached it to my body, dragging out the air and the blood and my organs and my muscles and my flesh. I felt a sudden weakness and thought I would faint; my skin was empty and unable to hold itself up.

I fell to my knees and then shuffled across the floor towards the spot alongside the sofa where Harriet was lying. I realized that she was positioned only a few inches from where previously I had awoken, but her stillness had prevented me from seeing or feeling her.

At first it was not even possible for me to make out which way she was facing; her long and curled brown hair was in disarray. For that moment, God help me, I had an image of her lying underneath me, when we were in the throes of our lovemaking and her hair was wild and uncontrolled, sometimes falling and flowing forward over her face as she was overcome by our passion. In that moment I would reach out for her, pushing her hair aside with my hands, gently, to be able to see her lovely face in her ecstasy and to be able to find her mouth and draw it towards me.

In the stillness and unusual silence, my fingers lightly touched her face and pushed back the stray strands from her forehead. Mercifully her eyes were closed, and there was no indication on her face of the trauma which must have been her last moments. She did not look alarmed, or hurt, or in fear. She just looked like Harriet. My Harriet.

In an instant I wondered how I knew that she was dead. For the first and only time I had a moment of hesitation. Could I be wrong? Was the blood from something else? But the idea was there and was gone just as quickly. It was her stillness that put the matter beyond doubt. No reaction to my hand on her face. No sign of life or breath.

I sat on the floor, leaning back against the sofa, and lifted Harriet's head onto my lap. I could feel the soft squelch from the area behind her ear where the bones had been shattered and the flesh was damp from oozing blood. With the tips of my fingers, I traced the contours of her lovely face, as so often I had done in life. Beginning at the top of her forehead, at the point of her widow's peak, the end of my index finger traced down towards the bridge of her nose, along its length, onto that area above her mouth which I had so often kissed, and then all around the edges of her beautiful lips. Then around her tiny chin, small and shaped like a doll's, and onto the nape of her neck, where I had pressed my face after we had made love and were falling asleep.

No one who has not experienced it can ever understand the physical pain of such a moment. No poet, no novelist, no historian, no film-maker – no matter how erudite or eloquent or empathetic – can ever begin to convey the sense and depth of desolation and despair. There simply are no words, and every one of us, every member of the human species who has experienced that moment, knows that what I say here is true. Nothing I have known or read or seen or experienced before or since comes close. Thank God, because I would not know how to survive it twice.

I think I may have passed out again, because I remember regaining my senses once more, and feeling a renewed sting of loss. I felt my head starting to spin and tried to recall how much wine I had drunk. It was a lot – far more than would have been safe and sensible – and I wondered whether the alcohol was having an anaesthetic effect on my pain. I shuddered at the terrible prospect of eventual sobriety.

Here was the love of my life, lying dead in my arms, and I had killed her. To one side of me, still, was the top of the broken bottle, covered in blood. I could tell now that there was no cut on my hands. The blood which had congealed there was from the fatal wound in Harriet's skull.

I cannot be certain how long I sat there, maybe it was a few minutes, maybe an hour. I was stunned and paralysed by my grief. I felt an irritation on my neck and touched it, to find it soaking wet from the rivers of tears which were still running freely. Now and then a huge welter of grief would rise up and wrack me uncontrollably, as if my own soul was trying to escape from my body, and I had to swallow back hard to remain alive.

Now, and only now, did I begin to think about the consequences of what had occurred. I had killed my wife. Yes, unbelievable though it seemed, I was a killer. A few hours ago I was a man, and now I was a murderer, someone who had taken the life of another person. It all seemed so strange, so surreal, that all these events which had happened in our private lives now also would be played out in public. My wife's adultery had been a personal matter, and somehow, in a way I cannot explain, my wife's death also seemed to me to be our business and our business alone; something which existed between her and me. But my wife's murder was not just going to be a matter of our business, it was going to be everyone else's business. Adultery was a private matter, but murder most certainly was not.

While for all these weeks I had been left alone with the torment which arose from discovering my wife's unfaithfulness, now my pain would become of consuming interest to the outside world. People I had never met would be privy to my most intimate feelings. Everyone would have an opinion. The neighbours, the newspapers, their readers, everyone would have their little piece to say. No one who read our story would care that I loved her as much as I did, or that at this moment I would gladly change places with her. No one would believe it or care about it if they did. All they would see is a killer, a man with blood on his hands.

However intense and sincere my private shame and regret, however real my grief, was a matter of no consequence. Society demands that justice must be done, and that it must be seen to be done. The law would have to take its course, the murderer must be punished. But there, in that flat, with Harriet's lifeless head resting on my legs, it all seemed so inappropriate. Still it seemed to me to be a private tragedy, in which the loss of her was my punishment, and would be for the remainder of my life.

For now, though, the woman who had given me a reason to live was lying beside me, utterly lifeless, and never to return to me. People say they feel that a part of them has died, and something like that is how I felt now. My life could never again be whole. I was bereft.

But Harriet was not my sole reason to be. I had another important role in my life, another responsibility, and now my thoughts turned back to Roger. In a very few hours he would be waking. I did not know exactly when he had returned to the flat, or indeed why. Entering through the front door and going directly to his bedroom, it was entirely possible that he might have seen nothing. Perhaps he had heard raised voices and done exactly that – put himself directly to bed. The look of serenity on his sleeping face gave me hope that this might have been so. Equally, even if he had come in at the end of my argument with Harriet, it must be questionable what, if anything, he would remember in the morning. It was by no means unknown for Roger to experience events which might seem traumatic to others, and for them to have been entirely erased from his mind by the following day. Then I began to think, and instantly to become alarmed, about how he would be likely to react to the present scene. Most probably he would be confused and then thrown into a panic, and then the situation would be beyond recall.

What then? When the police arrived, I would be taken away. What would happen to Roger? Difficult though it must be to believe, at that moment I was instantly more concerned about what would befall my brother as a consequence of the previous night's events than about what would befall me. My path was obvious and inexorable. Even at so young an age, I knew that clearly. I was going to be arrested, I was going to trial, I was going to prison, and that would be the end of me. There was no "after that". That was it, my lot, the unavoidable consequences of what I had done. Roger's destiny was something else. I began to consider the possibilities. Probably he would be taken immediately into some compulsory care facility. He would be confused, lost, and heaven knows what trauma he would go through in his mind as he failed to comprehend what was happening to him. The idea appalled me.

Eventually Roger would no doubt be placed in an institution of some kind where he would be surrounded for all of his time, for ever, by others with problems parallel to his, or worse. This thought horrified me even more, and instantly I rebelled against it. Then I thought about my parents, our mum and dad who had always allowed themselves some consolation in knowing that I would do whatever I could to look after Roger. I had a momentary flashback of the original case conference at the hospital which would have consigned him to an institution, and which had impelled me to take over responsibility for Roger's care in the first place. Now I would be unable to do so, and my older brother would pay a higher price than I would for my terrible crime.

After I had been completely in a daze, a stupor, these thoughts began to galvanize me. Was there any alternative to the horrors which currently seemed inevitably to flow from my actions? Were there any choices to be made? Was there, in short, any way that I might be able to get away with what had happened here in my flat this evening?

As I looked around, down at Harriet's inert body, across at the bloodstains on the rug, over to the bloodstains on the wall by the light switch, at the bloodstains on my clothes, I thought that there was nothing to be done. It was 3.30 a.m. and evidence of a violent crime was everywhere. In a very few hours it would be the dawn of a new day, and with it would come unavoidable discovery.

With a growing sense of urgency, I began to move in what now may seem like a surprisingly controlled way. I knew that I had to think quickly. The first issue was Harriet's body. From having viewed it only moments ago with overwhelming regret, I was now very quickly looking at it as a problem to be resolved. If she was still here, in the flat, by the time Roger awoke, all would progress beyond salvation. I knew immediately that I had to get her out of here to somewhere safe, where she would remain undiscovered while I returned to clear up, and then have time to consider a longer-term plan.

Instantly I knew that I had a single option. There was only one place outside of the flat over which we had any control, and that was the insect farm. If I could get Harriet's body there, it would give me a chance to clear my head and to think about what to do next. I swear that my motivation at this point was not about me; now I was utterly preoccupied with what would happen to Roger, to his welfare, to his life, if I was not around to take care of him.

It was a distance of less than 250 yards to the allotments, and I knew that the chances of being able to take Harriet's body all that way without meeting anyone, without being observed and without leaving any trace, were close to zero. Still, if there was any chance at all, it was better than the alternative. If I did nothing, discovery would be inevitable. It might be a very slim chance that I could get away with it, but it was better than no chance at all. The only thing I had in my favour was that it was December, bitterly cold outside, and no one with any choice in the matter would be likely to be out in the small hours of the morning. Anyone who was on the streets would be going about their business and, with any luck, might take little notice of anything else going on around them. Or so I could only hope.

Most of the blood from the wound in Harriet's head had spread on the rug in front of the sofa, and so I knew that this had to go too. I remember thinking it was fortunate that the rug was just a bit longer than Harriet's body; amazing how quickly, in emergency, we can start changing our perspectives. I dared not allow myself to look any more at Harriet's face, and was grateful that once again her hair fell to conceal it as I began to roll her over. One turn, two turns, and now what had just hours ago been a lively and lovely human being, my beautiful and most loved wife, was a parcel, bundled up and ready for disposal.

I have heard people before and since say how heavy a dead weight can be. I have to say that this was not my experience. Harriet had never been a big or heavy person, and had become even more slight since the summer. Also I think that my state of desperation and the powerfully flowing adrenalin may have given me additional strength. In any event I had less difficulty than I had imagined in hauling my newly wrapped bundle up to a standing position and then over my shoulder. I looked around, decided that I had no choice but to leave everything else until I could get back to the flat, and opened the door. I grabbed the keys to the insect farm off their hook, and walked out.

The hallway was in almost total darkness and immediately I was in a dilemma about whether to push the button which turned on the staircase lights. Even in normal circumstances it was not unusual for the switch to turn itself off before visitors reached the ground, and I did not want to risk having to feel for the next button at the first-floor landing. I stood in my doorway and waited a moment for my eyes to adjust, and decided to risk the darkness. Harriet's body was bent at her waist and draped over my back in a fireman's carry, leaving both of my hands free to steady myself on the banisters. I was about to take the first step down when I felt a movement at my feet, and looked down to see Olly the cat brushing past my ankles. I had to restrain myself from swearing out loud. Treading as lightly as I could, I was acutely aware of every tiny creak of the wooden floorboards. At one moment, as I turned on the next landing, the edge of the rug which was wrapped around Harriet's body brushed against one of the doors, and I held my breath, remaining still for long enough to be certain that no one had heard. Thankfully I was able to open and close the main door to the street silently.

Had someone stopped me on that short walk to the allotments – had a police car drawn up, or even had a passer-by stopped and looked with curiosity at me – I probably would have given up there and then. As I turned every corner I fully expected to meet whatever would be the instrument of my discovery. The early-morning milkman whose decision to take a short cut would change the course of the rest of my life. The postman who decided to turn right and not left at the junction and bumped into me bearing my load. Like a high-wire artist beginning to wobble and speeding up in order to reach the rope's end before he falls, I felt myself trying to accelerate as I neared my destination.

I glanced around me as I walked. The streets were lined with rows of Victorian terraced houses, some of two stories and some of three. I looked especially carefully at any window with a light on inside, but at no point did I see anyone looking out, nor any twitch of a curtain or blind.

A few minutes later, astonishingly, I had reached the allotments and had been seen by no one that I was aware of. Of course I could not guarantee that I had not been spotted by someone in the distance; maybe a neighbour heard or saw me go out of the house. Maybe someone made a mental note which would be recalled only later when the police appealed for witnesses. "Oh, there was that bloke acting oddly in Rosemere Street," they would remember, and their husband or wife would urge them that their civic duty was to call the police.

The allotments were surrounded by metal railings designed to keep out the vandals, and the gate was locked with a heavy padlock. I had to use both hands and bend my knees to reach it, but even now I cannot say that I was finding my burden unduly awkward or heavy. I was even able to close the gate and replace the padlock before turning inwards and heading towards the shed which housed Roger's insect farm.

It was another twenty yards from the gate to the shed, and I remember thinking that I was walking on soft earth, and that the patterns on the soles of my shoes would be likely to leave a distinctive print. Probably an expert would be able to tell that the person wearing the shoes was carrying a weight.

I was easily able to open the door and, once inside, I found an open area and gently placed the rug and Harriet's body onto the floor. It seems ironic now that I took great care that her head should not bump as I settled her. Crazy, of course, but then who could be other than out of his right mind in this situation?

I made certain that every inch of Harriet was covered by the rug, looked around to make certain that there was nothing apparently untoward, opened the door and walked out, being sure to lock the door behind me and to wipe any trace of blood from the padlock on the outer gate. I knew that I still had to be every bit as careful as I had been on my journey here. It was less likely that anyone would take notice of me now that I was not carrying anything, but all the same, if seen by someone who knew me, I would have little chance of producing a plausible explanation of what I was doing out at 4 a.m. on a winter's morning. I pulled up my collar and hurried back through the streets, retracing my journey of just a few minutes earlier. At one point I saw a light being turned on in an upstairs window, and could make out the shape of a man wearing a dressing gown coming into the room, scratching his head as he stepped forward to glance out into the street below. I walked just a little faster, keeping my head down and my collar up. I did not think that he had seen me.

Back once again inside the flat, I went immediately to the bathroom with the intention of splashing water on my face, but as soon as I was inside the door I felt an instant rising of nausea and could only just manage to get to the lavatory in time to lift the seat before I retched violently into the bowl. It was that sickness when you have thrown up many times before and there is nothing more inside you to come out, so that all you have is the pain of stomach contractions. As though my being was trying to express the horror of what was going on, trying to expel the monster from inside of me before it could eat me from within.

After a few moments I ran the cold tap and cupped my hands under the flowing water. I was about to put my face in it when I realized that my skin was still covered in dried blood. I reached for the soap and began turning it relentlessly, and then for a little nail brush that I kept on the sink and I began to scrub until it hurt. Only then did I feel I could rinse my face and, grabbing a towel and burying myself in it, I pressed the tips of my fingers into my eyes, as though to blur out the images that assailed them.

In the mirror, my skin appeared pale and puffy and looked as though someone had shaded large dark semicircles beneath my eyes. My lips seemed to have had the blood drawn from them and had vanished into a thin horizontal slash across my face. For the first time, I felt that I could not recognize the person that looked back at me. It was the face of a murderer.

I had to focus. I needed to set about clearing up the flat, and especially taking care of any of the more obvious signs of dried blood before I would have to wake up Roger. I filled a plastic bucket with hot water and, in the absence of anything more suitable, added a handful of the soap powder I used for washing clothes. Most of the stains from the immediate area had been absorbed by the rug, and so I made a tour of light switches and door handles. I wiped away the smears from the leather sofa, and then saw a splash of deep red just above the skirting board a few feet away. I knew I would have to clean more thoroughly later, but now my most urgent priority would be removing what I could of any sign that Harriet had been here. Even as I did so, I understood that my efforts were almost certainly completely futile. It seemed inconceivable that no one had noticed her coming to the flat last night; that none of my neighbours had heard her on the stairs, that no one had heard what must have been the crash of breaking glass which killed her. Still, by now it was as though a survival instinct had taken over my actions and I was proceeding on a kind of autopilot.

The way last night had unfolded had given Harriet very little opportunity to unpack the bag she had brought with her. It was a large black canvas holdall with a zip across the length of the top. The zip had been opened and I could see her bathroom bag, T-shirts and underwear. Again I felt the nausea rising in me, but this time was able to control it. I knew that I had to be certain that there was nothing of hers which hadn't been here before. I checked every surface and could find nothing.

I looked at my watch. Now it was 4.45. Should I take the risk of going out again, and perhaps be spotted carrying a bag through the streets? I glanced out of the window to check whether it was yet becoming light. Beneath the streetlamp I saw the outline of a skip standing at the side of the road. Builders had been renovating the house opposite for some weeks, and I knew that they were close to finishing their work. As I looked more carefully from my window, I could just make out the shape of an interior door from the house, with frosted-glass panelling, on top of the discarded rubbish. I wondered if I dared press my luck, but then realized that I had very little choice. I found a black plastic rubbish bag under the sink and slid Harriet's canvas holdall inside. I tied the end of the bag in a knot, and then carried it back downstairs and crossed the road. I reached over into the skip and lifted the edge of the door. I was able to slide the plastic bag just beneath it, so that it was almost completely obscured. I looked about me once again to try to check whether I had been detected, but could see no sign to cause concern.

I would spend the rest of the time available to me before Roger woke up further cleaning and tidying the flat, and meanwhile trying to work out what to say to him. That would depend on what he had seen, on what he remembered, and on whether and how seriously he was traumatized by it all. I had no way to tell, but understood that I would know from the first words he spoke when he opened his eyes this morning whether or not my fate, and his, would be sealed.

Chapter Eighteen

At 7.30 I had a last look around the flat to confirm that there was no obvious trace of Harriet's recent presence, and then went into Roger's bedroom to wake him. I spent some moments looking at my brother's face in the semi-darkness. I have to say that he looked entirely at peace, as if there was nothing and no care in the world to disturb his simple existence. There was nothing in it to suggest that he was anything other than the innocent eight-year-old that he in part was; I don't think he was actually sucking his thumb, but he might as well have been.

Taking a deep breath, I put my hand on his shoulder and gently shook him.

"Roger. Roger. It's time to wake up now and to get your breakfast."

I have mentioned before that Roger always woke from his sleep as though he had been studying a scene from *The Sleeping Beauty*. He opened his eyes and looked around as if curious to know who and what and where he was. I sometimes thought that if he had woken up in the caves of Bora Bora or in a tent in ancient Egypt, he would never react any differently from the way he reacted when he woke in his bedroom in a flat in Clapham. Every day was a new day; every discovery seemed to have no point of reference from the past.

He looked up at me and smiled. I searched his expression for any signs of concern or trauma from the previous night and found none. Would he ask about Harriet? I wasn't even sure if he had registered that she was expected to be back yesterday, nor did I yet know why or when he had returned to the flat. It was equally possible that he had witnessed everything and knew more than I did about the violence I had inflicted upon Harriet, or that he had arrived back later, gone directly to his room and seen nothing. I waited and wondered.

"What's for breakfast?" he said.

"I thought that today we might have a thimble of the nectar from the queen of all honey bees, washed down with a mighty bucket full of lark's vomit," I said, and instantly Roger dissolved into his familiar fit of giggling, covering his mouth with his hand. I think we each of us loved our routine as much as did the other.

"I think just the toast and Marmite for me please," he said, "and then maybe a banana?"

"All right then," I said. "Just this once."

I brushed away the tear that was forming in the corner of my eye, leaving Roger to get out of bed and to wash and dress as I returned to the kitchen. So much to think about, but probably best to get him off to his day centre before I did so. I had put two slices of bread into the toaster when I heard the telephone ringing.

My instant thought was that it must be the police. Who else would be calling at this time of the morning? I imagined that a neighbour had heard something alarming and called them; but if so, wouldn't they more likely be knocking at the door? I tried my best to compose myself before picking up the receiver, but had little faith that I was anything like composed when I spoke. I said our number and waited.

"Hello, Jonathan?" I did not immediately recognize the voice. "It's Mr Harries. You know, Terry's father? I was calling to apologize about last night and to make sure that Roger is OK."

I felt a moment of relief that it was not the police, followed immediately by a new wave of concern at what Mr Harries might have to tell me.

"Oh yes, Mr Harries. Yes, I did wonder what had happened. Roger came in and went straight to bed, so I haven't had a chance to ask him, but he seems OK this morning. Was everything all right?"

"Oh, that's a weight off my mind," he said, and his voice sounded as though it genuinely was. "Everything was fine and there was no sign of a problem. Roger came home and had his tea with us. Beef burgers; he said they were his favourites." My mind was a whirl of impatience. "But when it was time to go to bed he started to become a bit agitated. He began talking about his farm and the creatures, and worrying about whether they needed him. I tried to reassure him, and for a little while he calmed down again, but then later he got agitated and said he wanted to come home."

"Oh, don't worry, Mr Harries," I said, "you should have just called me. I would have come to collect him."

227

"Actually, I did call you. About tenish I think it was, but there was no answer. I assumed you were out, which is why I couldn't bring Roger over right away."

"That's funny. I was here all night," I said. "I must have fallen asleep and not heard the phone."

"Then an hour or so later I could see he wouldn't settle here. He wasn't overwrought or anything, but he just kept on repeating that he wanted to come home. So I thought I had better bring him. When we got to the flat I could see the lights were on, and Roger insisted that he should come up alone. He didn't want me to come in with him for some reason. I told him to come straight back down if you were not there, and I waited downstairs for a while to make sure he didn't, so I assumed that everything was OK. Was he all right when he got there?"

"Yes, Mr Harries, he seemed fine," I said, thinking quickly. "He didn't say much, just that he was tired and had wanted to come back to sleep in his own bed. To be honest, that's why I was in two minds about having him come over to you in the first place. He likes his routine. I didn't want to ask him a lot of questions last night because he seemed so sleepy. Anyway, I am just making his breakfast and he seems fine this morning. Will we see you at the bus?"

He confirmed that he would be taking Terry to the bus as usual.

"Just one thing," I said, trying again to sound as casual as I could. "About what time was it when you dropped Roger off?

I was half asleep and didn't notice the time. I like to make sure he gets a good eight hours a night."

"I think it was just a little after eleven," said Mr Harries. "As I say, we saw the light on so thought it was OK for him to come up on his own. I hope that was OK."

I reassured him that it was and we ended the conversation. I breathed again, and then thought how close a call it had been. If Mr Harries had chosen to come up with Roger, as opposed to dropping him home and letting him come up alone, I would by now be in a prison cell. Equally, I had no precise idea of what time it was that Harriet and I had had our fight, but my sense was that it had been earlier. There must at least be a decent chance that Roger had come into the flat, seen and heard nothing, and taken himself straight to bed.

The toast had popped up and Roger came into the kitchen, fiddling with the top button of his shirt as he approached. It seems to me that someone somewhere decided at some time that people with learning difficulties should have to have their shirts buttoned all the way to the collar, like a subtle sign of incompetence. It had always irritated me and I told Roger not to bother. Nonetheless, he seemed to spend a lot of his time trying to fasten the top button. He sat at the kitchen table and I put down the plate in front of him with his toast and Marmite.

"There we are, Roger. Pickled hog intestines on rye, just as you ordered. Would you like some crow's-feet soup on the side?" Roger was a perfect audience as always. I sat down and, once again, made a Herculean effort to sound as casual as I could. "So how was last night? You decided not to stay out after all?"

Roger shook his head, but looked completely unconcerned. He put a large corner of toast in his mouth and indulged his familiar habit of giving me a panoramic view of it being masticated.

"Miss Tresize at the day centre said that her son Billy has some spiders in a jam jar that they don't want. She doesn't know what sort they are, but she said I could have them if I wanted."

"That's nice, Roger," I said. "It'll be interesting to see what kind they are." I waited while Roger inserted another large section of the toast in his mouth, and gave him a chance to deal with it before trying again. "Was it nice at Terry's house? What did they give you to eat?"

"It was OK," he said. "We had beef burgers. They were horrible." There was a pause and a gear shift in favour of a subject he found far more absorbing. "I think they might be stag beetles. I don't think Miss Tresize knows the difference between a spider and a beetle." Roger giggled and put his index finger to the side of his head, pointing it and screwing it around vigorously. "She's a bit of a loony."

I was waiting for any reference to Harriet, but none came. I considered introducing the subject and then thought better of it. I had no idea what questioning Roger might at some time be subject to, and thought that it would be better if some time passed before anyone asked him to recall anything. At this moment I still had no clear idea what he had seen, if anything, or what knowledge he had of what had happened. My curiosity was immense, but for the time being I knew it had to take second place to my caution.

Though my head was in complete turmoil and my thoughts were an anarchy of fears, on a practical level everything passed just as it might on an average morning, and twenty minutes later I was walking with Roger down the road to meet the bus. We got there just as it arrived, but there was no sign of Mr Harries or his son Terry. The bus pulled up at the kerb and I said goodbye to Roger and watched him walk down the aisle, scanning all the faces he knew so well, but apparently also looking out for Terry. The driver was about to set off when I saw Mr Harries and Terry approaching from a distance, hurrying along the pavement, and I asked him to wait for a few moments. Roger was on the bus and looking out of the window towards the direction Terry usually came from. Father and son got to the door, and I saw Roger and Terry greet each other with their familiar overwhelming enthusiasm. Mr Harries stood beside me as the bus pulled away.

"So no sign of any problem with Roger then?"

"No, none whatsoever. He didn't mention anything except how much he liked the beef burgers."

"Excellent," he said. "So sorry about that confusion last night. It would have been good if it had worked out. Maybe we should wait and try it again some time? It would be good for everyone if Roger felt a bit more relaxed about breaking his routine." I thanked him and agreed. Actually, I knew he was right, but my head was crammed full of far more urgent priorities than this one. I went to head off on my way when he spoke again. "When is that lovely wife of yours coming down again? Newcastle, isn't it? Is that where she's studying?"

I was momentarily taken aback. It hadn't occurred to me that he might know Harriet, or anything about her. Then I remembered that sometimes, when she was on holiday between terms, she took my place and walked with Roger to the bus. Being a more sociable person than me, she had probably chatted to Mr Harries.

"Actually, I believe she is coming back tomorrow," I said. "She's working very hard."

"Oh. Well do give her my best regards when you see her," he said. "She's a lovely girl she is. Lovely."

"I will," I said, and his description of Harriet as "a lovely girl" sent a distress signal through me. Yes, she was a lovely girl. I couldn't get away fast enough.

This was alarming. Already I had been forced into telling a lie when I hadn't even had a chance to think through my plans or my story. Instinctively I thought I would be bound to have to say that Harriet hadn't come home last night, but I knew I would need to give some serious thought to the details. There would eventually be a hundred questions, asked by people with far more expertise than old Mr Harries. I would have to consider every angle, every possibility, if I was to stand even the smallest chance of getting away with what had happened.

Who knew, for example, that Harriet had been due to come back to London last night? I remembered that originally she had been due to come down on Thursday, and her plan to come two days sooner had been agreed at the last minute. Whom had she told? I had no way to know.

When you think about the possibility of any of this happening now that we are all being watched and traced without being particularly aware or complaining about it, it must be obvious that there would be not the smallest chance of getting away with the deception. Harriet's journey south by train, and then from King's Cross to the flat, would be observed and recorded on scores of cameras. Her credit card would be registered at Starbucks or WHSmith or some such place, but back then none of those things was yet part of our lives.

I considered whether there would be any firm evidence that she had travelled two days earlier than her initial plan. Certainly Harriet was a lovely girl, as Mr Harries had said, and was the kind of person that people tend to notice. But this was the end of the autumn term, and hundreds if not thousands of young women with curly brown hair and long flowing coats would be travelling on the railways to get home for Christmas. I realized that my fate might well now be only a matter of chance. If she had been spotted on her journey by someone she knew, or had struck up a conversation with someone who would remember her later, I would be lost.

No place to hide. If not, then possibly my problems were containable.

In giving consideration to all the practicalities, I am in danger of creating the impression that I was oblivious to the terrible tragedy of Harriet's death. I most certainly was not. I was traumatized, and as I looked back on it much later, I realized that I was probably in shock and exhibiting the clinical symptoms of being so. I felt disorientated in all of my thinking and in all of my actions, as if suffering from jet lag or sleep deprivation.

When I returned to the flat after dropping Roger at the bus, I walked up the stairs and found that once again the tears were flowing liberally down my cheeks and splashing onto the collar of my jacket, making dark stains like heavy rain on a summer day. I felt a sudden weakness and thought I might pass out on the stairway. My head was spinning, and then I heard a noise behind the door of the flat below me, and sprinted up the last few stairs to avoid a meeting or any need of explanation.

I also did not know what, if anything, had been heard by my neighbours, but I knew that I did not yet have my story sufficiently straight to be able to provide answers to any questions. The flat at the bottom of the house had been rented by a Polish couple, with whom I had only a slight acquaintance, but enough to know that they had recently returned to their homeland following a death in the family. I knew none of the details and felt no need to know. On the floor immediately below lived Mrs Chambers, former owner of Olly the cat. As I've mentioned before, Mrs Chambers had originally occupied her own floor and ours as well, and when we first moved in she had given me a rundown on some of the best and worst previous occupants of my flat. Several of the stories contained oblique references to strange activities, and I thought her remarks were designed to let me know that not much could go on above Mrs Chambers without her knowing about it.

If I was asked about any unusual noises, then something like "Sorry, I must have fallen asleep with the TV on" would be about the best I could do. Not very good, and certainly not good enough if faced with tough and searching questions from a tough and searching policeman. On balance I thought it best to say nothing, in the hope that if questions were ever asked, some while would have passed and Mrs Chambers's memory of anything suspicious might have faded.

Back and alone in the flat, at last I had the chance to think a little more clearly. I walked from room to room, examining every surface for any sign of Harriet's recent presence, and all the while thinking. All this was important, and all this was manageable, but what on earth was I going to do with Harriet's body?

Even today, so many years after those original events, I am not able or willing to write down here the detail of what happened in those next few hours. If the events surrounding the moments of her death are traumatic for me, at least they were blunted by the effects of shock and alcohol, and the fact that my loss of consciousness had removed from me any clear or detailed memory of the incident itself. I was completely sober during everything that had to be done to dispose of Harriet's body. All of it was carried out in the light of morning, with no dark places in which to disguise the detail, no way to divert my own imagination from the realities, no intoxicant to dull the sharp edges. The removal of her clothes, the blazing heat from the fire of dry dead leaves, the smell of burning from her Afghan coat. And even today, frequently my sleep is shattered by marauding images of soil being piled onto Harriet's lovely face, falling into her nostrils and into her mouth, piling into the corners of her now half-open eyes. Oh my Harriet. My beautiful, simple, purest, most loved girl. The single love of my life.

When all my instincts would be to reach over and remove a speck of dirt that might threaten to go into her eye, here I was piling deep-brown and damp clods of earth onto her beautiful face. When all my motivation would be to keep her soft and tender flesh safe and untouched, here was I taking earthworms by the handful from a tank in Roger's collection and putting them into the six-foot-long wooden tub which he and I had made months earlier.

Heaven knows it was all a very long way from the perfect crime. Even then I knew that if I was ever seriously suspected, I would have had no chance whatsoever of getting away with Harriet's murder. But, difficult and hazardous as it was, the matter of what to do with Harriet's body was far from being my only or even necessarily my major problem. On that first day I still had to deal with Roger, and with the inevitable enquiries which would ensue as it became clear that Harriet was missing. Very quickly I realized that it should be I who was the first to instigate them.

It would not be unusual that Harriet and I might not have spoken on the telephone every day. This was Wednesday, and I decided that, as far as the world was concerned, my story was that I was not expecting her until the following day. No need to raise the alarm before then. Of more immediate concern was Roger. All day I was turning over in my mind what he might have seen or heard from the previous evening, and I wondered why he had said nothing about Harriet at breakfast this morning. Not that her name came up in every conversation between us, but if he had witnessed anything at all from last night, then I felt that surely he must at the very least be curious.

Among the blur of horrors and images from that terrible time, I felt a flicker of recall of Roger's face, with an expression of apparent alarm. I had no idea whether my impression was of something real or imagined; and if it was real, what had he seen? Was it the argument? Was it the blow I had struck with the bottle? Had he seen the bottle breaking on the back of Harriet's head and had he watched the blood begin to flow as she fell to the floor? Had he even lost consciousness, as I must have done? And if so, how had he managed to put himself to bed and sleep so soundly?

I turned the matter over and over again in my mind, agonizing in my indecision. At one moment I was able to convince myself that he had seen and heard nothing and was blissfully unaware of any problem. At the next I was worried that he had seen and heard everything and was traumatized and in shock; that what he had witnessed must have done him emotional damage. Feeling unable to cope with the uncertainty, I determined to ask him more questions, but then just a few moments later I decided the opposite. It would take a supreme effort of will not to do so, but in the end I felt sure that it would be best to wait until he or other circumstances brought up the subject. Prompting him could easily be counterproductive, and the longer it took, the better were my chances that he might forget or be confused about what he had seen and when he had seen it.

All this time, I was still feeling the stomach-churning aftereffects of all the alcohol I had consumed the previous evening. I had already felt nauseated as I cleared away the broken glass and the empty wine bottles, but now I experienced a further wave of disgust at the thought of myself as a violent and wretched drunk. I reflected on the need for clear thinking in the days and weeks ahead, and the mix of self-loathing and pragmatism made me resolve there and then to curb my drinking habits.

Eventually I pulled myself together enough to call the office and speak to the branch librarian Mr Waddington. I told him that I had a touch of a flu virus and that I would be unlikely

to be back at work until the following Monday. He said not
to worry – obviously more concerned that I should not bring
flu into the office than by my absence.

"When is your wife coming down for Christmas?" he asked,
and it occurred to me that he might suspect that my sudden
need for a day off was to do with her return.

"Oh, not until tomorrow," I said. "That's why I want to
stay in bed today, so I have a chance of being on the mend by
the time she gets here." I felt that he probably believed me.
In the afternoon I walked down to meet Roger from the bus
as usual, and he and I walked back to the flat.

"I went down to the insect farm today, Roger," I said to him.
He seemed pleased. There was always a sense that he would
have liked me to be more interested in what was his obsession
than I sometimes appeared to be, so he no doubt regarded
the information as welcome. "Yes, I thought I might try to
spend a bit more time there with you. I made up my own box
to keep some worms in. One of those we put together a few
months ago. Hope you don't mind."

Roger didn't mind at all, and we agreed that after tea we
would go down to the shed to have a look at my work and
make some more plans. As we left the house and set off down
the street, I noticed that the builders' skip was full to over-
flowing with rubble, and that someone had tied a tarpaulin
over the top of it. I allowed myself a moment to feel hopeful.

Once at the insect farm, for the first half hour or so, Roger
seemed to be completely carefree. Maybe he really had seen

and heard nothing last night. Maybe the memory of his face was part of a subconscious nightmare which had afflicted me after the deed. I began to hope, but then gradually I started to become aware that something was darkening his mood. When I looked over towards him, he was standing next to one of the tanks and muttering to himself.

"What is it, Roger?" I asked him. "Is something troubling you?"

He did not turn, but mumbled something back to me. At first I could not make out what he was saying.

"These cockroaches."

I walked over to look more closely into the tank which was distracting him.

"What about them?"

"I've put them in with these termites, and I thought they would get along all right. But the cockroaches are eating too many of the termites, and if I am not careful we won't have any termites left at all."

"Can we put the cockroaches somewhere else?" I asked.

"Not easily," he said. "I think we are going to have to kill them."

"Really?" I said. I was amazed. I hadn't known him to kill any of his collection before, and was surprised to hear him say so.

"Yes. I've tried them in a few places, and they do have to be fed, but they are too greedy. They upset the balance."

And with that Roger put his hand into the tank, closed his

240

fist around one of the cockroaches, and simply squeezed it. I continued to watch as he pulled out the carcass, put it into the pocket of his jacket, and then repeated the exercise with another one. I heard the crunch of its body, like a dried leaf underfoot, as it was crushed to death. I looked at Roger's face and saw that he seemed to be sad.

"Are you OK Roger? I didn't know that was part of keeping insects."

"Not very often," he said. "Usually they get along and find some sort of way. But occasionally, if they can't sort out a way to live together, I have to sort it out for them."

Part of me at that moment thought that perhaps Roger was blanking out what had been a horrible experience. Another part wondered if he had seen anything at all. The only thing which did not seem possible was that he knew everything and had decided that the best thing he could do was to keep quiet.

On the following day, I took Roger to the bus, and then walked to the shops to buy enough groceries to make dinner and breakfast for three people. I was never a great cook, but I had made something of a speciality of chicken casserole, and at lunchtime I put all the ingredients into a dish and put it in the oven on a slow heat. At 1 p.m., I took a last look around the flat and, God help me, I made a banner which I strung across an alcove that read: "Welcome home Hattie". I never called her Hattie, always Harriet, and perhaps I felt guilt about even writing her real name. As luck would have it, when I left the flat on my way towards King's Cross, I met my downstairs neighbour Mrs Chambers on the stairs.

"On my way to meet my wife," I said, and then wondered of this seemed a bit forced. Too late, it was out.

"Oh, do give her my best regards," she said. "I hope you'll all have a lovely Christmas." I detected no sign of anything untoward in her manner. Another huge hurdle cleared. "Oh, there is just one thing," she said, and my heart missed a beat. "I have been meaning to say to you that if Olly is becoming a nuisance to you, you should shoo him out downstairs. I hardly ever see him these days." I said that Olly wasn't a nuisance at all and that he was good company for Roger and me. Mrs Chambers seemed to be content with that answer and went into her flat.

I took my usual public-transport journey to the station, trying to act exactly as I would have done in normal circumstances. I even considered buying flowers, but as I had never done so before, I thought it might be going a bit too far. Harriet had originally intended to come down on a train arriving at 2 p.m., and I was a few minutes early. A sign on the indicator board said platform 7, so I took up my position at that gate.

At this point I was trying to do my best to live the part I had set for myself, so that as much as possible of the story I would eventually tell would be true. I'm not proud of the fact that I cooked a meal and set the table for a dinner for three which I knew would never take place. Such was my turmoil and madness that there may have been a few moments when I even imagined how delighted Harriet would be at my efforts. Of course I had not for a second forgotten the trauma and nightmare of the last thirty-six hours, but it certainly is extraordinary what tricks your own mind can play.

As I stood alongside a gaggle of assorted parents and lovers waiting to meet the train from Newcastle, I found myself scanning the faces of the people leaping from the open doors of the carriages, keen to get a head start on the crowds. Yes, there were several girls of around Harriet's size and shape and hair colour and style, but there was certainly no moment when I thought anyone looked spookily like her. I continued looking until the majority of passengers had passed me by, many of them falling into the arms of their loved ones as Harriet would have done if all this had been for real. Now there were only some older people and a few stragglers struggling with oversized luggage.

I considered what to do. It was too soon to sound any kind of alarm or alert the police. What would I do if these circumstances were real? If I had really expected to meet her from this train and she hadn't been on it? Probably I would make a call to the house that Harriet was living in, just to check that she had left on time, or maybe to see whether her luggage was still in evidence. I knew the telephone number in my head and was feeling in my pockets for change for the phone box, when I sensed the presence of someone at my shoulder. The person seemed to make no move to greet or touch me – but was standing closer than a stranger would normally stand.

I looked up and saw that it was Brendan Harcourt.

For an instant I felt that my knees would buckle beneath me. Of all the eventualities I had anticipated, this had not been one of them. I looked straight into the face I so despised; the face which I had imagined so many times in intimate relationship to the woman I loved. So much and so long, in fact, that now the reality seemed somehow less real than the imagined images. His features were less sharp than they were in my mind's eye. His hair colour less flaming. His skin colour less vivid. His eyes less serpentine. Taking in all this in a few seconds, I realized that I needed to say something quickly, but was still collecting my thoughts when he spoke first.

"Jonathan. What are you doing here?"

By now I had caught up.

"I came to meet Harriet from the train. I didn't know she was coming down with you. Where is she? Did you leave her struggling with her luggage? That's not very gentlemanly."

"What are you talking about?" he said. "She wasn't on the train. She came down a couple of days ago."

"What are you talking about?" I said, an unconscious echo. "She didn't. She was due to get this train. She told me. She bought her tickets a while ago."

"I know she did," he said, "but then she got finished with something she had to do a bit sooner than she expected and said she was coming down earlier in the week."

"Well, why didn't she tell me?" I said, and paused, as if lost in thought. "But wait a minute. She can't have done that, because she would have turned up. If she decided to come down early she would have had to come home. Apart from anything, she doesn't have anywhere else to go." Immediately I began to wonder if I was getting ahead of myself and started to row back. "You must be mistaken. If she had been coming down early she would have told me. She must still be on the train or somewhere. I was about to call the house in Newcastle to make sure she left in time to catch that train. I left our flat a while ago, so if she had been held up for any reason, she might not have been able to get to a phone in time to tell me."

"Jonathan," he said, "you aren't listening to me. Harriet came down on the train on Tuesday."

"Brendan" – again I was unconsciously echoing him, but this time with growing dissonance – "she can't have. If she had, she would have told me, and she didn't. Why would she come to London ahead of her schedule and not tell me? It's not like it's my birthday or something."

"I don't know why she didn't tell you. I had assumed that she had, but I know for sure that she left Newcastle on Tuesday, bound for London."

"How do you know?" I asked. By now I could almost feel myself clambering into the driving seat. "Did you see her off on the train?" I sensed that he was beginning to flounder, perhaps remembering the need to lie, but confused about the truth.

245

"Of course not. It's just that she mentioned it to the three of us. On Monday, I think. Yes, Monday. She said she was going down on the following day instead of on Thursday. We had all planned to go out for an end-of-term drink, and she said she would miss it."

"That's a pity for you all," I said, trying to confine the irony. "So where the hell is she?" Should I seem worried, confused, more concerned than I was pretending? I was making this up as I went along, and was not sure how to get the mix right. What I did feel sure of was that Brendan believed me when I said I had expected to meet Harriet from this train. "I'm going to have a walk down the carriages just to make sure she hasn't fallen asleep or anything."

I was about to start walking towards the train when he stopped me. "Jonathan. There is no point in doing that. I just know that she came down on Tuesday."

"But I still don't understand how you could know that for certain unless you saw her off. Did you?"

"No," he said. The more uncomfortable he became in his role as a liar the more comfortable I became in mine. "I told you. But I did see her that morning, two days ago, and she was packing her stuff and shortly going to leave for the station."

"Were you round at her house then?"

"Yes," he said, "I popped round to return a book she said she needed for study over the holidays."

"Really?" Damn me if I wasn't beginning to enjoy myself. "What time was that? Because to get the train arriving at two she would have had to be at the station by nine. You must have been an early riser?"

"Yes, because it was a book I had borrowed and which she said she badly needed."

"Which one?"

"What?"

"What book was it that you returned to her because she badly needed it? I'm just curious."

I knew this was getting off track and, despite the pleasure I was beginning to have in making Brendan squirm, something told me that I was at risk of over-playing my hand and should return to the question of Harriet's whereabouts. Brendan's lies might be useful to me later, and so maybe better not to give him a chance to get his story straight right now. I could tell that he was as concerned as I appeared to be about what might have become of Harriet. It's just that we both had our own very different reasons for not saying everything we knew.

"Well, I'm going to call her house in Newcastle. Who knows, maybe she left the precious book behind, got off the train at Durham and went back. We just don't know. Why don't I do that, and you ring Martin and Jed at their parents' houses to see if they know anything? Then we can compare notes."

Obviously still totally bewildered, Brendan agreed. As I began to turn over the situation in my mind, I guessed that he had spent the night with her on Monday, and then maybe had walked her to the station the following morning. Probably he saw her off from the platform, and I could imagine their tearful farewells.

Perhaps he had been urging her to leave me and she had been saying that she would, but not quite yet. I would never know, and I had to hope that no one else ever would know either.

So there we were, an odd couple, making our calls from adjacent telephone booths on the station platform, each holding on to his secrets about what he knew of the other. Brendan, worried about his lover, but also worried that I may soon discover that he had been having sex with another man's wife – my wife. I, not at all confused about what had happened to my wife, but preoccupied with playing the role of the anxious husband with no idea that his beloved was being unfaithful with another man. I had to hope that his lies would get him into difficulties before mine would have the chance to catch up with me.

"I think we need to inform the police," I said.

I don't want to give the impression that I had worked out some sort of masterplan to enable me to get away with killing my wife and was carrying it out step by step. I had not. At this point my mind was still plagued at every moment by nightmare images and by the horror of what I had done. I have seen this sort of thing described as a living hell, and it was something like that. Experienced as though you are an unwilling witness to events over which you have no control; a world in which the bizarre becomes the everyday, the surreal becomes familiar. And in and among all this I felt that I had no choice but to do whatever I could to keep myself safe from the consequences of my actions.

Proscriptions on both murder and adultery are among the most fundamental of human laws; as old as the Ten Commandments themselves, and no doubt older than that. Only a fool would put them on an equivalent level, but nonetheless both Brendan and I had each committed a mortal sin which we were now trying to conceal. While my purpose was simply to appear to know nothing about the disappearance of my wife, his imperatives were far more complex. His instinct to conceal his infidelity was in direct conflict with his concern about her whereabouts, and that was bound to lead him into making mistakes.

The very first questions the police were likely to ask would probably reveal that he had lied about when he had last seen her, and the chances are that his thoughts were going crazy trying to work out the ramifications of whatever he might say. If a few questions from the police revealed that he and she had been lovers, and then she turned up within hours with some innocuous explanation for her absence, their secret would be blown. I cannot know whether or how Harriet had planned to tell me about her love of several different types of music, but whatever her plans were they certainly would not have included a police inquiry.

"Surely there's no need to alert the authorities just yet," Brendan said. "I'm sure there must be an obvious explanation we haven't thought of."

"What, like she got off at York, went shopping and fell asleep?" I said. Again, I don't now know if I was getting agitated for effect, or whether I was just naturally taking to the part of a distraught husband. "People don't just vanish, Brendan. If, as you say, she left Newcastle on Tuesday, why hasn't she turned up here?"

He had no answer. His calls to Martin and Jed had revealed nothing new. Neither of them had a clear idea of what her plans had been. They vaguely thought she was travelling down on Tuesday, but had no way to be sure.

"I thought you said she had told the three of you that she was travelling down sooner than her plan? How come you remember that so clearly and they don't seem to remember it at all?"

"Oh, I don't know. Maybe they weren't paying close attention."

"But you were?"

"Look, Jonathan," he said, "there's nothing to be gained right now by going into why I know it. Let's just accept that I know she left Newcastle on Tuesday. Today is Thursday and she is not here."

"So you say, Brendan. I hear you. The trains from Newcastle are notoriously useless, but even they don't take two days to get here. She is my wife and I am worried about her. I am going to the police. You can come with me or not, as you like."

Chapter Nineteen

Walking along the road towards the police station at King's Cross, I inhaled as deeply as I could to try to get the oxygen flowing through my body. I was about to take yet another action which would affect the rest of my life. Obviously I had already embarked upon an unstoppable course two days ago in my flat, but until this past hour no one knew that Harriet was missing. What I was about to do would inevitably begin a chain of events over which I could have little if any control. I knew that I had not had time to think things through properly. I also knew that, even if I had the time, I had no experience or knowledge relevant to the concealment of a serious crime. I had no idea then, and have no idea now, if it really is possible to plan and to carry out the murder of another human being and get away with it. But if it is, then surely it would take days or weeks of thought and preparation. No doubt there would be many elements to get right – time, place, method, absence of witnesses among them. The death of Harriet had been unplanned, it had several potential witnesses and many different routes to the truth; but regrettably there was no going back. I had to deal with the situation as it was, and all I wanted to do was to stay out of jail.

The impression that most of us have of the inside of a police station in the 1970s comes from watching cop dramas on the television. We envisage a counter and a friendly bobby drinking tea from an enamel mug. When I went into King's Cross police station on that Thursday morning in December 1972, I guess I thought I had an idea of what it would be like inside, but found that my expectations were wildly inaccurate.

The station was housed in an old Victorian building right in the heart of the notorious red-light district, and even at that time of day it was full of drunks and prostitutes, all of whom were in various stages of desperation. I waited in a general holding area, looking around me at the collection of sad humanity gathered by whatever circumstances into this thoroughly depressing scene.

I found myself gazing, probably for too long, at a girl who could not have been much older than I was. I realized that I was being rude, but her stare back at me was not defiant or offended. Her drooping eyelids seemed for all the world to be every bit as dead as were Harriet's lifeless eyes the night before last. There was time for the thought to cause a pang of pain as it flickered across my mind before I could dismiss it, trying once again to focus on what was about to unfold.

The place seemed to be full of cages. Not cages designed to incarcerate prisoners, but apparently to protect the police from the general public. In contrast to my mental image of an open area with a friendly bobby standing on the other side and writing in a big ledger, what I actually discovered was a series of spaces enclosed by heavy-duty wire mesh, the function of which was to ensure that no one could get within striking distance of an officer. Instantly I felt uncomfortable and out of place, like a civilian in a war zone, and I could see a look of slight surprise on the face of the policeman who peered at me through a hole in the wall. By the time I managed to negotiate my way through the obstacle course which got me to the porthole, the young policeman on the other side of the wall had lost his initial interest and did not even glance up as he asked what he could do for me.

"My wife has gone missing," I said. It felt like a milestone, and it was one. The start of a process which instantly, now it had begun, was unstoppable. The policeman was still finishing off writing what appeared to be some notes about the last thing he had dealt with, and clearly I did not yet have his full attention. For some reason, just at that moment, Harriet's last words to me once again came flowing into my head and pulled my concentration away from what I needed to be saying. As though she was tugging at my sleeve.

"*Your first love is the blues. If you could only ever listen to one type of music for the whole of the rest of your life, this would be it. Right? But it isn't the only type of music you can ever hear, is it? There are other types. Not as fulfilling or transporting or wonderful to you, but still enjoyable for what they are.*"

Involuntarily I heard her words replaying as though spoken by someone standing behind me, and at the same moment I saw Harriet's lovely face swimming before my eyes. I turned round and saw the young girl with the dead eyes looking at me, and her face began to float in my imagination and merge into Harriet's. I put out my hand to lean on a small ledge in front of the opening, and I think my sudden precarious state finally caught the attention of the officer.

"Are you all right?" he said. He looked around as if to get a second opinion, but he was alone in his cubicle. He pushed a button on the desk in front of him, and in the distance I heard the sound of a buzzer. Just a second later a door opened and another officer, an older man, came into the public area.

The policeman came over to me and took me by the arm. He turned and guided me back to where he had come from, and I looked up and saw the face of the young girl receding into the distance. The curl of her lip suggested her conclusion that I was just another drunk. Inside the door I was immediately in a long corridor with straight-back chairs to one side, a machine for coffee and another selling crisps and chocolate. It seemed more like an NHS hospital than a police station, and I guessed that it was geared to a lot of people being made to wait for a very long time. The officer guided me to one of the chairs, keeping a firm hold of my elbow until I was safely seated.

He asked if I was all right, and I said that I was, but had just come over a bit dizzy.

"I don't know if I am making a big fuss about nothing, but my wife seems to be missing. She was due to travel home from Newcastle on the train arriving at 2 p.m. and she wasn't on it. I wouldn't worry so much, except that a friend of hers who was on it says she actually left Newcastle on Tuesday, but she hasn't shown up anywhere."

It was a big moment for me, but I saw not a flicker of anything from the officer. He seemed to be about fifty years old, and for a moment I thought he reminded me of my dad. He had the same pattern of lines in his face, the same slightly downtrodden expression, maybe careworn from experience.

"I'm sure it's nothing to worry about," he said. His response had the air of routine to it – he'd probably spent years of dealing with scores or maybe hundreds of hysterical spouses. "I'm sure there is an innocent explanation."

He went off to try to find a vacant interview room, but returned after a couple of minutes and said he would be unable to find one free for a quarter of an hour or so. I told him that I was concerned because I had to be at the bus stop to collect my brother at 4.30. I saw the puzzled look and explained.

"My brother has a mental handicap. I am his only carer and I have to be there to collect him from the bus. If I'm not, he'll be stranded and helpless."

"Well, how about this then?" said the officer. "Chances are that by the time you get home, your wife will have turned up safely. We don't start worrying about a missing adult until they have been gone for twenty-four hours anyway, so why don't you go and meet your brother, and if your wife hasn't turned up by tomorrow, come back here and we will see what we can find out. How does that sound?"

It sounded perfectly all right to me. I had achieved my main objective and was very glad to get out of there; a chance to collect my thoughts and maybe to plan ahead.

My next major concern was Roger. I had a little time to spare before I needed to collect him from the bus, so I planned to pop back to the flat to start preparing his meal. As I turned the corner into my road, my heart stopped and so did my legs. A police car was parked at the side of the road, opposite my house, and two uniformed officers were speaking to a builder. One was writing in a notebook. I could hear and feel the blood being pumped through my veins. I had no choice but to go on walking, and I proceeded as slowly as I could without drawing attention, straining my ears to try to tune into the conversation. As I got near I could hear the builder speaking. "...but I haven't got anywhere else to put it. We've got to get rid of the rubbish somehow. No one said we needed permission..." By now I was level with the skip and was able to glance over the edge. It was empty. The original must have been taken away and replaced. I breathed again.

I got to the drop-off point just in time to see the bus arriving, and still had not made up my mind how to handle things when Roger stepped off and fell into line alongside me.

"Have you had a good day, Roger?" I asked him.

"Yes," he said, instantly full of life, "we had modelling and the teacher brought in some clay and I made a rocket ship and Terry made some spacemen and we put them together and she said it was marvellous and they are going to keep it to show at the next open day. What do you think about that?"

As I listened to Roger speak and watched his face, full of enthusiasm and animation, I felt a sudden and entirely unexpected wave of envy flowing through me. Lovely, lovely Roger. He had no worries to speak of at all. He could enjoy whatever was happening right now without the need to think about the past or the future. His life was entirely straight-forward and apparently without outside concerns. Roger had no inkling whatever of the mayhem that was likely to unfold around him very soon, and truly seemed to have no memory of any of the events that had made it inevitable. There had been no mention whatsoever of Harriet either yesterday or today so far, and so I decided to play it straight and see what happened.

"I was expecting Harriet to get back from university today. I went to meet the train, but she wasn't on it." I half-turned so as to be able to watch Roger's face very carefully as this information was absorbed. The little frown of confusion was exactly what I would have expected and indicated no special concern. Clearly he had no immediate idea of what could be an explanation. Eventually he shrugged his shoulders and appeared to relax.

"What's for tea?"

"Well," I said, "I was expecting Harriet to join us so I have made one of my special chicken casseroles. It'll be ready to eat by the time we get home." I thought I would press my luck just a little bit further. "And maybe Harriet will have turned up by then and we can all eat together."

Roger seemed to like this idea, and within a few minutes we were back at home. Usually any post and packages which had been delivered for anyone in the house were left on a table in the front hallway, and Roger seemed especially delighted to have received one of the little boxes which contained some new specimens.

"I didn't know you had been expecting anything. Did you send off?" I asked him. He did not respond directly, but asked if he could go down to the insect farm later to house his new arrivals properly. I was happy for him to go on his own, and said that I felt I should wait in the flat just in case there should be any news from Harriet. He appeared to be unconcerned, and his main preoccupation was whether he would be allowed to eat her share of the chicken casserole if she did not turn up.

After our meal, Roger took his new specimens and set off for the insect farm. I was content for him to do so in order that I could clear out as many of the other thoughts which were crowding into my head and make my plans. Tomorrow I would be returning to the police station to renew my report that Harriet was missing; but what else would a husband in my circumstances be doing?

My phone call to the house in Newcastle had yielded only monosyllabic responses indicating ignorance of anything helpful, other than that there was no sign of Harriet. Her holdall seemed to be missing, but no one there appeared to know or to care when she had left or how long she had been gone. I decided to call again, but this time the phone in Newcastle was not answered. It was the end of term, and I guessed that the house was empty.

I wondered if there was evidence in Newcastle of Harriet's relationship with Brendan, and now, for the first time, I also wondered if Martin and Jed knew of it. If it eventually became known that she had been betraying me, this could be seen as a motive for her murder. Certainly, it had led to her death at my hands. That said, I was as sure as I could be that no one other than Roger knew that I had any inkling of her infidelity, and I felt reasonably confident that I could act the part of an amazed cuckolded husband if it became necessary.

My main objective had to be to stay above suspicion. I knew that the moment a serious investigation started I would have little or no chance of remaining safe. Though I had done my best to clear up in the house – I had washed the paintwork thoroughly, thrown out and burnt the rug, laundered the towels – there were bound to be minute traces of blood or of the violence in the flat. I also did not think it likely, unless they started a serious investigation, that the police would find out about the existence of the insect farm. However, if they did, I would be under arrest within minutes.

It was clear that all my efforts must be focused on evading any question falling upon me, and so I needed to do everything I could to ensure that all my actions were those of a husband whose wife had gone missing, and who had not the smallest idea about how or why it had happened.

As I thought more about it, I thanked my stars that I had managed to remain quiet in those last few weeks about what Roger had told me. If I had raised the matter on the phone with Harriet, Brendan would then have known of my suspicions, and I would have had an obvious reason to be angry with her. As it was, so far as I could tell, no one other than Roger knew. I very much doubted whether he, even under questioning, would reveal what he had told me. Any pressure would be more likely to make him close down rather than be forthcoming, and even if he were I reckoned I could shrug it off as a misunderstanding which I had taken very lightly.

Roger returned home on schedule at around 8 p.m., and I asked him if he had been able to house his new insects as he had wanted to.

"Yes," he said happily, "I think they will be right at home." Then he seemed anxious to get off to bed.

I began to think more about Brendan; about how he had found it necessary to lie about the last time he had seen Harriet, and about the complications of his affair with her. They provided a possible opportunity. At 9 p.m. that evening the phone rang, and I thought I knew who it would be. I had prepared my lines and was ready.

"It's Brendan. I was calling to see if you have heard anything from Harriet."

"Oh, Brendan, it's you," I said quickly. "I'd hoped it was Harriet. Bugger. You just got my hopes up. No, I haven't heard anything at all. I don't know what to do. I went in to see the police, but they said they wouldn't be interested until she has been missing for twenty-four hours, so I have to go back there tomorrow. I don't know who else to call. I'm at my wits' end. No use in calling her parents – they're still in Singapore, and I'd only scare them half to death. I wondered if there were any other friends you could think of who might know something? Anyone else we can ask?"

"I've spoken to Laura, who is one of the girls who shares the house with her in Newcastle," he said. "I tracked her down at her parents' house in Sevenoaks. She didn't have much idea, but said she thought she was due to come down today."

"What about any of the other girls in the house? Or maybe other friends she might have that I don't know about?"

"There are two girls other than Laura, but she's not especially friendly with them. And apart from Jed and Martin, I honestly don't think there is anyone else she is close to."

I remained silent for a moment, as though considering how to phrase my next thoughts.

"Brendan," I said, "I'm not sure quite how I should ask this, and I wouldn't put you on the spot if it wasn't so serious. However, obviously my mind is roaming over every possibility." I hesitated again. "Would you be able to tell me if she was seeing someone else?"

"What do you mean?" Was there a trace of alarm in his voice, or was I mistaken?

"I have no reason to think this, and ordinarily it's the last thing I would imagine. Harriet is as loyal as anyone could ever be. But she's missing, for God's sake, and the police are bound to ask me. Is there any possibility that she could have gone off with someone else? I mean, with another bloke?"

Neither of us spoke for what seemed a long time, and I thought that perhaps the call had been cut off. Then I could hear breathing and realized that what I was hearing was the sound of a guilty man panicking. "Brendan? Are you still there?"

"Yes, I'm still here. It's just that I was shocked by what you said. No." He was stuttering and stammering like a schoolboy caught stealing apples. "Of course not. I can say that for sure. I would know. There is no one else. She only has any interest in you."

"But how can you be so sure? She probably wouldn't have confided in any of you guys, would she?" Was I enjoying myself? I hope that I could not be said to have been enjoying anything so soon after the tragedy with Harriet. On the other hand, the idea of torturing Brendan, this bloke whose infidelity and deception with Harriet had indirectly led to her death, had its own appeal.

"Trust me, Jonathan," he said, "I would know. One way and another the four of us spend quite a lot of time together, practising and performing. If she had had another man, we would have known. Take it from me that whatever the answer turns out to be, that won't be it."

"Well," I said, "you do sound very sure. It's just that the police are bound to ask me, or maybe I've been watching too many detective series on the telly. Anyway, I can't think of anything else to do, other than to wait to see if she calls or turns up. If she hasn't done so tomorrow, I'll go back to the police at King's Cross. I guess they will want to speak to you, as you seem to have been the last person to have seen her. Do you want to hurry things up by coming with me?"

We agreed to wait to see what the morning brought and decide tomorrow if he should come with me to see the police. I, of course, knew what the morning would bring and went to bed that night, totally exhausted, but completely unable to sleep for more than five minutes together.

Chapter Twenty

I kept wondering whether and when Roger would ask about Harriet. On one hand, I was mightily relieved that he clearly was not at all traumatized by anything he might have seen or heard on Tuesday night. On the other hand, it was unusual that he had not seemed interested in when we might see her, nor had he shown much of anything when I told him that I didn't know where she was. But that was Roger. Even after all these years of knowing him, indeed, of never having known any life without him, I still was unable to read with any reliability what was going on in his head.

It would have been useful for me to have had some idea of what Roger might say if and when anyone asked him, but I remained certain that the longer it was before that happened the better it would be. With any luck there would seem to the police to be no reason to ask Roger anything, and if ever anyone thought there was, his thoughts would be confused by the passage of time.

After dropping Roger off at the bus on that Friday morning, I decided to go back to the insect farm for one further look around before returning to the police station. It was the location of my most likely vulnerability, and I knew that the current situation could only be temporary, until I could think of a better idea.

I had the keys to the outside gate and to the shed in my pocket, and so went straight there from the bus and looked around carefully to check that there was no one in the area when I let myself through the locked gates. Not that I was not a familiar sight on the allotments, but now I was thinking about how any of my actions now would square with those of an increasingly distraught husband of a missing wife. I let myself into the shed and closed the door behind me before turning on the lights. Half a dozen fluorescent bulbs flickered to life, each one a few seconds apart, and my eyes began to adjust. My plan was to see if I could stand back and look at the contents of the shed as a newcomer might who had no idea what to expect. Where would your eyes go? Would it be obvious to any suspicious person where they needed to start looking? Put another way: was there any way to persuade myself that, if the police asked me to show them this place, they would not be taking me out in handcuffs?

Standing back and viewing the insect farm for the first time, you had the impression of a big area full of rows of tanks, crates, boxes and equipment. It was amazing how Roger had grown and developed this project since he began with that first tiny converted aquarium all those years ago. I thought back to that very first day when I had been trying to get his attention because I was just back from my camping holiday, and all Roger could think about was his new universe. I began to walk slowly along the sides of the tanks, one stacked upon another in racks, each one housing within it its own differentiated environment and civilization; each containing its own little ecosystem, its own unique version of paradise. In some there appeared to be little more than a muddy sludge pressing against the glass wall, broken up only by the odd cavern and twig. In these it seemed that there was little if anything to be seen. In others though, it was much easier to make out an environment and a pattern of behaviour, and in these cases it was possible to begin to see how and why the hobby was such a fascinating one for Roger.

I was in a kind of trance as I walked around the perimeter of what seemed destined to be Harriet's mausoleum, struggling to adjust the focal length of my eyes in an effort to identify and study the creatures that lived in the half-light. I found myself leaning against one of the tanks stacked at head height, and was pressing the side of my face against the glass. There was condensation on the inside, and I had to move my head to try to get a clearer view inside it. The tank was laid out with coloured gravel in the bottom, with an arrangement of twigs and small branches bridging the gaps between rocks of different shapes and sizes.

At first it seemed that the tank was empty of animate life. All I could make out was a few green leaves and some pools of water resting in the hollows of the stones. I looked harder and strained my eyes in the gloom, and only after a minute or two did I begin to discern the shapes of the ants, which I could now see advancing up and down the branches. Once they came into focus, it quickly became hard to believe that they had not been obvious from the start. First I could see dozens, and then gradually I could make out what must have been hundreds of them, apparently organized into their brigades and battalions and armies, marching across the twigs and branches, and all heading with uncompromising determination in the footsteps of their comrades. Round and round they went, back and forth, in an apparently endless stream of motion. There they were, going about their business, evidently entirely in command of their world.

If it could be possible to ask them, undoubtedly they would say that they had all the answers. They were the most intelligent and advanced creatures in their world. They knew it all, and what they didn't know for sure they had very plausible theories about. They could chart the extent of their universe. They had understood and had dominated their environment. They looked up, and they could see everything to the limit of their understanding, and when they looked up, they saw no God. They felt self-contained, no doubt self-satisfied, entirely in charge.

I stood up and struggled to regain my composure. All the while as I glanced around, I had tried to prevent my gaze from going directly to the large oblong box tucked away below the far stack of shelves, with the mesh over the top of it. But of course I could not unknow what I knew, and my eyes were drawn irresistibly in that direction. Once it came into my sight I could look nowhere else, and it was obvious to me that this was the first place anyone searching for a dead body would look. I had to conclude that the only possibility of not being caught was to prevent the police from learning about the insect farm. If they did learn of it, I would have to try to deter them from taking an interest. Once an enquiring officer was inside this building, my chance of evading detection and arrest would be zero.

I felt a sudden pain in my stomach from hunger and I glanced around for a final time before locking the door. I queued at a sandwich shop next to the Underground station. The idea of eating in the street was always frowned upon in my family, and it was one of the liberating things about being an orphan that I felt no fear of being caught by my mother cramming food into my mouth as I walked along. Even so, I could hear her displeasure. What would she be thinking if she knew about what was really going on with me now? Perhaps she did know. I felt a further huge wave of nausea as the idea struck me, and I had to stand to one side of the pavement for several moments to collect myself. If there was any way that my mother or father knew what was happening to me, I decided that they would also understand my current actions. Their first concern now, I felt certain, would be for Roger, and that was my first concern as well. I took a little comfort from the idea.

I had not been in touch with Brendan to see if he was going to the police station with me today, and wondered what to do. I decided that I would go alone, but be sure to let them know that I had asked him to come along. If I had been told it, I had not remembered the name of the policeman I had seen yesterday, but when I briefly described him to the officer behind the porthole he immediately knew whom I meant.

"That'll be Sergeant Norris," said the officer. "I'll just see if he is in. Who shall I say wants him?"

I told him my name and said it was about my wife who seemed to be missing. The young officer picked up the phone, and I saw him mouthing the words which asked Sergeant Norris to come out to see me.

The sergeant looked as though he had not left the station since the last time I had seen him there twenty-four hours earlier. Come to think of it, there was never anything about him to suggest that he ever left the station. Maybe they put him in a cupboard and plugged him in to recharge overnight.

"Still not turned up then?" he said. He was using a plastic spoon to stir the cup of brown liquid which he had obtained for himself when I had asked for water. He placed it on the table. We were in what I learnt was called an interview room, which is where they put you whether or not you are suspected of a crime. What that means is that there is toughened glass with wires running through it, and there are plenty of metal hoops and brackets to which to handcuff you should it become necessary.

"She hasn't, and now I'm worried sick." I spoke hurriedly, blurting it all out. "No one who shares her house in

Newcastle knows where she is. A bloke she's friendly with in Newcastle says he is sure she left there on Tuesday. I wasn't expecting her until yesterday, but either way there is no sight nor sound of her."

Sergeant Norris had brought a standard form with him, and methodically we went through the essential details of Harriet's life. Name, address, age, place of birth, names of parents, occupation, where last seen. It felt strange talking about Harriet in this context. The flesh and blood of the woman I loved was now being expressed as a set of stark data.

"Did you bring a photograph?"

"Pardon?"

"A photograph. Did you bring a photograph of your wife?" he asked. "The next stage would be for us to circulate a photograph of her to other police stations and eventually, if she doesn't turn up, maybe on some posters. We'll need as clear a photograph as you have."

I shook my head and apologized. It should have been obvious to me that they would need one. I had plenty at home. I would bring one in.

"One thing I am sorry to have to ask you, but I hope you'll understand why I need to."

I nodded. "Go ahead."

"Do you think it's possible that your wife has met someone else – another man, I mean – and maybe gone off somewhere with him? I'm not saying she has left you or anything. It's just that it wouldn't be the first time that a young woman has got carried away with a romantic fling."

I had anticipated the question and mentally rehearsed my performance.

"You know, in the last twenty-four hours I've obviously thought of that, and I know everyone must say this, but really, you don't know Harriet. She just wouldn't do anything like that. She's not that kind of girl."

"No one is that kind of girl," said Norris, "and yet somehow or other lots of wives leave their husbands, and lots of husbands leave their wives."

"And anyway" – this was the part I had to pitch carefully – "she seems to have been very close to a few blokes in Newcastle, one in particular called Brendan, and he was absolutely vehement that she hadn't been seeing anyone else. He was close enough to her to be certain, he said. He absolutely assured me."

I saw Norris writing on the back of the form he had just completed. "And what is this chap's name? And where might we be able to find him if we need to?"

I gave them Brendan's name and telephone number. No, I did not know the precise address. "But we always drop him off at the end of a place called Essex Road in Croydon." I said. "I wonder—"

"You wonder what?"

"Nothing, just a stupid idea. But as I think about it, Brendan was just a bit evasive about why he thought that

Harriet had travelled down on Tuesday. I just wondered for a moment whether she might be at his place, but honestly, that's ridiculous. She couldn't be."

Sergeant Norris told me that in the absence of any evidence that a crime had been committed, there was little they could do for the moment, other than to circulate details of a missing person. If I brought in a photograph, they would add that to the details. He was still quite sure there was nothing to worry about, he said. He had seen dozens of cases like this, and most often the missing person had just wanted to take a few days alone to think about life.

"Nine times out of ten they turn up safe and sound and usually embarrassed that everyone has been worried about them," he said. "I'm sure that will happen here."

I told him that I hoped this would turn out to be so, repeated that I was worried half to death, and stood up to go. "There is just one thing I'd like your advice on." He raised his eyebrows in enquiry. "Do you think I should alert her parents? They live in Singapore, and obviously there is nothing they can do right now to help. I don't want to worry them unnecessarily if there turns out to be no reason to be concerned."

The sergeant did not hesitate. "I think you should," he said. "Firstly, they may have heard from her – who knows, she could even have taken it into her head to pay them a flying visit and she might answer the phone. More likely they have no idea, but I think they need to know that their daughter is missing anyway."

272

I said that I could see the sense in that and undertook to let him know straight away if they had any information, or if anything else turned up.

"You really still don't think I need to worry?" I said, as he showed me the way back into the maze of cages in the entrance lobby.

"I shouldn't think so. To be perfectly honest, we won't start to worry unless there is no sign of her for another week or so. Even then, if there is no evidence that anything bad has happened to her, she'll just go down on the list as a missing person. You'd be amazed how many people just go walkabout for their own reasons, but almost all of them turn up in the end. There is a lot of this sort of thing about, Mr Maguire."

I thanked him and walked away. Once outside and in the street I breathed deeply and found I had to lean against the wall for support. I could feel my pulse beating in my head and chest, and hoped I had managed to disguise the reason for the stress I was so plainly feeling. Nothing in Sergeant Norris's manner suggested that he suspected anything untoward, but I guessed that he was much more practised at concealing his thoughts than was I.

Chapter Twenty-One

At this distance in time and space, I am not able to say for certain exactly when the focus of my efforts shifted from trying to keep myself out of trouble towards pushing any suspicion in the direction of Brendan. The seed was planted at that instant at the railway station when I realized that he was having to lie to me about what he knew of Harriet's intentions, and about how he knew about them. There was no telling how long, and to whom, Brendan would keep up his attempts to conceal his affair with my wife. If he started down that road with the police, who knew where it could end?

I think that, in those first few days, the idea of gently nudging doubts and concerns towards Brendan merely felt like an aspect of diverting attention from myself. In the days that followed, it became more of a mission. After all, there was a very plausible interpretation of events that in fact Brendan *was* responsible for Harriet's death. Obviously I know that immediately this sounds like special pleading on the part of a killer, but if anyone wanted to see it from my point of view for a moment, it has the ring of credibility about it.

I loved my wife. I had never been unfaithful to her – neither before nor since our wedding. I had never told a lie to her. For reasons which were not altogether selfish, I had made the sacrifice of not being with my wife all the time – with a view to being able to be with her permanently after a relatively short hiatus. I am not at this late stage going to try to suggest that there was any special virtue in my decision to give up studying to take care of Roger. I never have said that and I never will. He was and is my brother, I love him, and it is my pleasure to do what I can to take care of him.

Nor, if honest, could I claim that I was making any particular sacrifice in forgoing romance or sex with other women. Neither my work nor my daily life away from work threw me much in the way of other women my age, and even if they had, I had never taken any interest in them. Not any of them, not ever since I met her. That part of my life was all about Harriet. Again, it always had been and always would have been.

So perhaps the least that could be said on my behalf is that my reasons for not being with Harriet were not unworthy ones. I was a dutiful husband, waiting for her, patiently, and was entirely ready to love and to cherish her, in sickness and in health, forsaking all others, for as long as we both should live.

That was the plan.

Then along came Brendan. Brendan fucking Harcourt. Harriet's jazz to my blues.

I had cast my mind over the events of that evening, now four days ago, hundreds and hundreds of times. No, not hundreds and hundreds of times; that implies that there were gaps in between. I cast my mind over them constantly, still never really understanding what had happened. But the one thing I was sure of was that it was that comparison – that analogy of my love for Harriet, and hers for me, with some favourite type of music – which had tipped me over the edge. Sure enough, music was important to me, but I knew that her appreciation of it was far more profound than anything I could ever have experienced. I had seen her enchanted during *Jazz on a Summer's Day*, I had seen her entranced during the Clapton solos of 'Have You Ever Loved a Woman' and I had seen her quite literally enraptured as Rodolfo and Mimi fell in love over a lost key. None of this was within the realms of my personal experience.

Maybe in her mind, therefore, a comparison of our love with her most loved music was not as demeaning as it so certainly felt to me. Maybe comparing the soaring ecstasy of lovemaking with the soaring joy of listening to a favourite aria was not as crazy as immediately it had seemed. But it was too late to worry about any of that now.

* * *

I waited until much later that night before telephoning Harriet's parents. There was an eight-hour time difference between London and Singapore, and so I decided to delay until it was early morning there before calling. I had only ever seen photographs of the house they occupied, and I imagined the background to their lives more as part of a film set than as something real; something convivial and colonial, involving white panama hats and lots of deferential servants. I knew that even to find that it was me calling instead of Harriet would immediately cause them concern, so I tried to put the information in context as quickly as possible. After the briefest of greetings with Harriet's mother, I launched straight into it.

"I am sure there is nothing at all to be worried about, but I thought I had better let you know. Harriet seems to have taken herself off somewhere, and none of us knows where she is. I was just calling to see if by any chance she had been in contact with either of you?"

"What do you mean, 'taken herself off somewhere'?" she said. "Where is she?"

"We don't know, Mrs Chalfont." If we knew that, I was thinking, we wouldn't be calling you. I was surprised to find myself reacting already like a man trying to solve a genuine mystery. It would stand me in good stead for what I knew must be ahead of me. "She was due to come down from Newcastle on Thursday, and I met the train, but she wasn't on it. I've called her flatmates and spoken to a couple of her friends from college, but no one knows where she is."

Silence on the other end of the phone. I imagined that Harriet's mother's instant reaction was that her daughter had left me. No doubt she was trying to work out what to say which wouldn't make that instantly obvious.

"How long has she been missing?"

"As far as I know, it's two days. I had expected her to come to London on the train on Thursday. What's a bit more worrying is that one of her friends from the quartet was on the same train, and told me he thought she had left Newcastle on Tuesday. If that was true then she has been missing for five days."

"Which friend is that?"

Of all the questions Mrs Chalfont could have been expected to ask, I had not expected this one.

"Pardon?"

"I said which friend from the quartet told you that?"

"A bloke called Brendan Harcourt. Why, do you know him?"

"I know of him," she said. It was plain that this was the name she had been expecting. It was a turn of events I had not anticipated, and I realized that I had very little idea of how much or how little Harriet had been in touch with her parents. I always assumed that it was very little; she had only seen them twice in four years, to my knowledge, and I guessed that they were not constantly on the telephone. I also had no reason to know whether they had been in postal contact, or how frank or intimate Harriet might have been in any letters.

"May I ask how?"

"No, you may not," she said, then appeared to remember her manners. "I mean to say that of course you may, but that isn't my immediate priority. Have you informed the police?"

I told her that I had gone directly to the police station after Harriet failed to show up on the train as expected, but that they had been unconcerned and asked me to come back the following day if there was still no sign of her. Which I did, but even now they didn't seem to be taking the thing seriously, since there seemed to be no reason to think that any crime had been committed. "I think they think that maybe she has got fed up with me and gone off with someone else."

"And what do you think?" she asked.

"I just don't know," I said. "To be honest, I'd be absolutely amazed if that were so. Certainly if she was fed up with me, or if I have done something wrong, I don't have a clue what it could be. She gave me no hint of it."

The pause at the other end of the phone line was of someone with something to say, but weighing up whether or not to say it. When finally she spoke, it seemed as though she had decided not to.

"Can you give me the names and details of the policemen you have dealt with so far?"

I said that I had the information on a piece of paper and could get it in just a moment, but asked why she wanted them. "One of the few advantages of being in the service," she said, "is that one can still have a bit of influence over public servants back at home. I'm going to ask Geoffrey to make some calls. Maybe get things moving a bit. I'm sure there is an entirely innocent explanation, but we shouldn't be taking any chances."

"Sure," I said, "give me a minute and I'll get the name and phone number of the officer I've been dealing with." I read out the details I had for Sergeant Norris at dictation speed and she was about to end the call.

"Mrs Chalfont, one thing," I said. "I thought you were about to tell me something about Brendan Harcourt, but you changed the subject. Is there anything I should know about him? Anything about him and Harriet?"

"Why do you ask?"

"Only because I thought I heard something in your voice which implied it. And it's an open secret that he has had a thing for her for many years."

Once again she seemed about to say something and then to change her mind.

"No, there's nothing untoward that I know of," she said. "It's just that I have heard Harriet talk about all the boys in the music group, and for some reason his name stuck in my mind."

I knew that she was lying, but I also knew that I wasn't going to get any further information out of her in this conversation. When I put down the receiver, my mind filled up with a cascade of new thoughts. I wondered what Harriet had told her mother about Brendan and, whatever it was, might it be something which could help me to stay out of harm's way?

Chapter Twenty-Two

Roger's day centre opened on Saturdays mornings and he liked to attend, which meant that Sunday was ordinarily our only opportunity in the week to sleep just a little bit later. On this particular Sunday morning, however, I was awoken by someone pushing the bell at the front door on the street. The sound mingled with the hum of traffic from the high street at the top of our road and a single church bell tolling in the distance.

It was a long way down only to find a man offering free copies of *The Watchtower*, and so my habit was to ignore anyone calling unless I was expecting someone in particular. I waited for the fourth ring before putting on my dressing gown and scurrying the three floors down to open the door.

"Mr Maguire?" Instantly I knew that the two men in plain clothes at the door were from the police, and indeed after a moment or two I realized that I knew them.

"I am Detective Sergeant Wallace from Wandsworth CID, and this is Detective Constable Pascoe." These were the same two officers who had come to the house asking questions after the fire. I had no time to consider whether there was any significance in the coincidence. "We understand that you reported that your wife is missing," Sergeant Wallace continued. "May I ask whether you have heard anything from her?"

"No, I haven't," I said. "Do you have any news? Has she had an accident or something?"

"Why should you think that?"

"Because on Friday when I spoke to the police in King's Cross they told me that no one would be taking much of an interest in my wife's disappearance for a long time, if at all. Now I have a couple of detectives at my door, and so I assume that something has happened."

The two men exchanged glances.

Both looked straight out of central casting; as though they had studied at Pinewood rather than Hendon. One wore a gabardine raincoat, pulled together tightly at the waist with a tie-up belt. The other wore a shorter car coat, and both had trilby hats. I remembered the underlying hostility of our previous encounter and reminded myself that I would need to try to stay on the right side of these two, if at all possible.

"May we come in?" Sergeant Wallace asked.

I apologized and opened the door wider to let them come inside, then led the way up the stairs. When we reached the top landing before the door to our flat, I turned and spoke in a whisper.

"Just one thing before we go in. You will remember from the last time we met that I have an older brother with a mental handicap." I hated describing Roger in such bald terms, but felt that I should spell out the situation quickly and with no ambiguity. "Roger isn't really aware that there is a problem about Harriet. He knows that we have been expecting her and that she hasn't turned up, but he doesn't know how worried I am. If he did, he would be likely to get very anxious and upset. So I've been trying to keep it from him." I explained that he was asleep at the moment, but that if he should wake while they were still in the flat it would be good if they could avoid saying anything likely to cause him concern.

To be fair, both of them seemed to take this on board at face value, and said that they understood and would do their best. Perhaps it was a function of the differing circumstances, but on this meeting I had an early impression that these were decent men. Inside the flat, the two detectives removed their coats and placed them over the backs of dining chairs, while I put on the kettle. All of us spoke at subdued volume.

"So I guess you had to buy everything from scratch after the fire, Mr Maguire?" asked Pascoe. I confirmed that I had bought quite a lot of things from a charity shop, but quickly added that I was keen to know what had happened to merit this visit.

"I think that maybe I can guess what might have happened to put Harriet's disappearance higher up the in-tray," I said. "I assume that it's something to do with her father's status in the diplomatic service?"

"Let's just say that your wife's family has friends in high places," said Wallace. I nodded and gave them a half-smile.

"Well, I'm sorry if this is a nuisance to you blokes. If what Sergeant Norris at King's Cross told me is correct, then I'm sure you must feel you've got lots of more important things to be doing on a Sunday morning. But I think you'll understand why this feels like very good news to me. My wife has never gone missing before, and so while I'm sure it feels very routine to the police, it feels very far from that to me."

The two detectives assured me that their private thoughts were irrelevant, and that they would be taking this inquiry very seriously.

"We're just humble servants," said Pascoe, with what I felt was a slight trace of bitterness. "It is for others to point us, and we just go off in the direction we are pointed."

They sat alongside each other on the sofa. As we went once again through the banal detail of Harriet's life and our unusual domestic arrangements, I took in the faces of the two men. There was something about both which echoed what I had seen in the face of Sergeant Norris at the police station. Something a bit careworn, a bit harassed, a bit overworked and a bit underpaid. Faces of men who had seen too much of the darker side of human life, and carried some of the baggage in the crags and creases.

As we talked, I began to feel myself involuntarily affected by what seemed the surreal aspect of having these two men sitting here, just inches away from the location of the scene which, if they could only have been aware of it, would provide a complete and instant answer to the enquiries they were making.

Detective Sergeant Wallace was sitting with his feet on the spot where I had woken from unconsciousness five nights earlier with my hands covered in congealed blood. Detective Constable Pascoe's shoes were resting exactly on the area of the floor where, five nights ago, Harriet's body lay lifeless and inert. Lying on the chair in the corner was the cat, Olly, also a silent witness to what unfolded right here just a few days earlier. I had a brief mental image of the cat walking across and pawing the ground where Harriet had lain, but of course it did not.

I went in detail through the narrative of expecting Harriet to arrive on the train on Thursday, of meeting Brendan instead, and of only then hearing the suggestion that she had left Newcastle two days earlier. And all the time I was wondering how something as huge and traumatic as a murder could have happened in this same physical space such a short time ago and it not be instantly obvious to everyone present that this was so. The walls and furniture were silent witnesses which would never speak. Strange thoughts, confusing and bewildering.

We continued to talk, and I had to struggle to avoid glancing downwards onto the floor, as if to make further and final checks that there was no visible trace of what had happened. In my mind's eye I could see a drop of congealed blood caked into the weave of the carpet, but of course it was not really there. I needed to remain focused on what I was saying to the policemen, but at the same time my thoughts were invaded by the vividness of these recent images.

"May I ask you why you went to the police so quickly on Thursday?"

"What?" I was losing my fight to keep my attention on the conversation. "I'm sorry. I don't understand what you mean?"

"Well" – it was Pascoe speaking – "usually if people go to meet someone from the train and they aren't on it, they just wait for the next one or the one after that. They don't usually go straight to the police unless they know that something is wrong."

I hadn't had much time to think through the answers to every possible question, but this, at least, was one I had anticipated.

"I probably would have just assumed that she had missed her train and would come in on the next one, had it not been for the fact that at the station I bumped into her friend Brendan Harcourt, who seemed certain that she had left Newcastle two days earlier on Tuesday." As I was talking I had an odd sensation of being able to hear myself speak, almost as though I was listening to someone else. My brain and mouth were communicating, but the thing that was me seemed to be standing outside of either of them. I was conversing on autopilot, and meanwhile the actual me was finding it more impossible than ever to prevent my eyes from flickering downwards to the floor at their feet. In the involuntary machinations of my mind I could see the ghostly shape of Harriet lying prone and prostrate on the floor, and all the time I expected her to tug at the legs of their trousers, calling their attention to her. "Down here. Look down here."

"Are you all right, Mr Maguire?" said Wallace.

I squeezed closed my eyes, trying to rid myself of the ghastly spectre which affronted my imagination. I pressed my thumb and forefinger into my eyelids, gently shaking my head. Pascoe went to the sink to get a glass of water and returned to put it down on the table beside me.

"I'm sorry," I said eventually, and sipped from the glass. "It's just that it's been a very stressful few days. My wife is missing, I have no idea where she is, and nor does anyone else. It's not at all like her. Ask anyone who knows her. People seem to be implying that she has just taken herself off for a few days and not told anyone where she is. Or maybe that she has gone off with another man or something. But she just isn't that kind of girl. She just isn't. I think something must have happened to her."

Neither man had spoken, and when I looked up I could see that both were looking over my shoulder towards the bedroom door behind me. I knew what had caught their attention and wondered how much he had heard. In the second or two before I turned, I struggled to transform the expression on my face.

"Hello, Roger, I didn't hear you come in. How long have you been there?"

Roger was standing in the doorway, still wearing his pyjamas. Nothing in his expression gave any clue as to what was going on in his head. The few seconds that passed before he spoke were just enough to send my already rising tension to fever pitch. In those moments I imagined that his first words would be that he knew the whereabouts of Harriet; a full explanation to be given in the light of my apparent lapse of memory. I felt as though the ground would open up beneath me as I saw his lips begin to move.

"Have any parcels arrived for me?"

Whatever I may have expected to be going through the enigma that was Roger's mind at that moment, this was not it. I closed my eyes and shook my head, recalibrating my response. In recent weeks there seemed to have been a constant stream of packages and boxes addressed to Roger, and indeed two or three had arrived the day before. I confirmed that they had, and Roger headed towards the hallway to collect them. Moments later he reappeared, holding one of the boxes and examining the label which indicated that it had arrived by Air Mail. He seemed pleased. "What's for breakfast?"

I breathed, and then I smiled. "I thought we might have a nice fried stoat with a pickled-onion glaze and a snail purée?"

Roger grinned back at me. "No thanks, Jonathan," he said, "I think I'll just have toast and Marmite today." His face cracked into a still broader untroubled smile, and then he turned around and went into the bathroom. Moments later I could hear the sound of taps running.

I explained our little breakfast joke to Wallace and Pascoe; they smiled and gave me business cards, and then asked me to contact them if and when Harriet reappeared. I gave them contact numbers for Martin and Jed and Brendan. They said that they did not need to be told how to contact Harriet's parents.

"Do you think that something bad has happened to her?" I asked as I showed them to the door. "Tell me the truth."

"I don't think so," said Wallace, "not for a minute. As I believe the sergeant at King's Cross said to you, sir, there is usually an innocent explanation for these things. Most likely she'll turn up in a few days and everyone will be embarrassed but relieved and we can get back to solving crime."

"Yes, like I say, I am sorry if this is a waste of your time." By now I had collected myself and was refocusing. "But I think you'll understand why I am glad that you are taking it seriously. I know you've probably got lots of cases, but I've only got one wife. And I love her." The final few words caught in my throat in an upsurge of emotion. I was aware of the two officers looking at me with what seemed to be genuine sympathy in their faces.

"I'm sure you do, Mr Maguire," said Pascoe. "And I am sure she will be back with you very soon." The two men walked onto the landing and were about to start down the stairs when Wallace turned back and spoke at a low volume. "By the way," he said, "I was just wondering, more from curiosity than anything else, but did anything further ever come to light about the cause of the fire at your home? I think we left the file open, but I don't recall seeing anything new."

"No, it didn't," I said. "The fire service could never offer a satisfactory explanation, so I've always just assumed that it was electrical or something."

"And Roger never said anything more about it?" His tone seemed to acknowledge that he was touching on a sensitive area.

"No, sir," I said, and just for a moment I saw again the image which had haunted me, of Roger crouching in the darkness of the insect farm while the flames from the burning house lit up the night sky outside. "Roger has never said anything more about it, because Roger doesn't know anything more about it. Never did, never will."

Wallace shrugged and glanced at Pascoe. The two men turned and walked slowly down the stairs.

Roger and I had our breakfast together, and an hour later I walked with him down to the insect farm. He had a lot of maintenance, cleaning and feeding to organize in the shed, and so I agreed to come back for him in a couple of hours. Again he seemed unconcerned and asked no questions about the two men who had visited. When later on I returned to the flat, I found the numbers for Martin and Jed at their parents' homes which I had given to the two officers. Martin was not at home when I called, and I left a message with his mother asking him to call me back. When I called the other number, Jed answered the phone. I sensed the tension in his voice as soon as he knew it was me.

"Oh hi, Jonathan. What's going on?"

"I wondered if Brendan had told you that we can't find Harriet anywhere. I went to meet her train on Thursday and she wasn't on it. I met Brendan at the station and he thought she had been intending to travel down last Tuesday. I know he called you from there. I don't suppose you have heard anything from her?"

He confirmed that he had spoken to Brendan on Thursday, but had not been able to recall Harriet saying anything about when she was coming back to London. "I thought it was Thursday, as you did, but Brendan said that she told the three of us that she was coming down a few days early. I have to say that I can't remember her telling us that, but if he says so, he's probably right."

"Why?"

"Why what?"

"Why is he probably right? Why is what Brendan remembers more likely to be right than what you remember?"

"Well, because..." those first two words were the start of a sentence which was clearly intended to have gone on to say that "the answer is obvious". However, Jed checked himself just in time and his voice wavered as he searched for an alternative ending. "...because both Martin and I have only a vague recall of the conversation, but Brendan says he remembers it specifically."

"Any reason why he should?"

"What do you mean?"

"I just wondered if there was any reason why Brendan should have been paying so much closer attention to Harriet's plans than you and Martin were? After all, the four of you hang out together most of the time, don't you?"

Again I could sense the tension and a slight hesitation as Jed struggled for an answer. My curiosity about who knew what was in danger of getting the better of me. It would be necessary for me to insist that I had no idea about anything going on between Harriet and Brendan, so to do or say anything to indicate suspicions at this stage would not be smart. By now I was sure that both Jed and Martin must have known about the affair, and I guessed that neither of them would have been comfortable about it. I thought it unlikely that either would conceal it for long if questioned by the police.

"I think the police may be in touch with you quite soon," I said.

Now he sounded even more concerned. "I didn't realize they were involved. I thought she must have just gone off for a day or so. I didn't know she was, like, really missing."

"Be honest," I said. "You know Harriet pretty well. Do you really think she is the kind of girl who would just head off on her own for a few days, not telling anyone where she was going? She'd know that we'd be worried sick. She'd never do that."

"No, but I just assumed. What else can have happened to her? It's not like she can have been abducted or anything, is it?"

"No," I said, "I don't think she can have been abducted. Her parents are fairly well off, I would imagine, but they're by no means loaded. But maybe she had an accident or something? Maybe banged her head and is in a hospital somewhere and hasn't been able to tell anyone who she is."

"But then she would have had some identification on her, and the hospital would have contacted you."

"I guess," I said. "I'm just thinking out loud. The fact is that I don't know what to believe. Was she acting strangely in any way in the last few weeks?"

"In what way?" said Jed.

"I don't know. I guess that if she has gone away on her own to think about whatever it is that might be on her mind, I was wondering if here had been any indication of it that you've seen. Remember that I haven't seen her at all for a month."

Once again I was sewing the seeds of a suspicion that might point to Brendan, but still I think that at the time it was partly subconscious – a by-product of my instinct for self-preservation.

Jed had no answers or theories, or if he did have them he did not share them with me. I wondered how long he and Martin had known about Harriet and Brendan. I wondered too about the nature of friendship among men, and of the strange loyalty that allows us to overlook or permit others to be subjected to outrages which we would hate to be the victim of ourselves.

Chapter Twenty-Three

It was four days later when I was awoken by the persistent ringing of the telephone. The handset was in the living room, and I was always anxious when it rang at an unsocial hour, because the sound seemed to reverberate through the entire building. I glanced at the clock beside my bed and saw that it was 5.45, and so I tried to collect myself as swiftly as possible in order to be able to get to it before it woke up everyone in all the flats below. I wore only a T-shirt and underpants to bed in those days, and I slipped out from under the covers and padded through the flat.

"Hello. Hello."

A remote crackle on the line told me that the call was long-distance, and my mind worked out the answer at exactly the moment that it also arrived through my ears.

"Jonathan? It's Mrs Chalfont. Harriet's mother," she added, as if I didn't know who Mrs Chalfont was. I guess it may seem odd that I referred to my mother-in-law so formally. I had met her only twice, once shortly before and once during the wedding, and then only for as brief a period as they could respectably manage. My father had always referred to his own mother-in-law as "Mum". I was about as likely to do that with Mrs Chalfont as I was to refer to the Pope as "Dad".

"Oh yes, Mrs Chalfont. What can I do for you?"

"I just wondered if you had any more information about this arrest that has taken place?"

I was stunned. "Arrest? What arrest?"

There was a pause. "Obviously you don't know. The police have arrested someone in connection with Harriet's disappearance. Her father and I are flying home tonight. We'll be there tomorrow morning. The police don't seem to be able to give us any further information, so I assumed that you would know more."

"They've arrested someone?" I know I was being unusually slow on the uptake, but this information was such a surprise to me that I was having difficulty taking it in. "Who have they arrested?"

"Well, that young man you mentioned. Brendan Harcourt. I still cannot understand how you haven't been told. Haven't you been keeping in touch with their inquiries? We don't even know if they are charging him and, if so, with what."

"They've arrested Brendan? Why?" By now my brain was finally kicking into sense. "Have they found Harriet? Is she all right? She hasn't been harmed, has she?"

"No," she said. "They haven't found anything so far as I know, but I understand that they have been making inquiries in Newcastle and they think that Brendan Harcourt knows more than he has let on. They've been told things by some of the other students."

"What things?"

"I can't say right now. That is, I don't really know for sure. Perhaps best just to say for the moment that he seems to have known her a lot better than he said he did."

"What? What does that mean? Does he know where she is? If so, why wouldn't he say?"

"I don't want to say any more right now, Jonathan. I haven't got the full picture myself. That's why I was calling you. Anyway, as I say, Geoffrey and I are flying back tonight. We arrive in the morning and we'll be checking into the Connaught. Meanwhile, maybe you could contact the police so that you can find out whatever they know and bring us up to speed when we get there?"

My thoughts were racing. I said that I would find out what I could, and that they should call me when they had arrived and checked into their hotel. "Whatever time it is," I added, though I wasn't sure why.

They had arrested Brendan. What could it mean? Now my mind was going at a hundred miles an hour as the few available facts were extended by speculation into a theory. I guessed that the police must have been making inquiries in Newcastle and would have learnt very quickly that Brendan and Harriet had been having an adulterous affair. By now he was probably admitting that he had slept with her on Monday night and had put her on the train on Tuesday. Since she apparently hadn't arrived in London, he would be assumed to have been the last person to have seen her. Add the fact that he had no doubt continued to lie about his relationship with her, and hence, presumably, the reason why Brendan would have fallen under suspicion. It seemed a bit flimsy, but at short notice it was the best I could do.

I went to the table to find the business cards the two detectives had left and called the main number. It went straight through to the CID room at Wandsworth, where a bored and very young-sounding officer told me that neither Detectives Wallace or Pascoe were in the office. It was still only 6.30 a.m.

"Can I take a message for them?" he asked.

"Yes, please ask them to call Jonathan Maguire. Please tell them it's urgent."

"Shall I tell them what it's about?"

I hated this at the best of times, and at my current level of stress it was all I could do not to yell down the phone that it was about my fucking missing fucking wife and that the two fucking detectives who promised me they would let me know of any fucking developments hadn't fucking done so. But I did not.

"My wife is missing and these are the two detectives looking after the case," I said instead.

"Thank you, Mr Maguire. I'll be sure to let them know."

So preoccupied was I now with this latest development that I could barely get through my usual routine of waking Roger, exchanging our morning jokes about breakfast, and getting him off to the bus. But Roger didn't seem to notice. He just spent the morning wittering on about the batch of cockroaches he had been promised by a new teacher at the centre, and how he might have to rearrange the tanks to accommodate the new arrivals.

"It was bad enough with the last ones," he said. "This time I need to find somewhere for them where they won't be eating all the other creatures in their tank." As I watched and listened to him, cramming soggy toast into his mouth and talking as he chewed, I could not help but wonder for the millionth time what went on in that strange mind of his.

On one hand, Roger was capable enough to be able to take on board and remember a vast amount of detailed information about the feeding and care of a wide range of creatures, many of them natives of foreign countries and requiring at least a simulation of their natural habitat for their survival. On the other hand, his brother's wife had gone missing, one of his favourite people in the world, and he hadn't even mentioned her name for a week. I found myself looking at his face as he spoke, paying no attention to the meaning of his words, but wondering if this person was any more or any less likely to alert the authorities to what had happened just a few feet away from where we now sat than would be the walls or the furniture, or indeed Olly the cat.

After dropping Roger at the bus, I hurried back to the flat and waited. I paced and worried and speculated and paced some more, until 10 a.m., when I felt certain that my impatience would blow a hole in my head if I didn't do something quickly. I put on my coat and set off to the police station at King's Cross.

I was asked to wait among the pattern of cages which formed the outer area of the police station, and wondered if someone wanted to keep me outside so that I would not see or meet Brendan. After ten minutes or so Sergeant Norris came out to see me and escorted me into the same interview room where he and I had first spoken.

"The two detectives looking after the case are on their way here from Wandsworth," said Norris. "I believe there has been a development in the inquiry."

"And what is that?" I said. I was trying to get the balance right between anxiety to know what had happened and whatever would be the appropriate levels of irritation at not having been kept informed. "Detectives Wallace and Pascoe promised me that they would let me know anything that happened."

Norris was about to speak when the door opened and in walked Detective Sergeant Wallace. Before he could say anything, I stood up.

"Detective Wallace. I came because I heard that there had been a development in the search for my wife?"

"Yes, Mr Maguire, there has been."

"I thought you said you were going to keep me informed. What has happened? Has she turned up? Is she OK?"

"No, Mr Maguire, I am afraid she hasn't. There is no good news, but also there is no bad news." He let that thought sink in. "However, there has been a development in the last few hours. It doesn't help us to know where Harriet is, but it may be relevant." He stopped speaking.

"And it is?"

He paused again, and I saw that he was looking squarely at me, but that the precise direction of his eyes bounced from one of mine to the other, as though trying to weigh up how I would react to what he was about to say.

"There is no easy way to say this to you, Mr Maguire," he said at last, "but I'm afraid that we think your wife was seeing another man."

I stared straight back at him and counted five in my head before I spoke.

"What?"

"Like I say, I am sorry that you have to hear it like this. Sorry that you have to hear it at all actually, but we think your wife was romantically involved with another man."

"And are you saying she has run off with him?"

"No, we're not saying that. It's someone you know well, but he swears that he doesn't know where she is."

I was thinking hard and fast, and knew that it was dangerous for me to appear to have no clue about Brendan. It might at some point come out that Harriet's mother had told me of his arrest. I looked at Norris, whose eyes reflected the same sympathy for me as I could see in the face of the detective.

"And is this Brendan?"

"Why do you ask that?"

"Because five hours ago I got a phone call from Harriet's mother in Singapore to tell me that Brendan Harcourt had been arrested. I didn't believe it, partly because you assured me that I would be the first to hear of any developments."

Wallace's expression told me that he could guess what had happened and was dismayed.

"I apologize to you, Mr Maguire. I certainly did not tell her before we informed you. Because of what I might best call the wider interest in this case, we are under strict instructions to keep our boss in touch with any developments. He must have told Mr and Mrs Chalfont without letting me know he was going to do so. I'm not happy about it, and can only say how sorry I am."

"Thank you," I said, and assumed that the "wider interest" was Wallace's way of describing the influence Harriet's parents were exerting. "But that doesn't matter now. Are you saying that my wife Harriet and Brendan are lovers?" I laughed, with disbelief rather than with any humour. "Because if so, you are wrong, Sergeant. I can assure you that there is absolutely no chance whatsoever that this could be true."

"Why do you say that?"

"Because there isn't. For one thing, Harriet and I have only been married for a short while. For another thing, she loves me. And for a third thing, Brendan bloody Harcourt has fancied my wife for years, but I know her well enough to know that she finds him repulsive."

Wallace and the sergeant looked at each other for a moment, and then Wallace glanced down at the table, apparently with some sadness.

"I am so sorry, Mr Maguire. In my experience, very few men in your situation ever believe that their wives could be unfaithful to them, but many are, and you won't be the first husband to have been led up the garden path." It was an old-fashioned expression even then. "But I regret to have to tell you" – he interrupted himself – "may I call you Jonathan?" I confirmed that he could. "I am sorry to have to tell you, Jonathan, that there can be no doubt about it. Harriet's flatmates have confirmed it. The other musicians – Martin and Jed – have also both confirmed it, and finally, Brendan himself has admitted it."

I put my head in my hands and sat quite still. By now my focus on acting a part was once again becoming overwhelmed by the shock and grief at the whole run of recent events, and I felt the balance of my mind going out of control. Images of Harriet crowded in, one moment laughing, one moment sad, and at another moment slipping off her dressing gown so that I glimpsed the incredible beauty of her body before she climbed into the bed beside me. I shook my head violently, trying to push out the unwanted pictures, and in an instant I once again found my body wracked with convulsive sobs, the tears falling liberally from my eyes, trickling down my cheeks and landing in a series of splashes on the table in front of me. This was no act. I am not sure if I was grieving for the unfaithfulness of my wife or for the loss of her, or for her murder. Or for the torment of what most probably was lying ahead of me. My mind was still spinning when the policeman spoke again. I felt a hand on my shoulder and saw that Wallace was standing beside me.

"It seems that your wife Harriet and Brendan Harcourt have been having an affair for a few weeks at least. Your friends confirm what you say about him having been interested in her for a long time, but they say that she only recently gave in to him. However, it seems that he has been much more keen on her than she is on him, and there has been a dispute between them about whether or not she should leave you to be with him."

Once again my emotions were split. Part of me was trying to take in the news that there was even a question of Harriet leaving me. The other part was trying to react like someone hearing all this for the first time. Fortunately both emotions produced the same monosyllabic expression.

"What?" One one thousand, two one thousand, three one thousand. "I just don't believe it. I don't believe any of it. There must be some misunderstanding. This couldn't be my Harriet. She wouldn't." My words pressed my face into my cupped hands, but now I was regaining control. Of course, I had not anticipated this turn of events, or that things would move so quickly, but I had realized from the moment that Brendan started to lie to me at King's Cross Station that suspicion might fall on him. My careful hints about the direction they should look in had borne fruit faster than I could have imagined. "But if what you say is true," I said, "and I don't believe it is – then where is Harriet? Are you saying that she is staying with him? What is he saying about it?"

"He says he doesn't know. It seems that he spent the night with her on Monday and walked to the train with her on Tuesday morning. He had to go to a lecture himself, so he says that he didn't actually see her get onto the train. But he is adamant that she must have done so, which is why she didn't come down on the train you went to meet on Thursday."

"But had they had a row then? Why do you think he might know where she is?"

Wallace sat back in his chair and looked at the ceiling. It was clear that this was the point where what he knew for sure ran out, and that going forward he was into territory he could only guess at.

"It's only that he was the last person we know of who saw her before she vanished. And we are also told by Martin and Jed and the girlfriends that Brendan was putting a lot of pressure on her to leave you." Now he sat forward, his elbows on the table in front of him, the palms of his hands cupped together like a child at prayer. "The most probable explanation is that she was in a dilemma, and couldn't work out what to do. Most likely she has got off the train at a station between Newcastle and London and has checked into a guest house somewhere while she clears her head and works out whether to stay with you or to leave you and go with Brendan. But also" – and now he paused again, separating his palms but keeping the ends of his fingertips together – "it must be possible that she told him that she wasn't going to leave you, he got mad and something very bad has happened."

Abruptly I got up from my chair and walked to the back of the room and stood facing the wall behind me. Wallace was sitting at the table and Sergeant Norris was standing in the corner of the room. Again I put my head in my hands, an involuntary gesture while my brain teemed with a thousand thoughts. At times I could hear Harriet's voice breaking through, speaking or laughing but expressing nothing intelligible. I turned to face the sergeant, as though he was an independent arbiter, my arms crossed in front of me, protecting my body from further battery.

"I just don't understand any of it," I said. "I don't believe that Harriet was having an affair with Brendan. I quite believe that he was putting pressure on her to leave me and go with him. Hell, he's been doing that for about five years." Now I turned back to face Wallace. "The bastard is well known to have had the hots for her ever since we all met. But any of her friends will tell you that she never ever responded to him. She has always tolerated him because they are in the quartet together, but I just don't believe that she gave in to him. If you knew how many times she has told me that she is not interested in him…"

Wallace was looking back at me, and I saw nothing in his face which expressed anything other than sympathy.

"I know, son," he said, and it was the first time he had addressed me in that way. "And I'm sorry. But some people can be very convincing, especially when they are ashamed of what they are trying to hide. I've seen it a thousand times. You're down here, looking after your sick brother, and she is up there having an affair with one of your mutual friends. Maybe it's little wonder that she didn't tell you the truth about it."

I wanted to say that my brother wasn't sick and that Brendan wasn't a mutual friend, but resisted the urge. Having this policeman's sympathy in this way was bound to be helpful to me and, to stand back from it, what he was saying wasn't all that far from the truth. I had been taking care of my brother, and I had been betrayed.

"So what happens now then?" I said. "Can you get officers in the towns where the train stopped to check hotels and guest houses? Is that the next thing to do?"

"It isn't, I'm afraid," said Wallace. "As I have mentioned to you before, with no direct evidence that a crime has been committed, it's not justifiable to commit the resources that that would involve. Like I say, chances are that Harriet is walking on a beach somewhere, throwing stones into the sea and thinking about how to come and tell you that she has been a silly girl. Up to you what you do then, of course. Personally I think that'll happen in a few days, but until then, we have no direct evidence against Brendan Harcourt. We held him overnight because he had originally lied to us about when he had last seen her, but this morning we will be letting him go."

I sat down hard again on my chair. The police had arrested a man they suspected of knowing what had happened to my wife and immediately were releasing him. "But Harriet's parents are flying in from Singapore because they believe the arrest means that you know something."

"That's unfortunate," said Wallace, and I could tell he knew that he would have to expect even more pressure from above to find a solution. "As I say, with no evidence that anything has happened to her, even with her family connections, we just wouldn't be able to justify a nationwide manhunt for a girl who has been missing for only a few days."

Sergeant Norris said goodbye to me, and Wallace showed me the way out to the foyer. I noticed that he had put his hand on my shoulder as we walked. It was not the hand of a policeman arresting a suspect, but that of a man of experience and wisdom supporting a younger man who was just finding out some sad and unfortunate aspect of the real world. I walked with my head down, playing my role in the mini-drama, which was that of cuckolded husband, idiot lover, deceived spouse. What it was not, thank heavens, was the posture of a husband who has killed his wife and is on the brink of being discovered. Once out on the street, my stride lengthened into a jog and then into a run, and then I was sprinting down the pavement, filling my lungs with the deep breaths of relief and release.

Chapter Twenty-Four

The Connaught Hotel is not a place where people like me stay when they come to London. It's a place where people like Harriet's parents stay. The kind of place where they assume that you are unable to open a door for yourself and that you are willing to pay some inflated gratuity to someone for hailing you a taxi and seeming to be very subservient.

I have been to many more places and seen more things since the events I am now relating took place, but in 1974 I felt that hotels like the Connaught were designed, in part, to make people like me feel uncomfortable. My own parents had not had cause to frequent hotels, and if and when they had, it was more likely to be at the guest-house end of the market. No liveried flunkey to salute and open the swing doors at the Pentewan Hotel in Salcombe where we used to stay for our annual holidays when Roger and I were kids. Seven years in a row we stayed there, largely because the owner, Mrs Burrows, was very welcoming and in particular always seemed to be very pleased to see Roger, who was equally pleased to see her.

But that was ten years earlier, and now, as I walked along Carlos Place approaching the Connaught, the doorman caught my eye but gave no impression that he thought I was about to enter the hotel.

"Morning, sir," he said finally, and saluted smartly as he pulled open the door. The flag above his head snapped in the wind. I can't say if he was actually looking me up and down, but he may as well have been.

There were half a dozen people waiting, and I was not sure which desk to queue at, or whether it would be appropriate to ask any of the men in various levels of what looked like paramilitary uniform where I could find Mr and Mrs Chalfont. I waited for a while, long enough to take in the old masters of galleons on the staircase and the deep leather of the armchairs. Eventually I noticed a young man of about my age wearing a grey uniform and a pillbox hat.

"I want to speak to some people who are staying here. Do I have to queue, or can someone else give me their room number?"

"Follow me, sir," he spoke with a strong East End accent which was trying to be posh, and led me to a corridor to one side and pointed to a row of telephones. "Easiest fing is to call the operator and ask to be put through to the room."

I was not fully prepared for the meeting I was about to have with Harriet's parents. Partly this was because I felt that I did not really know them at all or how they would be reacting, but much more of course it was because I was the man who had murdered their only daughter. How does one even begin to come to terms with something like that? No doubt they were distressed already, and would become even more so whichever way events were about to unfold. I, and only I, knew the information they were in search of and I, and only I, was responsible for the heartache they were going through now and would go through in the future.

I forced myself as best I could to put those thoughts to one side, and to organize in my mind the practicalities of the situation. I had no way of knowing how much they may have heard about Harriet and Brendan before all this happened. Certainly Harriet's mother had seemed to be more familiar with Brendan's name than I would have expected had he been only a run-of-the-mill friend of Harriet's. Yet somehow I doubted that she could name many of her other friends. The switchboard operator called the room, and then I heard Harriet's father say, "Please send him up to room 324." Perhaps the lack of enthusiasm I detected in his tone was more in the way I heard it than the way he said it.

I took the stairs, up and round and up and round again the huge atrium, and made no sound along the thick carpeted corridors. Eventually I knocked and wondered if they would make use of the spyhole before admitting me. The door was opened by Harriet's mother, who might have embraced her daughter's husband, but who instead retreated into the suite. I went in to be met by both of my in-laws, standing as though they had rehearsed our meeting.

"Hello, Jonathan," said Harriet's father, as I shook hands with both of them. "Bloody awful business this." It was not a question.

I was shocked at the sight of both of them. No doubt the long journey with little sleep, and also the worry about their daughter, had made their contributions, but both seemed to have aged a decade since I had last seen them less than three years ago. It occurred to me only now that I could see nothing of Harriet's features in either of them, and for a second I found myself considering if in fact Harriet had been their biological daughter. The thought had never occurred to me before, but I wondered if it explained what I had always felt was their unusual level of detachment from her.

"Never mind about that, Geoffrey," said Harriet's mother. "Let Jonathan tell us whether there has been any developments since we last spoke. Jonathan? Has anything further happened?"

"Nothing helpful," I said. "I went down to the police station after you called me and spoke to Detective Sergeant Wallace, who is handling the case." All three of us were still standing, as though the urgency to hear the latest news outweighed normal courtesies. "Harriet still hasn't turned up anywhere so far as they know, but he did tell me something which, to be honest with you, knocked me sideways." It seemed that I had already imparted the only thing they regarded as urgent, and that they knew that the next part was uncomfortable territory. Mrs Chalfont gestured towards two chairs and a hideous Regency sofa which were crammed uncomfortably in the bay window. We all sat.

"Mrs Chalfont, may I ask you," I said, "did you know about Harriet and Brendan?"

She was pouring tea from a bone-china pot which seemed far too small for the purpose into cups which were also inexplicably miniature. Plainly they had ordered room service in anticipation of my arrival. She added tiny splashes of milk before responding to my question.

"Harriet told me some time ago that there was a young man who had shown an interest in her for a very long time, and that her marriage to you had had no effect of reducing the enthusiasm of his advances."

"He's has fancied her for a very long time, that's for sure," I said, and I watched them both wince slightly at the expression, "but she always gave me the impression that his feelings were not returned."

"I think that would be right," she said. By now Mr Chalfont was half turned and looking out of the window, as though disengaged from the conversation. "But if I am not mistaken, in the last few weeks the pressure from him has been growing, and I wouldn't rule out the possibility that, partly in respect of the long periods apart from you, she might have let her guard down just a little."

The quaintness of her expression seemed to be straight out of a romantic novel, and I realized immediately that Harriet must have told her everything. That she had finally conceded to Brendan's long-term advances. I doubted, however, if she had told her mother that sleeping with Brendan

312

was her "jazz" in comparison to my "blues". I felt sick at the thought.

"So now the police are saying that they think it's possible that Brendan might have been pushing her to leave me, and that they quarrelled. He obviously lied to them about what he knew, and so they arrested him and kept him overnight. However, in the absence of any evidence that any harm has come to Harriet, this morning they have had to let him go."

"What?" It was the first time that Geoffrey Chalfont had spoken since greeting me, and he seemed genuinely surprised by this news. "But he is the last person to have seen her. What the devil do they think they are playing at?" He seemed to be asking his wife as much as he was asking me, and neither of us had any clear idea of the answer.

"Presumably if there is no direct evidence that a crime has been committed," I said finally, "they have no choice but to let him go. They seem to think the most likely thing is that Harriet got off the train on the route, checked into a local hotel, and is walking along the beach somewhere contemplating her options."

"After a week?" said Mr Chalfont. "They must have taken leave of their senses. Obviously I know less about what is going on in my daughter's mind than my wife does." He turned to me, his eyes meeting mine for the first time since I entered the suite. "I knew nothing of all this with Brendan, by the way. Clearly I have been treated to information only on a 'need-to-know' basis. Bloody awful for you, and I am sorry for it.

Don't know what the girl is thinking of." Now he resumed his original point. "But I do know her well enough to know that she would realize that by this time we would all be worried sick, and she would have let us know she was all right. Something has happened to her. There can be no doubt of it."

"I agree," I said quickly. "It's enough of a shock for me to find out about Harriet and Brendan. Obviously I thought I knew her better than I do, but I am sure that I know her well enough to know that she wouldn't just take off without telling anyone. Apart from anything else, she would know that you two would be worried half to death."

My little speech seemed to thaw some of the frost between the three of us, and it was almost as though we were accepting for the first time that we were all on the same side, all worrying about the same thing. Harriet's mother turned to me.

"I am so sorry for this, Jonathan. It must be terrible for you. Whatever else has happened, I know that you love Harriet, and I also know that she loves you. This is just an awful business, but I am sure it will turn out all right and that she will be back with you soon."

I put down my cup and pressed my face into the upturned palms of my hands. It was not a contrived gesture or an act. As before, I was finding the reality of what had happened, combined with the sympathy of those I was seeking to deceive, very difficult to cope with. And again, not for the first time, I found myself responding more like an aggrieved and worried husband than as a killer.

Plainly uncomfortable at any show of emotion, Mr Chalfont stood up and began to pace the room. For a moment I thought that Harriet's mother was going to touch me, a gesture of sympathy or support, but she did not.

Mr Chalfont said that he was going to make some phone calls and see if he could "get someone cracking a whip". I thought about Wallace and Pascoe back at King's Cross police station and about how welcome that would be. Harriet's mother said that they planned to take a nap to get over the journey, and wondered if I would like to come back later to have some dinner with them.

"It's very kind of you Mrs Chalfont," I said, "but I want to stay around the flat as much as possible just in case Harriet rings me there, or in fact turns up. Besides, I have to be there for most of the time to take care of Roger."

Her face was a picture, the perfect transition from recollection to distaste.

"Ah yes, Roger. How is the dear chap? So brave of you to take care of him."

In normal circumstances, hearing someone like Mrs Chalfont referring to Roger as a "dear chap" in her patronizing manner might have provoked me to tell her to fuck off. However, having achieved more today than I had expected, I was keen to keep Harriet's parents on my side. The more they witnessed my anxiety and distress the less likely they would ever be to suspect that I knew more than I was saying about what had happened to their daughter.

"Oh, Roger is fine. He is taking the bar exam next month."
No, that's not what I said. I said he was fine, but was miss-
ing Harriet, as we all were. That seemed to be all that Mrs
Chalfont needed to know about Roger, and we moved on.

"No doubt Mr Chalfont's intervention will bring the police
back to my door," I said, "which will be very welcome. If we
don't do something about it, before we know it Harriet will
just become another statistic in the 'missing person' file, and
that's the last we will ever hear of it."

Chapter Twenty-Five

The general feeling of dislocation which framed all of my thoughts was exacerbated by the all-pervasive preparations for Christmas which were going on in the shops and offices on all sides as I returned home. Every few steps along the high street were accompanied by the unrelenting noise of some terrible Christmas song merging into the next jangle of carols sung through a synthesizer by characters from a cartoon.

On the corner next to the pub car park was a man selling Christmas trees from the back of a white van. All around him there were couples and families with small children, holding up this one or that one as they tried to envisage a particular tree in the corner of their hallway or living room. The sight of them made me fall into a profound sadness about what might have been and what was now never going to be. I visualized Harriet's face superimposed on the smiling faces of the young mothers, and the imagined faces of our putative offspring on the excited grins of the young children. But there was no Harriet and there never would be any children, and all of it was my fault and my doing. Her life had ended, theirs had never begun, and mine was all but over.

Maybe I would get away with her death in the sense of escaping society's idea of justice, or maybe I was hours, days or weeks away from being arrested and thrown into jail for many years. In either case, the worst that could happen to me had already happened. I had lost the love of my life and would never get her back.

I turned off the main road into our street and was about fifty yards from the house when suddenly I became aware that someone had fallen in to pace alongside me. Before I looked, I knew who it was.

"Brendan."

"Jonathan."

I stopped in my stride and turned to face him. "What the hell?"

Obviously he had been waiting in the cold wind, and the skin on his face was pallid and taut. Traces of his brilliant red hair crept out from beneath a brown beanie hat. Immediately I could see that his expression was tense with anger.

"We need to talk."

Instinctively I turned again to continue my journey, and he began to walk alongside me.

"You've got a fucking nerve to turn up here." I barked at him. "Why aren't you under arrest?"

"I was under arrest. You know I have been under arrest, but you also know that I don't have any idea what has happened to Harriet."

I stopped again and turned to face him.

"And how would I know that? I have just been told by the police that you were having an affair with my wife, and that you have been putting her under pressure to leave me. She wouldn't, and so you've probably done something to her, you fucking nutcase."

The look on Brendan's face said that he wanted to admit the relationship, but even now some instinct was preventing him from doing so. Evidently he was caught between a reluctance to face the husband of the woman he had been sleeping with, and the need to find out anything which might cast light on her disappearance.

"Look, I don't know what to say about any of that. You know I have loved Harriet for as long as you have, and obviously I know that has pissed you off. I don't blame you but, for what it's worth to you, I haven't had any choice in the matter. I never have had a choice. I've always been head over bloody heels in love with her. Just as you have."

"Except that she married me!" Instantly I was shouting, distraught and losing control. "We both loved her, but she chose me, you bloody madman. It's just that you could never accept it." Out of the corner of my eye I could see that some passers-by had heard me, a man and his two young children, and were scuttling away as quickly as they could. "You couldn't accept that, could you? You just kept on grinding her down and grinding her down until eventually, when I was three hundred miles away, looking after my brother who has only me in the world, she finally gave in."

"Yes, I did," he said. His voice was also raised, but to a level many decibels below mine. "You're right, and I think you would have done the same if the thing had been the other way around. I didn't have any choice. Surely you of all people can understand that?"

By now I could see that some other people, two women walking together, had noticed us and were slowing down to see what was happening. I realized that Brendan and I must have looked as though we were about to come to blows, and I began to collect myself enough to start thinking about what I needed to achieve from this situation.

"So what have you done with her?"

"What?"

"What have you done with her? The police know that you were trying to persuade her to leave me and that she wouldn't. Obviously you have done something to her. Where the hell is she?"

"I don't know. If I did, what would I be standing in the street talking to you for?"

"So why are you standing in the street talking to me? I don't bloody well know anything. You know I don't. I was expecting her off the train on Thursday. That's all I know."

"But that's what I can't work out," he said. "You know now that I saw her off at the station in Newcastle. I left her outside of the Central Station. The truth is that she was looking forward to spending some time with you. She was happy."

I looked back at Brendan's face as he spoke to me and, hard though it is for me to say it, for a moment I felt a hint of sadness for him. I guess he really was as much in love with

Harriet as I was, and here he stood, distraught and confused by her sudden and unexplained disappearance. A few seconds later however, my sympathy evaporated and I felt the need to reassert myself. I spoke more quietly.

"And she had no plans to leave me?"

"None whatsoever. You can believe that or not, but it's true. You know Harriet, she took everything as it came along. She had finally said yes to me, and she seemed perfectly happy. I believe that she saw no reason why the present situation could not continue. I think that in the end she might even have planned to tell you about it – but despite my best efforts, she had no intention of leaving you, not now and not in the future either."

I stood silently while the import of Brendan's words circulated around my brain, and I thought about Harriet and about what she had said to me on that evening. Jazz and blues. Blues and opera. No reason why they could not coexist. No reason to have to make a choice. No reason why one needed to impede on the other or why enjoyment of one should invalidate enjoyment of the other. They were just different things. Instantly I felt the tears well up in my eyes as I wondered whether all this had been necessary. Whether I could ever have seen things as Harriet had seen them. Whether I could have found some acceptance and have lived the rest of my life with her, enjoying having the warm glow of her sunny and smiling face around me every day. I felt a renewed sense of loss and sadness at what now could never be.

Brendan was still looking at me as the tears rolled down my face. I could not speak, and after several moments he began to take small shuffling steps backwards.

"I'm sorry, Jonathan. I truly am. It was never about you. It was always about Harriet and how wonderful she is. But you know that."

"Yes," I said, and even in the profundity of my sadness I still heard a little voice at the back of my mind reminding me of the need to get the tense right. "She is. Harriet truly is a wonderful woman."

Chapter Twenty-Six

For the next two weeks leading up to Christmas, Detectives Wallace and Pascoe appeared to work full-time on trying to solve the mystery of what had happened to Harriet. They called Brendan back in for further questioning, and they interviewed Martin and Jed at their parents' homes. They also travelled up to Newcastle to look around the room in the house where she stayed, and they visited the homes of the girls with whom Harriet had been living.

At no time in those weeks did it seem to occur to anyone that Harriet had indeed travelled south on that Tuesday and had come to the flat. I was never told whether the police assumed that Brendan was lying about having seen her off at the station, or that she had taken the train but got off at some station en route. I was never asked any specific question, thank Heavens, which involved that particular evasion. I had gone to the station on Thursday to meet the train I expected her to arrive on and that, it was assumed, was the beginning and end of what I knew. If anything, I was treated as the poor idiot whose wife was cheating on him and who never suspected.

In the middle of all this, on a Friday just about a week before Christmas, I received a call from Mrs Chalfont asking me to join her and her husband for dinner. I had no wish to go, and it was perhaps one of the few advantages of my situation with Roger that I had a ready excuse.

"I could bring him along, if you like, but that might make it less easy to talk."

Mrs Chalfont did not consider the offer for long, and we agreed instead that I would drop Roger off at his bus in the morning and go over to their hotel. I arrived on time at 10.30 and discovered that a buffet breakfast for three had been delivered to their suite.

For most of the next hour my parents-in-law went through a comprehensive account of the measures they had been taking since their arrival in London to ascertain what had become of their daughter. These seemed to consist almost exclusively of lobbying senior civil-service mandarins of their acquaintance who, for the most part, had only tangential if any relationship to any relevant government department. Indeed, I think that at one moment Mr Chalfont even referred explicitly to "the old-boy network".

We compared notes on what we each knew of the investigation being carried out by the police, and I told them of my frustration that there seemed so few other options. As far as anyone knew, Harriet appeared to have simply vanished into thin air.

"I have asked the police if there is anything further I can usefully do," I continued, "and they say not. However, I did think it might be a good idea to have some leaflets printed with Harriet's picture on them, and to hand them out around the stations in Newcastle and London."

Mr Chalfont said he thought that was a good idea, and suggested that it might be useful to offer a reward for information which helped us to find her. "We can put up £500 if you think that would be helpful?" I said that I did, and that I would add the offer to the information on the poster.

When our time together seemed to be nearing an end, Mr Chalfont suddenly stood and began to pace, as if hesitating to broach an awkward subject. He went on to explain that what he persistently described as "our family crisis" could not have come at a worse time. The Foreign Secretary was due to visit Singapore over the New Year holiday, apparently, and so they had little choice but to return there at the end of the week to make the necessary preparations. He said that they would of course return to London at a moment's notice should there be news, but that in the meantime perhaps I would be kind enough to keep them closely in touch with any developments by telephone?

Possibly I was lacking in sensitivity, or more probably it was the way their sort of people chose to cope, but for the life of me I could not detect anything resembling the kind of distress which one might ordinarily expect in such a situation. Harriet was their only daughter and was missing, perhaps dead. While tears and hysterics might not seem appropriate at a Saturday-morning brunch, I might have expected some sign of emotion.

"What, in your heart of hearts, do you think has happened to Harriet? Do you think she may have left you and gone off with someone else, or do you think she is dead?" It was the most direct question of the morning and, in the whole time I had known him, it was the closest that Mr Chalfont got to anything personal in asking it. I paused and searched the ceiling with my eyes.

"Do you know what?" I said finally. "I just do not have a clue."

Eventually I said goodbye to them for what I imagined might be the last time and found myself outside on the busy streets of central London. I reflected that there were two possible explanations for their apparent detachment. One was that it was a façade for what was really going on in their emotions – an exhibition of the stiff upper lip which had helped Britain to build the Empire. The other was that they thought they knew exactly what had happened to their daughter, and that she had left me to go off with another man. I was not able then to decide which of these thoughts was uppermost in their suspicions, and do not know to this day.

After a stay in London of a little more than two weeks, on Christmas Eve, Mr and Mrs Chalfont flew back to Singapore. I did not go to see them off at the airport, and they did not feel it necessary to say anything in a brief telephone call very much more than goodbye. I think they realized that even if they did ever see their daughter again, the chances were that they would never again be seeing me.

Days followed upon days, and weeks spread into weeks, and we heard nothing from the police beyond a phone call from Sergeant Norris which came on more or less every Tuesday or Wednesday, asking if we had heard anything from Harriet. I would usually find something new to say about how I was busy trying to track down one of her old friends from school, or how someone in the newsagent had told me he thought he had seen her when he was spending a weekend away in Devon but had been mistaken.

"Anything new at your end?" I would ask.

"We've circulated the photo to every police station in the UK, and we're following up a few possible sightings, but to be honest we've not heard anything which I would regard as promising."

We would each agree to alert the other if anything of interest transpired, but gradually I felt any residual hope and energy dissipating from his voice. I guessed that we were moving into a phase which the police would probably call "managing expectations". I had my expectations well under control, and had to remind myself from time to time of the need to show impatience.

"Have you people given up? Are you assuming that she's dead?" It was coming up to three months since I had reported Harriet missing, and something told me that I ought not to be acquiescing so quietly to the idea that the mystery would remain unsolved.

"I understand your frustration, Jonathan," said Norris. "Perhaps I should pop round to see you and I can put you in the picture about the way these things usually develop."

I was never keen to have the police visit the flat, so I made up a reason to be passing Norris's office at King's Cross later that day and offered to drop in. When I arrived there at 2 p.m. that afternoon, yet again Norris was wearing the same clothes and the same downtrodden expression as he had worn when I first met him. We sat in the same corner of the waiting area where we had spoken all those weeks before.

"You're an intelligent man, Jonathan, so I won't try to deceive you." I found myself wondering how I would feel about being patronized in this way if I really was the distraught husband of a missing wife that I was acting.

"I have always appreciated your frankness," I said.

"I think I've said before that in a case like this, in the absence of a body, and without any compelling reason to think that any crime has actually taken place, there is a limit to the resources we can expend on looking for your wife." He went on to say that the intervention of her influential father had already forced them to dedicate more time and manpower to the inquiry than would be usual, but that influence could only have so much effect, and in this case it had more or less run its course. "You have to understand that at any given time there are literally hundreds of people who have just walked out of their houses and are never seen again. People just decide one day to start a new life for all sorts of reasons.

I know you will probably never believe it, but the chances are that something like that has happened here."

I dropped my head into my hands and ran my fingers through my hair, clawing at the scalp.

"Sergeant Norris, I understand what you are saying to me, but you've got to understand that I will never be able to rest until I know what has happened to her."

Norris reached across and put his hand on my shoulder. "I understand that, Jonathan," he said, and I believe he meant it. "I really do. I will continue to do what I can, but I'd be lying to you if I said I had much hope of finding an answer to the mystery."

That evening I sat in the tiny flat I shared with Roger, contemplating our lives in the months and years ahead. The imperative, I knew, would be to find a way to come to terms with what had happened, and move on to whatever would befall us next. My priority was to ensure that Roger felt safe and content, and also of course to stay out of prison myself in order to be able to take care of him. I was unable to focus on making any plans, hoping only that the passage of time would offer a route forward and an answer to the nagging question of how and whether I would ever again be able to achieve some kind of peace of mind.

* * *

It was a Sunday afternoon, just about six weeks after my meeting with Norris, and my brother and I were down at the insect farm. Roger had been urging me for some months to help him to implement a number of improvements, and I had found it a useful distraction from my mental anguish to get stuck in to some manual labour. In particular he seemed to have been sending for lots of new species recently, and so we had constructed a number of new and differently shaped containers in which to keep and display them. This day was cold and blustery, and Roger was anxious to check that the rudimentary heating system we had organized was working. It was, and the shed provided a warm and even quite cosy refuge from the biting wind. Roger was sorting out a tank for a batch of some new kind of beetle that he was expecting to arrive any day. I honestly cannot remember what I was doing, but when I looked up and glanced through the cobwebs which obscured the already grubby window, I saw the two detectives, Wallace and Pascoe, coming through the wire gate. They were asking one of our neighbours, old Mr Bolton, for directions. As I looked I saw him wave and point his finger in the direction of our hut. My chest went into paralysis, and for an instant I could scarcely breathe. Roger did not appear to notice anything, and so I had a few moments to try to calm myself as they approached. Just before they knocked at the door, I spoke to Roger.

"Those two policemen who have been looking for Harriet seem to have found us here. I wonder how they did that." My anxiety was entirely in contrast with Roger's apparent total lack of concern, and he hardly paused in his work as the two men knocked at the wooden door. "Oh hi." I tried to sound unsurprised. "How are things? Do you have any news about Harriet?" They said that they didn't. "Sorry you had to come down here. Roger and I were just pottering about. If you had called me I would have come down to the station. How did you find us?"

I regretted the remark. Did the two officers exchange a glance? I could not be sure.

"We called at the flat and met your downstairs neighbour coming out. She said she thought you might be down here." By now both officers were scanning the tanks and boxes. Obviously neither had a clue what they were looking at.

"It's an insect farm. It's Roger's hobby." I thought that it would be good to emphasize that there was nothing secret about it. However, I lowered my voice so that Roger would not hear. "I think you know about it because you once thought that our parents had threatened to close it down. Do you remember?" Roger was still behaving as though he had not noticed the arrival of the two detectives, and now I felt the need to compensate for what might have been my earlier caution. "Roger has been building it up since he was a small boy. Have a close look if you like. Roger doesn't mind. Some of it is fascinating. Roger," I turned to my older brother, "you don't mind if the officers have a look at the insect farm, do you?"

Still Roger completely ignored us, and although he could often become totally immersed in his own world and apparently oblivious to surrounding events, I thought it unusual that he did not respond. He was cleaning the glass on the inside of a tank and, to all intents and purposes, he may as well have been quite alone.

"Go ahead," I said, and by now I could feel a cold and clammy wetness under my arms, and wondered if my anxiety would shortly be obvious. I wiped my face on my sleeve.

"Are you OK, Jonathan?" asked Pascoe.

"Sure," I said. "We've just been working hard before you came. I'll be fine in a minute."

I watched as the two detectives shuffled slowly along the rows of tanks, Wallace walking on one side nearer to where Roger was working, Pascoe on the other side, closer to me. Both men progressed carefully, each of them stopping from time to time to take a closer look and to draw the attention of the other to what was going on in these strange worlds. Pascoe seemed especially fascinated by the ants, and several times he called Wallace across to point out some aspect of their activity. You could tell that Pascoe was more interested than was Wallace, whose comments were polite and peremptory.

All the time both of them were edging closer to the far end of the shed, so that in a few moments they would be standing within just a very few inches of the coffin-shaped box which was full of earth and covered with a fine-wire mesh and which contained the last mortal remains of Mrs Harriet Maguire.

I tried to look out of the window, willing my eyes not to fall onto the casket, and perhaps hoping to see something

which would justify me calling the two men over. I saw a robin
land on the corner of an upturned bucket and was about to
speak, but instantly thought that the diversion would be seen
for what it was.

"What's in here?"

I could feel the strong pulse of my heart beat vibrating
through my body and into my brain. My ears were full of
the huge swish-swish of rushing blood, and I thought that I
would pass out. My breath caught in my throat and I turned
my head in what seemed like slow motion. As I looked I saw
that Wallace was standing above the wooden crate into which,
just three months earlier, I had ladled handfuls of dark soil
onto the smooth pink-and-white flesh of the woman I had
loved so very much. He was even tapping the box with his
right foot so that I could see tiny movements of vibration
across the wire mesh which covered the layer of soil. I tried
to speak, but the words would not come out. I have no idea
what they would have been anyway.

"It's a new wormery," Roger spoke for the first time since
the detectives had arrived, and now was walking a few paces
across to where Wallace was standing. "It's Jonathan's, actually. Do you want to take a closer look?"

The sudden animation from Roger drew renewed attention
from Wallace and Pascoe, and now both men stood alongside
him and were bending down to crouch over the wooden crate.
I swear to God that an image suddenly flashed into my mind
from all those horror films in which a white and ghastly hand

appears out of the grave, reaching to grab someone by the throat. But it didn't. What actually happened was that Roger was reaching for a pitchfork, and was getting ready to plunge it into the earth which scarcely concealed Harriet's body.

"I don't think they want to see that, Roger," I said, and was about to move forward and take the fork from him.

"I am sure we do," said Wallace. "Go on, Roger, we'd love to see what Jonathan has been up to."

Was it a nightmare? Was this really happening? After so many weeks, my original pessimism about getting away with murder had gradually faded, and by now I had allowed myself to believe that the mystery of Harriet's disappearance might never be solved. Just ten minutes ago my life and my future and that of Roger seemed to be straightforward and predictable. Now I was just moments away from a disaster which would turn our lives upside down. And then Roger was lifting the fork inches above the level of the soil, about to plunge the sharp tines deep into it, at just about the point where I calculated that Harriet's neck would be.

"Stop," I said. Such was the urgency and vehemence of my interruption that the three of them all looked at me at the same time, their faces full of enquiry. "I've only sorted that a few weeks ago," I said. "The worms will just be getting settled. They won't want a bloody great fork turning them over." For just a split second I saw Wallace about to mouth something which might have been acquiescence. He could be content, it seemed, not to have the soil turned over after all, but a moment later I saw Roger once again lifting the fork and prepare to plunge it downwards.

"Nonsense," he said, "worms and beetles enjoy a little earthquake," and with that I saw the fork go down, sharp blades entering the soil, and I closed my eyes tight shut and brought up my hands to cover my ears, entirely expecting to hear the crunch of bone as the fork juddered to a halt.

But it did not. The message of my senses stood in complete contrast to the confident expectations of my mind, and I watched in total amazement as Roger pushed the fork downwards so that it scraped off the bottom of the casket, and then bent it towards himself so as to be able to gather up a complete clod of the earth. As he did so he turned the fork over to reveal twenty or so fat worms, each of them wriggling and writhing as if in protest at the disruption, and all mixed together in the soil with a concentration of beetles of a type I had never seen before.

"See?" said Roger. "Happy worms and happy beetles, driven into action by visiting catastrophe" – and as I stood gazing transfixed at Roger's face while he was speaking, I saw for the first time since then that same look that I had seen in the garden at David Frost's party. He was partially in a trance, speaking as though someone or something else was speaking through him. The two detectives noticed it too, I think, because both seemed to be momentarily transfixed, and now Roger was turning, and looked straight at me as though we two were alone.

"We move," he said softly, "in mysterious ways."

Chapter Twenty-Seven

It strikes me that I have not recorded much about my life at the library and, truthfully, that's because there is very little about it which is memorable or worth telling. Like most petty bureaucracies, it was overrun with tiny politics about who was in line for promotion and who had incurred the displeasure of the branch librarian. One thing that the big experiences of my life has taught me has been not to sweat the small stuff, so I more or less irritated all of my colleagues by basically not giving a damn about all the things which preoccupied most of them.

I did not care much, for example, about who was in and who was out of favour. I did not get over-anxious to extract a huge fine if a kid or a pensioner brought a book back late. And I didn't risk evacuating my bowels if a reader or "client", as we were required to call them, threatened to complain that the service I provided was less than totally grovelling.

I only mention the library now because it was the day after the police had visited us at the allotments, and I was sitting in the staff room taking my morning tea break, when the deputy librarian, a spotty youth just a bit older than me called Nigel Hollingsworth, came in and told me that I was wanted on the telephone. It was someone calling from Roger's day centre.

While it's true that not much got me terribly anxious, this kind of news was guaranteed to do so, and so I leapt to my feet and more or less ran down the corridor to the Chief Librarian's office. I knew that the day centre would only ever call in an emergency, and they had never done so in all the time I had been Roger's main carer. The office was empty and the receiver was lying next to the phone. I grabbed it and spoke.

"Hello? It's Jonathan Maguire. Who is this please?"

"Oh, Jonathan." Immediately I recognized the voice of Mrs Flaherty, who was the head teacher at the day centre. She sounded terribly anxious. "I am so pleased they have found you. Something has happened."

"Yes, I assumed so. What is it? Is he OK? Has he been hurt?" There was a pause, as though she didn't know quite how to put what was coming next. My breaths came in short, sharp bursts. "Mrs Flaherty? What is it? What has happened?"

"Well, I'm afraid that I think that Roger has been arrested."

"What?" Of all the things I might have expected her to say to me – maybe an accident or a fight or a sudden illness, this was not up there among them. "He's been what? Arrested? By whom? What for? When?"

I realized that my barrage wasn't helping, but I could not stop myself. My mind was a cloud of confusion, tempered with an instant burst of indignation that the police would do something like this without first informing me.

"Yes, two detectives came this morning and asked to see him. I told them that I wanted to inform you, but they insisted and said that they had a warrant and that I had to get him immediately. They spoke to him for a few minutes in my office and then they took him out. I'm afraid that he was in handcuffs."

"What?" I could feel my temper rising up inside me uncontrollably. "Mrs Flaherty? They did what? You allowed the police to speak to Roger? What were they asking him about?"

"I don't know, Jonathan," she said. "They wouldn't let me stay in the room while they spoke to him."

Instinctively I knew it was a mistake to alienate Mrs Flaherty, but at that moment my frustration and sense of impotence overflowed. I felt so protective about Roger, so responsible for him, that the idea of him being confused or upset by things he would never understand, without me or someone else he knew and trusted being present, sent me into orbit. I asked if the officers had left their names.

"Yes," she said, "I've written them down somewhere. If you just hang on a minute I can find them."

"Never mind," I said. "Was it Wallace and Pascoe?"

"Yes," she confirmed, "that's it. I've found my note. DS Wallace and DC Pascoe. They're at King's Cross. They left a number if you want it?"

"I know exactly where they are." By now my surprise had transformed completely into anger. "Thank you, Mrs Flaherty. I know what I need to do."

I considered calling the police station, but knew that I would not be able to remain patient enough to wait until

Wallace and Pascoe were found, and that in any event whatever they said would involve me getting down there as quickly as possible. Without hesitating further or telling anyone, I walked straight out of the library and directly into the street to try to find a taxi. Five minutes later I was in the back of a black cab on my way to King's Cross.

As we edged through the busy streets of south London, I had time to try to calm myself just a little and to process the unexpected turn of events. It had all been too easy at the insect farm. One moment I had felt myself to be seconds away from the discovery of Harriet, and a minute later I was astounded at the realization that somehow, at some time, Roger must have discovered and dealt with the disposal of her body. How had he done it? When had he done it? I had no idea.

I had not even begun to be able to consider the implications arising from the revelation that Roger must have known about Harriet's death. Needless to say, I had taken the first opportunity after the policemen had gone on the previous evening to broach the subject with him. I knew from experience that it could be counterproductive to ask him directly, but my anxiety and impatience had got the better of me, and all my questions were met with a blank stare. Several times I tried allowing a little time to pass and then creeping up on the subject by asking about projects and reorganization at the insect farm. I fared no better. This was one of those occasions when none of my usual strategies got me anywhere at all. Just as when I had questioned him about what happened at David Frost's garden party, Roger's response to any enquiry about Harriet was met either with a facial expression which was impervious to interpretation, or by a complete change of subject. Eventually I had no choice but to give up and wait for another opportunity.

Now, however, I could scarcely believe my own stupidity in allowing myself to believe that he could have discovered and moved Harriet without anyone seeing or suspecting. That must be what had happened. Maybe the detectives had started asking questions in the vicinity of the insect farm after their unexpected visit, and someone had told them they had seen Roger acting suspiciously.

I was less than halfway to King's Cross when I knew exactly what I had to do, and that I had to do it instantly. The idea of Roger being interrogated about Harriet's murder was too horrible for me to contemplate, and I had no choice but to end it as soon as I possibly could. I would find the two police officers and tell them what had happened – then straight away I would call a solicitor and make a formal complaint about the police arresting a mentally handicapped person and interviewing him without a responsible adult being present. I had only a sketchy idea of the law, but I felt entirely certain that this must be illegal. Anything he might have confessed would doubtless be inadmissible.

I paid off the cab – a sum equal to what I earned at the library in a day – and burst through the doors, ignoring the usual collection of prostitutes and tramps in the waiting area, and went directly to the counter.

"I need to see Detective Sergeant Wallace and Detective Constable Pascoe. Straight away please."

The constable on duty looked about the same age as me, and was conspicuously unimpressed by my need for urgency.

"Will they know what it's about?" he asked.

"Yes, they will. Tell them it's Jonathan Maguire. They have arrested my brother, Roger. I want to see him and them immediately."

Making no apparent effort to respond to my peremptory tone, the constable picked up the phone and dialled. I began pacing, unable in my still-growing anger to remain in one place. Within two minutes the side door opened and DC Pascoe beckoned to me.

"What the hell is going on?" I said instantly. "You've arrested my brother. What the fuck do you think you are doing?"

I knew that this was not the recommended way to speak to police officers, but I was so close to being out of control that I knew no better. And by now I felt that I had nothing to lose anyway.

"Calm down, Jonathan," he said, "and come inside."

"I want to see him," I said. "Immediately. The poor bugger must have no idea what is going on. He'll be terrified."

By now we were in the corridor, outside of the row of interview rooms. I knew that Roger was likely to be in one of them.

"Actually, he's very calm," said Pascoe. "He hasn't minded helping us a bit."

341

"I'll bet he hasn't. Roger will say anything he thinks you want him to say just to keep you happy. You should know that. Anything he has confessed to won't be worth a damn if it comes to court. You should know that too. Anyway, now I want to see him."

Pascoe said nothing more but turned and walked along the corridor, past three or four of the interview rooms, until he reached the last one in the row. He turned the security bolt on the outside, opened the door, and stood back to allow me into the room. I was aware of him following me inside. Roger was sitting at the desk, facing me, and apparently in a daze. For a moment I was unable to get his attention until I spoke his name.

"Roger, are you OK? It's Jonathan. You will be all right now. I've come to clear everything up."

Roger looked up at me, his eyes moving only slowly, as though he was coming out of a trance. Instantly he smiled and his face lit up.

"Jonathan. Hello. How are you?"

"I'm fine, Roger, but it doesn't matter how I am. How are you?"

"I'm OK, thanks," he said straight away. "The two police-men have been very nice to me."

"I'll bet they have," I said, and I glanced around at Pascoe. "You haven't told them anything silly have you? You haven't told them you have done anything just to keep them happy?"

"I just told them that I was hiding in the insect farm. I don't know anything about it. I was hiding in the insect farm."

I was confused.

"What do you mean 'hiding in the insect farm'? When were you hiding in the insect farm?"

I swear that my next sentence was going to be something like "you were in bed when Harriet was killed", but I was interrupted by Pascoe from behind me.

"During the fire," he said. "Roger has just been confirming to us what we had already believed. That he was hiding in the insect farm during the fire."

"What bloody fire?" I said.

Pascoe looked back at me. Now it was his turn to be confused.

"The fire that killed your parents," he said.

"What? What's that got to do with Harriet?"

"Harriet?" said Pascoe. "Mrs Maguire? Nothing. Why do you ask that?"

"Why? Because as far as I know, that's what you and Wallace are investigating. My wife's disappearance. You've arrested Brendan bloody Harcourt and had to let him go, and now you have arrested Roger. Are you saying that that's nothing to do with Harriet?"

"Sit down, please," said Pascoe. "Let me explain."

I didn't want to sit down, but I reckoned we would get to the point sooner if I obeyed, and so I did. And all the while Roger was sitting alongside me, saying nothing.

"We are investigating the disappearance of your wife. But as you know we have also kept open the file on the fire at your parents' house. The fire was never explained, and your dad did have quite a big insurance policy, so it has remained an open inquiry. We don't have any choice in the matter. You also know that at one time we had an idea that Roger might know more about it than he let on. We asked you about it at the time, but you were adamant that it couldn't be the case, and so we let the matter go."

"Yes, I remember all that," I said. "So why are you raising it again now?"

"Because of something Roger said to someone else at the day centre which caused them to think he knew about something criminal. They were sufficiently concerned about it to inform us, which they did earlier this morning, and so we reopened the file to take a look."

"What?" I said. "What did he say? Who did he say it to?"

"I am not at liberty to tell you that," said Pascoe, "but I can tell you that we felt we had no choice but to ask Roger about it. And when I tell you what it was, I hope you will understand why."

"And why didn't you wait for me?"

"Because, Jonathan," he said slowly, "if you don't mind me saying so, it seems to us that you will do anything to protect your brother, and if you were here you wouldn't be able to stop yourself from interrupting every question we asked. As it is," and now he looked pleased with himself, "your brother Roger has cleared up the mystery, and we can all go back to the way we were before."

"Cleared up the mystery of the fire?"

"No," said Pascoe, "cleared up the mystery about what he said at the day centre."

"And what was that?"

"He told one of the other pupils there – is that what you call them? Pupils? Anyway one of the other men – that he had been involved in a killing."

"What? He can't have."

"I know, but you can see why we had to take it seriously. Anyway in all the circumstances, we had to ask Roger about it, and we now have done so. It took him a while to tell us, but it turned out that he was talking about something or other living in the insect farm. Something that had been doing a lot of damage to some of his other creatures in the insect farm. Did he have to kill some cockroaches or something? I think he must have felt very badly about it, and so when he talked about it at the day centre, obviously it came out as something like a confession."

"And was it Terry, the Down-syndrome kid?"

"I shouldn't really tell you this, but as no harm has been done – he told Terry and Terry told his dad, so by the time it went through all the Chinese whispers, it came out as a killing. Anyway," he said, "I hope you understand why we had to check it out. And I hope you understand why we had to check it out without you being present. But Roger has cleared it up on his own now, and so, if you want to, you can take him home."

I felt a constriction in my chest and realized that I'd been taking short breaths since first seeing Roger in the interrogation room. I filled my lungs to capacity to get the air flowing through me. It tasted like freedom.

Chapter Twenty-Eight

More passing days turned into weeks, and the weeks turned into months, and on every waking hour I expected to receive the phone call or the knock on the door which would bring the news that someone had seen Harriet on the train on that Tuesday, or that one of the neighbours had seen her coming to the flat, or that I had been spotted in the early hours of Wednesday morning labouring under a heavy load, and that therefore I was now a suspect.

"Can you tell me what was in the bundle you were seen carrying at four in the morning, Mr Maguire?" Neither of my imagined interrogators were Wallace or Pascoe. The question was asked by the clichéd concave face of a man with wire-rimmed specs and a sweaty brow, and I could give no answer. I knew that any hope I might have of staying out of prison rested entirely on luck, and that it must be extraordinarily unlikely that anyone could have the amount of good fortune that would be needed for none of these things to come to light. I was also acutely aware that I was adding to the risk I was facing when I had a lot of leaflets printed showing Harriet's photograph with the message "Have you seen this woman?" with the reward of £500 proposed by her father. The last thing I needed was for someone who had travelled on the train on that Tuesday to remember her as a fellow passenger. Did I deliberately choose a photograph of Harriet where the light came from the side and slightly distorted the features of her face? I guess I did, but the police had no reference point from reality, and none of our other friends ever mentioned it.

Probably as much from their sense of guilt as from their concern, Martin and Jed helped me to distribute the leaflets outside King's Cross station. Both apologized for not telling me what was happening between Harriet and Brendan, and I used their embarrassment to squeeze out more detail.

"In the end I just think she was worn down by his persistence," Martin told me. We were in a burger bar opposite King's Cross station, taking a break from a session of stopping people in the street outside to show them Harriet's picture.

"You shouldn't really blame her," said Jed. "I know that sounds like a stupid thing to say, but you've got to try to understand. It was a very tough ask for her to be away from you for weeks and weeks on end. All the rest of us were going out and doing the normal pairing-off. She was being asked to live the life of a nun."

The pain these thoughts caused to me were not part of any act. I had no need to pretend to be a distraught husband – I was distraught. Hearing any detail of Harriet's infidelity cut me to the core every bit as much as it would have done had she been with me still.

We neither saw nor heard anything further of Brendan during this period, and I did not seek him out. Martin and Jed told me that he had taken the trip up and down on the train to Newcastle, apparently looking out of the window as if to do so might yield some clue as to what had happened to her. If he had ever had his suspicions, he was too shamefaced, I assumed, to come and ask me about them. Eventually Jed, Martin and Brendan returned to Newcastle and I went back to work at the library, where, for several months I had to endure the pitying glances of colleagues, before eventually my little tragedy became just another part of my pathetic life's story.

Ideally I would like to be able to record that Brendan was charged with Harriet's murder, found guilty and went on to spend the next twenty years in prison. In my mind, this would be a suitable punishment for having slept with my wife. The law, however, failed to see it that way. The absence of a body made it more or less impossible, the police kept on telling me, to prove that a crime had even taken place, let alone that Harriet had been murdered.

And so that was it. That was the story of Harriet Maguire, née Chalfont, born 1952, who went missing in 1973 and was never heard from again. I had no insurance to cash in, no funeral plans to make. As far as the wider world was concerned, it was almost as though she had never existed. I was back at my job, Roger went back to regular attendance at the day centre, and we all got on with our lives. I never managed to get anything resembling an answer from him about what happened to the body I had buried in a box full of soil and worms in the insect farm in a shed in the allotment site just two hundred yards or so from our flat. Every attempt at securing an explanation was met with a change of subject or a blank stare, and after a while I just gave up trying.

Chapter Twenty-Nine

In the few years after Harriet's death, I left the library service and opened a small bookshop in Clapham High Street. We specialized in travel books and have done reasonably well. I never married again – after all, I was already married, and never sought a divorce or an annulment. Harriet had been the single love of my life, and I never felt that I wanted to try to replace her.

Roger and I carried on in our own way. After another five years had passed, we moved to a small house just around the corner from the flat. It was a proper semi-detached; I thought our mother would have approved. We did not need to move the insect farm again, and the oversized shed on the allotment has continued to accommodate Roger's ambitions.

I lost touch with Martin and Jed, although one day, perhaps seven or eight years after what happened, I ran into Martin in the street and he told me that he thought Brendan had emigrated to Canada and was married with children. The news left me cold, and I felt no curiosity to know any more.

As expected, I never saw Harriet's parents again after that last Christmas and, in 1983, ten years after the disappearance of their daughter, I heard that Mr Chalfont had died in

Singapore, and that his wife was returning to England. She did not contact me and I made no attempt to contact her.

Last month, just a few weeks before my birthday, Roger and I were having breakfast in our small kitchen when, quite out of nowhere, he asked me what date it was.

"April 17th, I think. Why do you ask?"

"Two weeks from your birthday?"

"Yes, that's right, Roger. Another bloody birthday. Two weeks away."

"And how old will you be?"

"I will be fifty-seven. Why, what do you have in mind?"

"The same age that Dad was when he died."

"Yes, I believe so," and something rang a bell from a long long time ago. Something he had asked me about decades earlier.

Two weeks later, on my fifty-seventh birthday, my older brother Roger gave me a very unusual present. He woke up and changed whatever remains of the rest of my life. His was the gift of revelation.

The day began as usual – an early start for me, waking and listening to the radio. It was Saturday and I had been awake for half an hour before I remembered that it was my birthday. The years have brought me many acquaintances but very few friends and, as I come to consider it, there is no other person in the world, other than Roger and myself, who could spontaneously recite the date of my birthday. I considered waking Roger a little earlier than usual, just so we could do some silly birthday stuff, but then I remember thinking: fifty-seven? What the hell. It's not fifty, it's not sixty, it's not even fifty-five. No big deal. Let him sleep.

After an hour or so I swung my legs out of bed, put on my dressing gown, and ambled through to my older brother's room. For some reason I have got into the habit of looking at Roger for just a few moments before I rouse him from his sleep, and yesterday, not for the first time, I felt a little frisson of envy of the life that Roger leads. His appearance was of a man with no worries, no responsibilities, nothing to plan for or even much to remember. Yesterday seems very much like today, which will be very much like tomorrow.

I reckon that he looks younger than his sixty-three years. He has few lines for a man of his age, and his hair is thick and dark. Meanwhile I have no doubt that the cares and responsibilities which have thus fallen upon me have made me look older than my now fifty-seven years, and so I guess that Roger and I look more like twins than anything else. Now, as always since we were small boys, he is probably rather better-looking than I am.

For the very first time in his life – or certainly in the time that I have been taking care of him – Roger woke up and opened his eyes spontaneously. I had been about to nudge him awake as I always do, holding his shoulder and starting to move him gently backwards and forwards. Always Roger goes from totally asleep to totally awake in an instant, with no gradation in between the two states. However, on this occasion, as I was about to take hold of him, his eyes popped open, he beamed me a big big smile and said, "Happy birthday, Jonathan." I nearly fell backwards from the shock.

"Roger!" I said. "You scared the living daylights out of me. Have you been lying there awake and waiting for me to come in?"

"How old are you today?" he said, totally ignoring my question. "Fifty-seven, is it?"

"Yes, it is, Roger. Fifty-seven. How clever of you to remember."

Roger covered his mouth, just as he often did when something felt too exciting for him to cope with. His eyes shone, wide and innocent, exactly as they had half a century ago in anticipation of some treat or other.

"I have something for you."

"You do? That's great, Roger, what is it?" I began to anticipate what he might have made in his craft lesson at the day centre, and readied myself for seeming to appreciate a fly swat or a wooden device for making it easier to pull my feet out of rubber wellingtons. Instead of that, Roger leapt out of bed and a moment later he had pulled open the drawer in which we kept his pullovers. I assumed that he had secreted whatever it was at the back of a drawer, except that he kept on pulling until it fell out, and all of the folded-up clothes spilt onto the floor.

"Roger?" I said. "What on earth?" But I didn't have time for any further enquiry because Roger had turned the drawer upside down, and I saw something that looked like an envelope attached with Sellotape to the bottom. Roger was picking away at the corners of the tape and soon had released the envelope. He turned and handed it to me. I looked down at it, genuinely and utterly confused. The paper was yellowing and brittle with age, and I did not have the smallest clue as to what it could contain. I turned it over and saw some words written in ink, as from an old-fashioned fountain pen. A moment later I felt an echo from a distant time, another life, a long long time ago. I recognized the shaky handwriting as my father's and squinted in the half-light to read what it said.

"To be given to Jonathan on his 57th birthday."

I continued to stare down at the envelope in total amazement, and then I looked back at Roger, lost for words. I had so many questions that I did not know where to begin. All I was getting back from Roger in response was the sunshine of an almighty grin, as from a small boy who has been sworn to secrecy and, despite many temptations and all the odds against doing so, has managed to keep his promise. Here I was, looking at my supposed mentally handicapped older brother, who had managed to keep a secret for not far short of forty years.

"Roger? What the hell?…" I tried and failed to find the right words. "Is this from Dad? You've kept it all this time?" Roger was too excited to answer, but just stood still, smiling and nodding vigorously. Clearly he was beside himself with delight that he had completed a task that he must have been asked to undertake all those years ago. "And has this letter been stuck to the drawer since Dad died?"

Roger shook his head, and now I remembered that we hadn't even bought the chest of drawers until after the fire in which Mum and Dad had been killed.

"He told me to keep it in the insect farm and so I did. I put it underneath the drawers when we bought the flat."

"So how long before he died did he give it to you?"

"One day," said Roger, and sat back on the bed, as though tired after the completion of his life's work. He looked neither happy nor sad to recall the day our parents had died.

Oddly enough, I could not bring myself to open the letter there and then. These events were so unexpected and weird for me that I felt that I needed to take them on board before I did so. My eyes were blinking to try once again to focus on the stale yellow pages and the watery lines of blue ink.

"What's for breakfast?" asked Roger.

"As it's my birthday and therefore rather a special occasion," I said, "I thought we might have a pickled bat brains on walnut bread with stale doughnuts."

Roger put one finger to his lips as though considering the offer, and then shook his head.

"Nice idea, Jonathan," he said, "but I think I'll just have toast and Marmite and then maybe a banana."

"Coming right up," I said.

Fifteen minutes later, as Roger ate his food and stared into the middle distance, I was looking again at the envelope and thinking. I was still reeling at the idea of Roger keeping it safe and secret from me for all this time, and had not the slightest notion of what could be in it. I glanced again at Roger, saw that he was in something of a trance, and inserted my thumb under the flap of the envelope and slid it along, tearing as I went. Inside was a single sheet of A4 paper, covered in tiny writing in the same trembling hand. I put on my specs and began to read.

My dear Jonathan.

If things have gone as your mother and I intend, you will be reading this on the morning of your fifty-seventh birthday. There is nothing especially significant about the date, except that I wanted to choose a moment a very long time from now, but one that Roger would have a chance of remembering. I am thinking that if he waits until you are the same age as I am when I am writing this, it might stick in his mind. I hope that it has. If not, and you are reading this sooner, then so be it.

As I write this, your mother and I are making our final preparations to end our lives. I assume that this will be a shock to you, and hope that it will be. If so, it means that we will have achieved our intention.

This will be confusing for you, but I hope that by now you yourself might be a parent. If you are, you might understand why, for all of your lives, your mother and I have worried what would become of you both after she and I have died. As you might imagine, our main concern is about Roger. We know that you will always be able to take care of yourself, and your promise to take care of Roger has given us enormous comfort.

However, we know that this will be difficult even with help, and may be impossible without it. So our priority in recent years has been how to raise enough money to give you a head start financially. I am sorry to say that we haven't had much success in being able to do that. I think you have noticed that in recent months my hands have begun to shake, and I have been diagnosed with an early onset of Parkinson's disease. No one at the office has noticed it yet, but as soon as they do, I will need to give up work, which will set us in the wrong direction altogether.

So last month your mother had an idea. (I am only telling you that it was your mother's idea so that you don't think that she was ever under any pressure from me. She wasn't, and isn't.)

For many years we have had the usual life insurance, but six months ago I increased the policy and our premiums as far as we possibly could, without giving rise to undue suspicion. By now you will have worked out the rest of our plan. On some night in the near future, maybe even tomorrow, we are going to give this letter to Roger and ask him to hide it in the insect farm, and then to remain in the shed until morning. We are confident that we have prepared carefully enough for the fire to be considered an accident of some kind. We cannot afford to have it believed to be suicide, because then the insurance will not pay out.

I have made every effort to persuade your mother that her plan to provide you both with security could involve me alone, and she need not also lose her life. She would not hear of it. We have always done everything together, she reminded me, and we are going to do this together too. She said that she would have no interest in going on in this life without me, and to be honest I don't think I have the courage to head off into the next one without her.

So, if things go according to plan, you should receive enough money in a lump sum to set you and Roger up – if not for life, then at least to give you a decent start. I apologize for the bad timing – you are in the middle of university – but with the increasingly obviously shaking hands, I just don't think we can wait any longer. If I lose my job, I would also lose any death-in-service benefits that go with it. I know you will make the best of everything.

If our plan has worked, this will all be a distant memory for you. Your mother and I are sorry for the distress it will no doubt have caused you at the time, but we hope you understand why we have done it, and why we thought it best to keep it a secret from you. If ever our plan is discovered, we need to be certain that it never rebounds on you. This letter would be evidence of it. By the time you are reading this, no one will know or care.

So your mother and I thank you from the bottom of our hearts for whatever you have been able to do for Roger. If not much, we understand and forgive you. If you have been able to do what we know you intend, then God will bless you and will forgive you for anything bad you have ever done in your life.

Who knows, maybe one day we will be a family once again in heaven, whole and reunited.

As ever, Dad

My eyes were streaming with huge tears as I read the final few words, and I had to swallow hard to suppress the cry that was welling within me. I looked up and was glad to see that Roger was still staring into empty space, no doubt mentally down at the farm among his creations. I dried my face and tried to compose myself.

"It's so great to receive that from Dad after so much time has passed, Roger. Brilliantly well done to you for saving it all these years." Suddenly his face lit up with pleasure once again, but now I had a question which I had to ask, even though I already knew the answer. "Do you have any idea what is in this letter?" The expression on my older brother's face changed again, and instantly he was more serious. He shook his head like someone being asked if they knew a particular party game. "That's good, Roger," I said. "Dad was just remembering what it was like to be fifty-seven and wanted to wish me a happy birthday. A lovely thought."

Lame as it was, the explanation seemed to Roger to be perfectly satisfactory and, having kept the secret for so long, he seemed quite ready to get on with the day as though nothing special had happened.

My father's handwritten words were echoing across the decades and around my brain, and I felt sharp surges of pain to think of the anguish which he and our mother had endured, and how desperate they must have been to feel that the best thing was to devise and carry out their plan. To be in a situation in which the best service you can perform for your children is to take your own lives must surely be as desperate as anything can get in this lifetime. It struck me that we often talk about people making "the ultimate sacrifice", and that's exactly what our parents had done for their son.

I guess that, once they decided on their course, it was impossible for my parents to go on living with it looming over their future. However, as so often in our lives, there were unanticipated consequences from the timing of their action. Their preoccupation must have been – understandably – the end of their own lives and the long-term financial security and welfare of their children. I also had little doubt that the prospect of advancing Parkinson's disease must have been a terrifying one. They thought they were doing their best. From my point of view, of course, the timing could scarcely have been more unfortunate, and despite myself I felt a flash of anger that a decision which would have such a profound effect on the rest of my life had been taken by them alone and without my knowledge or consent. Their suicide had taken place while I was still at university, completely derailing my own plans, which had led directly to me having to live apart from Harriet. It was living apart from her which had thrown my wife into the arms of Brendan Harcourt, with all the dreadful and tragic consequences that had followed from that. I thought about how so much of what we do with one intention in our minds can so very easily turn into something completely unexpected and undesirable, and I wondered what my parents would have thought had they ever known what would be the aftermath of their personal self-sacrifice.

A little later on that morning, Roger asked me if I wanted to go down to the insect farm. His enthusiasm for his hobby had remained undiminished over the years, and quite often I would go down there with him. Some years ago I had commandeered a little area of unused ground just outside of the shed and turned it into something resembling a garden; nothing serious, just a few slightly sad-looking flowers and a little patch of shingle. Some friendly council workers digging up the road outside had looked the other way while I made off with half a dozen paving slabs on a wheelbarrow, and over the course of a couple of weeks, Roger and I had manhandled them into place to create our own little makeshift patio. We had a pair of folding canvas chairs which remained propped up against a wall inside the shed, to be pulled into use on any day when the sun broke through the clouds. On this day, my fifty-seventh birthday, there was a watery sun, and so I packed a make-do picnic of pies and salad, and made up a flask of tea. I could hear Roger pottering about inside the shed while I sat outside, enjoying the fresh air and reading the *Observer*.

After an hour or so I took my chair and went inside to see what Roger was up to, and found that he was kneeling on the floor and bending over one of his glass tanks, apparently motionless, and peering inside. For a few minutes I watched him, as unaware of me standing behind him as the insects in the tank were unaware of his looming presence above them. Funny how something so potentially powerful, so awesome in relation to yourself, can be just outside of your ability to perceive it. These creatures owed their existence to Roger, and yet had no knowledge of him. They went about their business, eating, working, reproducing and occasionally massacring their enemies, without awareness or thought that they may be answerable to a greater being. Most often his presence was entirely benign and life-giving. Just occasionally however, if the situation demanded it, he would intervene, invisibly, and turn their lives upside down.

"So the police were wrong about you all along," I said at last. Roger turned to look at me and raised his eyebrows. It was a facial expression suggesting a level of comprehension and enquiry which I do not think I had seen before, and it was this which made me continue. "For a long time, you know, I think they thought that maybe you had started the fire at Mum and Dad's house." The corners of his mouth drooped down slightly, and I kept on talking. "Someone had suggested to them that perhaps they had threatened to close down the insect farm, and that you had become angry and started the fire." I don't really know why I was saying it after all these years, but it seemed to me that if I did not do so now, I never would. I stopped speaking and allowed the words to percolate around the mystery that was Roger's brain. Who could ever know if they were doing so in a way anyone else would recognize? It seemed entirely possible that at this moment he was considering what I had just said; equally it seemed just as likely that he was in a far off land of ants and beetles and spiders, or his mind could be in some third place that I might never know anything about.

"Yes," he said finally, "wouldn't it have been funny if I had got into trouble for the wrong one?"

Now it was my turn to raise my eyebrows.

"'The wrong one'? What do you mean 'the wrong one'?"

"Just saying, wouldn't it be funny if I had got into trouble and had to go to prison for the wrong murder?"

My mind turned a somersault, but very quickly I recalled the confession he had made at the day centre all those years ago about killing the cockroaches which had come so close to getting him into huge trouble at the time. I was about to warn him that careless talk of that sort could be dangerous.

"Oh, I don't think you'd go to jail for killing insects, Roger," I said.

"Not for killing insects," he said slowly, and looked directly at me. "For killing Harriet."

Once, when I was a small child and my mother was hoovering the carpet on the stairs, I played a game which involved plugging and unplugging the vacuum cleaner from the electric socket. Evidently I must have found it amusing to confuse her about the reason why the machine kept stopping and starting. My game was interrupted by a huge bright blue-and-red flash of electricity which burned my hands and knocked me across the hallway, leaving every part of my body numb as it decided whether to live or whether to die. Eventually, gradually, it decided to live – but only just. I lost count of the number of adults who took the opportunity to share their view that I had had a miraculous escape. That, as near as I can describe it, was the effect on my mind and body of the three words just spoken by my brother.

Slowly, as the breath began to refill my lungs and the oxygen began to filter back into my bloodstream, I gently took Roger by the cuff of his jacket and led him outside. I picked up the two seats, clattering clumsily against the frame of the door as I unfolded and set them out. My foot caught the step and momentarily I stumbled, nearly falling headlong. My initial shock was even further exacerbated by the momentary jolt of tripping over. I put one chair to one side of the patio and one on the other, half-facing each other. I sat down and gestured for him to sit opposite me.

"Would you like some tea from the flask, Roger?" My throat was tight, and the words were uttered through a strangulated larynx. I rubbed my neck as though to loosen the sinews which had made it feel constricted. We sat down together while I poured the tea carefully into two enamel mugs, and for a few moments we remained silent, two old men, our lives inextricably intertwined by circumstances, and yet in so many ways there was such distance between us.

Over the next two hours, inch by inch, minute by minute, thought by thought, I slowly extracted from Roger the individual elements which, once rearranged, made up an account of the events of that night well over three decades earlier. It did not come out in the form of a story, nor any kind of narrative with one thing following another. It would not have been possible for Roger to relate it in such a way. Instead, he was able to give me a series of memories and impressions and images which made little sense in themselves but, when taken in the context of what I knew already and could remember myself, allowed me eventually to understand and piece together what had happened. His recall was not linear, and not logical, but what is so strange is that, when all put together, Roger remembered everything so much more clearly than did I.

Roger had understood, it turned out, that Harriet was due back from Newcastle on that Tuesday. Even that was a revelation to me. He had been excited at the prospect of seeing her and secretly had been disappointed when I arranged for him to spend the evening with Terry and his father. He had not known, or certainly had not understood, anything about the turmoil filling my mind regarding Brendan. Even now, as

Roger's vignettes of recollection were emerging, I was careful not to allow him to realize the impact on events of what he had told me about having seen Harriet and Brendan kissing, and having heard his words: "I love you, Harriet."

Roger had worked out that I arranged for him to stay at Terry's house because I wanted to be alone with Harriet, which is the reason he had not complained. But he had also been missing her himself, which was why he had started to become restless at Terry's house, and had pestered Mr Harries to bring him home.

In fits and starts and with arbitrary and maddening diversions, Roger conveyed how he had told Mr Harries that it would be quite all right to drop him at the front door of the house. We seldom locked the door at the top of the stairs and Roger was quite capable of letting himself into the flat. He had not heard or thought anything untoward until he reached the top landing, at which point he had heard raised voices. Very gently and slowly, he had pushed open the door. Then he paused for a moment, stopping in his tracks, because he could hear a sound he had not heard for many many years. He had remained still and listened for a few minutes, unable to work out what the sound was. Only then had he realized that it was the sound of his younger brother crying.

The glimpses into his mind and thoughts that Roger allowed were enough for me to work out what had followed. The sound had set off in him an instinctive reaction, just as it had in the local streets many years earlier when I was being bullied by a bigger boy. Now, just as then, Roger had lost control. He had entered the room determined to intervene, only to be confronted by the sight of Harriet and me – her alongside me, apparently calm and in possession – but me sitting and sobbing and in a level of distress that he was not able to describe, and presumably therefore he was still less able to cope with. When he came to speak about this moment, his jaw seemed to seize up, and he struggled to form the words. His instinct to protect me from harm was overwhelming. He had picked up the first thing that came to hand, a wine bottle, and had done what he needed to do in order to take away the thing that seemed to be hurting me. When he turned back to me, it seems, I had passed out, and, seeing that I was no longer apparently suffering, he had left the room, washed, changed into his pyjamas and put himself to bed; which is how and why he was sleeping peacefully when I came to a little later and went into his room.

I will not attempt to convey the whirlwind of thoughts and impulses scrabbling over one another for priority and attention. "But when I woke up, Roger, I had a broken bottle in my hand." Roger shook his head. He had no explanation.

"I could tell that she was hurting you. I just had to stop her from hurting you."

Of course it is not possible for me to work out, let alone to express, what I felt and am still feeling. Is it anger? No. How could I feel angry that I had an older brother whose sole instinct was to save me from distress? Relief? Hardly that:

Harriet was still taken from me, still I never got her back and never came close to replacing the part she had played in my life. Bemusement? Probably that. I felt a sensation of profound emptiness, maybe better described as numbness, as I tried to unpick in my brain all of the ramifications and baggage which had resulted from the fact that for all these years, all these decades, I had thought myself to be responsible for the murder of Harriet Maguire.

If someone is a thief – steals something from his friend – but later returns it, is he still a thief? Or if he takes a single object without permission and then takes nothing else for forty years, is it still fair to describe him as a robber? Perhaps not. But once a murderer always a murderer. It is a label which, once attached, can never be detached. Though this dreadful secret has remained within the torment of my own memories, it has been the constant reality accompanying every aspect of my life. A fact of my life. Every moment of every day of every year, I have thought of myself as a killer; someone who has taken another person's life. Perhaps we might compare it to having a missing limb: something you might eventually learn to live without, but still there will never be a moment of your life in which you do not have a missing part.

Though I could not place hand on heart and claim that Harriet's murder has been present in every single thought, it would be fair to say that she, and what happened on that night, have been present somewhere in every conscious hour. Her physical beauty has not withered with the passing years, the tenderness of her touch has gently caressed me through sleep and dreams. But the other side of that same coin is the memory of throwing shovelfuls of soil onto her flawless skin, and of watching her disappear under the earth. All these images are every bit as vivid as I write as they were on the day it all happened. Now, as it turns out, the label which has adhered to me like a tattoo branded into my soul turns out to have been based on a falsehood. It was not I who ended the mortal life of my wife, but a man who – as Harriet herself was the first to acknowledge – would go to any lengths to protect me. He would, and he did.

"You do realize, do you, Roger, that for all these years I thought that it had been me who had killed Harriet?" The expression on his face suggested no proper comprehension of the real import of my question; as though I had asked him to describe the taste of a strawberry.

"I thought you knew I had done it, and have been looking after me."

"I have been looking after you, Roger," I said. For a long time I looked at my older brother, my lovely older brother Roger, the friend and companion I have spent my life with, the warmest, most gentle, most loyal and loving person I have ever known. The creator of my universe, and the person who had killed my wife. "I have been looking after you, Roger, but equally, my friend, it seems that you have been looking after me."

Once again we both sat quietly, each with our own thoughts. I considered the secret lives that we all lead inside our minds, the thoughts we have which remain unknown to those around us as we go about our business. How I could have managed to live my life, apparently an average and normal sort of guy, and all the while with the concealed belief that I was a killer. And I was at a loss to know how my brother, so close to me and so open in so many ways, could have retained so huge a secret in that space just behind his eyes.

"You must have wondered," he said at last.

"Wondered? Wondered what?"

"I thought you must have wondered what became of her."

Of course I had wondered. I had wondered about it many times, and indeed had asked him many times, but had never managed to get an answer. Always he had responded with a total blank, or instantly had changed the subject to something completely unrelated. Now though, my older brother Roger stood up and went inside the shed, emerging only a few seconds later carrying a brown heavy-duty cardboard container, about the size of a large matchbox, which he handed to me. It was damp and discoloured, and had signs of having been delivered by Air Mail. I slid my spectacles into place from their usual resting place on my forehead and screwed up my eyes to read the label, turning it into the light. My mouth shaped the words as I deciphered them. "Fragile. With care. Live specimens. Genus *Osedax*."

"They are found in the area of Monterey Bay near San Francisco," said Roger. For a moment I thought we were experiencing another example of Roger changing the subject completely when confronted with a question he preferred not to deal with. No doubt the expression on my face indicated clearly that I had no idea what he was talking about, or what could be the relevance of his words. Then he spoke again, slowly, distinctly and, not for the first time, in a tone which suggested that he was speaking to an idiot. "I sent off for them just a few days after the last time we saw Harriet. They are the only species of beetle on the planet which eats bones."

In the space of a few seconds, the intervening years of ignorance and confusion were swept away like the seed heads of a dandelion blown into the wind. I remembered one Sunday in the flat when the two detectives had called unexpectedly, and I had been worried about Roger's reaction to news that Harriet was missing. All he had seemed to care about on that morning was whether a particular parcel had arrived. I recalled the day when Wallace and Pascoe had turned up at the insect farm, and the alacrity with which Roger had shown them the crate in which Harriet's body had been buried in soil. All the time he had known that this was her burial ground, but that by that moment there would be no evidence of her. "Amazing creatures," he was saying, "Seventeen different species, all with no eyes or digestive system, but they land on a skeleton and insert little appendages like roots down into the bone, and then suck out the organic material. After a few days, the whole thing disintegrates and there is literally not a trace left." He paused again. "They can be handy things, these insect farms."

Roger remained still for a while, and once again he seemed to be thinking, as I was thinking. I looked at the face I knew so well and, for the ten thousandth time, I tried to imagine what it must be like inside his head. How he might be processing the life-changing words and meanings we had just shared. For a moment I thought he was about to say something more, a further revelation about the death of Harriet. Then he stopped himself and seemed to consider for a few more seconds before he spoke.

"And now may I ask you a question, Jonathan?"

"Of course you can, Roger. What is it?"

"You won't be cross?"

"No, Roger" – and in the light of what he had just been telling me, I wondered what he could possibly be intending to ask me that he feared might make me cross – "you can ask me anything and I promise that I won't be cross."

"Tomorrow," he said, "could we have something different for our breakfast?"

Chapter Thirty

In the many years since those seismic events which shaped so much of the remainder of my life, I have made a number of attempts to write down some of what happened. I thought that the process of organizing the story into a continuous account might help me to come to terms with it all. I am not sure whether it did or did not, but when we got back to our house on the day of my birthday, I went straight to my desk to pull together the various starts I had made over the years. Somehow it seemed to me that these extraordinary revelations from Roger at last offered an opportunity for what I have sometimes heard referred to as "closure".

I have of course spent the days and nights since then turning over questions in my head. So many questions but, chief among them, how it was that Roger – my older brother, who has so many problems and handicaps – could have done everything he did and still managed to keep his secrets for all these years.

I have also thought much more in recent weeks about the insect farm and the implications for Roger of his role as its creator. It was he who had dreamt up and built this amazing universe, and he who was ultimate controller of everything that took place within it. Perhaps his omnipotence in this environment helps to explain why Roger felt it to be within his power to control events as he had in our world too. He, it turned out, was the silent and invisible mover behind what happened on the insect farm, but also in the lives of Harriet, himself and me.

I have no way to know whether any of these thoughts will help me to get a perspective on all that has happened, but one thing has become completely clear to me. It is that all the while the insect farm is a part of our lives, I will be destined to remained plagued by these events every single day. Again and again I have turned over everything in my mind, and what keeps coming back to me is that the insect farm has been a hidden player in so much that has happened – the continuing thread running behind so many of the milestones along the way.

It was Roger's place of hiding when our parents died in the fire; it was the place where I hid Harriet's body on that terrible night; it was the place where every last trace of her was consumed; and the place where I came within a hair's breadth of being arrested as Harriet's killer. It has taken me some while and a lot of agonizing to reach this conclusion, but to me it now seems perfectly obvious that there can be no chance of moving on – for me or indeed for Roger – while the insect farm remains in existence. It has become my firm resolve that we must finally be rid of it.

I realize that I will have to think very carefully about how to break this news to Roger. I do not underestimate that it will be very difficult for him. His first reaction could well be anger and confusion, and I must not forget how violently he responded when I hinted all those years ago that Dad had wanted to close it down. But I believe that in the end I will be able to make him understand why it is necessary. After all, as Harriet was the first to point out, Roger would do anything for me.

Anyway, that's a job for tomorrow.

Acknowledgements

The author would like to thank Alessandro Gallenzi, Elisabetta Minervini, Christian Müller and Clémentine Koenig at Alma Books. Also everyone at Curtis Brown, but especially Gordon Wise and Richard Pike. And of course Emily Banyard, Annabel Robinson and Fiona McMorrough at FMCM.

Apart from being one of the leading broadcasters and producers of his generation, STUART PREBBLE is an acclaimed writer of fiction and non-fiction. Among his publications are two novels, five comedy books based on the *Grumpy Old Men* TV series which he produced and, more recently, a book about the Falklands War, *Secrets of the Conqueror*, published by Faber and Faber in 2012. *The Insect Farm* is his latest novel.